ADVI
PL

ADVENTURES IN THE PLEASUREZONE

Delaney Silver

Nexus

First published in Great Britain in 1993 by
Nexus
338 Ladbroke Grove
London W10 5AH

A catalogue record for this title is available
from the British Library

ISBN 0 352 32845 2

Phototypeset by Intype, London
Printed and bound in Great Britain by Cox & Wyman
Ltd, Reading, Berks.

Dedicated to *The Transformer* . . .
. . . who transformed me.

THANK YOU

This book is a work of fiction.
In real life, make sure you practise safe sex.

Contents

1 *Home Coming*

'Oh God! Oh God! At last,' Josh moaned as his prick went deep. She was hot. Wet. Tight. Fabulous. On the beat of each attribute he shoved in heavily, and Julia bucked in response. She whimpered and he swivelled his hips, stirring his rod in the soft, pulpy pot. Oh God, he'd missed it so much . . .

Electric sex? Fantasy? Pleasurezone? Hell, the real thing felt just fine right now. He'd been starving for it, ravenous for sex. Hungry for the fat, silky hole between a woman's legs.

And yet, even as the climax built and the long-dammed pleasure came surging up, his imagination niggled him, and he knew he'd soon want – and get – something more. Much more. And as different from this as night was from day . . .

'Unngh! Oh yes, Josh, yes! There's no one like you,' his target groaned as he hit bulls-eye. 'Oh God, yes, do it! I'm dying!' Naked heels drummed his arse, and nails – inch-long and baby pink, he thought in an odd cool moment – scrabbled and scored at every last bit of him they could reach. A warm, fluid-lined vagina rippled around him . . .

'Oh yes, baby, yes, it's better than I remember,' he hissed against her throat, slap-bang in the hold of reality now, no time for conjecture or question. His prick was sliding in a smooth, stretchy glove. A glove lined thickly with melted butter.

'Oh Jesus, that's beautiful,' he groaned, dimly surprised by the strange, husky sounds coming out of his own mouth. It'd been so long, so very long. Not only had he forgotten what it felt like to be inside a woman, he'd even forgotten what his voice sounded like when he was.

It couldn't last long, of course. Josh was proud of his control, but after eight sexless months he was fighting a losing battle. For a minute he thrust metronomically, urged on by Julia's ecstatic yelps and the hot, liquid squelch of sliding flesh; then, like the beginning and the end of the universe – the Big Bang and Apocalypse all rolled into one – the familiar miracle began.

'Oh God, oh God, oh God,' he shouted as spunk powered out of his balls, along his shaft, then spewed into Julia's shuddering, climaxing cunt.

The feeling was sublime and loin-shattering, like nothing else known to humankind, and Josh couldn't believe that he'd managed without it. The few times he'd jacked off on Phobos – when his drug level had dropped and his prick had been twitching – hadn't been anything like this. Nice as it'd been at the time, you couldn't compare a damp squib with a supernova.

In a few moments, as he drifted slowly down, remnants of rational thought began to assert themselves. It was time, Josh realised, to relieve Julia of his weight. He was a lean man – hard, sleek and fit – but at just short of six foot and solidly muscled, he was a heavy burden for his petite partner. As he lifted himself clear and lay back on the crumpled sheets, she snuggled against him with a long, satisfied sigh.

Within a few seconds, she was asleep, her soft snores quite endearing in a way, and Josh, feeling peculiarly lucid and alert, was able to relax and take stock now his first screaming lust was sated.

A horny kid, then a highly sexed man, Joshua Jordan Mortimer knew that he'd never been as randy as this in his whole life. He was also beginning to suspect that this latest of his many homecomings was quite different from all the ones before it. But at least, as he stroked the warm damp skin of the woman beside him, he knew some things were the same and he liked them that way . . .

Julia was soft and pliant, warm and willing, with thighs like pillows and an ever-flowing cunt. She never asked

2

questions – she never asked for anything – she was simply the very first name in his computerised 'little black book'. He'd called her the moment he'd got in from City Field, almost before his flight bag had hit the mattress. But while he'd waited for her, even before he'd stripped off his travel-stained clothes, he'd discovered that 'something more'.

Scanning the flickering video screen, he'd scrolled quickly out of his own personal files and into Leisuretext and the general entertainment listings, where he'd found very little of interest. Eight months away on a rockball, and what'd changed? Absolutely zip. He tracked up through music and three-dee art. Still nothing. Finally he keyed in 'Services Available', and then the code for his newly enhanced financial status.

Virtually anything could be acquired through Leisuretext: bookings for sport or concerts; for drama or exhibitions; every conceivable kind of tuition, relaxation and amusement to either cheer up the miserable or wind down the overstressed.

Yeah, they can sort out every bloody problem but mine, Josh thought wryly, shifting uneasily and feeling the hard slide of tumescence in his pants. Come on, Julie baby, I need you, he thought, still flicking keys to take his mind off his prick.

Then suddenly he blinked in amazement and sat down, stunned, in his computer chair, his cock pulsing wildly as he stared.

I don't believe it.

It's impossible.

Josh had seen some exotic merchandise on sale in his time, but surely they weren't *allowed* to offer this to the general public? And yet they must be. The municipal approval code was flashing in the bottom left hand corner.

He cupped his crotch unconsciously as he read.

SEX ON THE BRAIN? LOOKING FOR SOMETHING UNIQUE AND SPECIAL? YOUR WILDEST EROTIC FANTASIES CAN NOW BE EXPLORED AND REALISED IN ABSOLUTE SAFETY. WE CAN MAKE YOUR MOST BIZARRE DREAMS REAL, AND,

3

Slightly dazed, Josh scrubbed at his eyes and shook his
head. But when he looked again, the extraordinary message
was still alive and glowing. Space-lag, man, he told himself.
But when he cleared the screen and re-keyed, he knew that
his tired eyes weren't deceiving him. The crazy ad came
zapping up all over again.

What did they mean? Was it some kind of brothel? A
role-playing club? He laughed out loud, then looked round
nervously. There was no one around to call him a nutcase
but he just couldn't imagine anyone playing out *his* 'wildest
erotic fantasies'.

And what did they mean, 'in perfect safety'? The sexually
adventurous were safe from disease these days, but there
were still scenes and practices that were physically hazard-
ous – not to mention being an emotional and psychological
minefield.

Off duty on Phobos, with nothing to do in his spare
time but read, he'd dipped into all sorts of esoteric science
articles. He'd read about 'structured dreaming', 'neural re-
creation' and other such mindgames, but had assumed that
the techniques described were either experimental or firmly
in the hands of the military.

Until now.

Was that what Pleasurezone Inc. were selling? Customised wet dreams for discerning perverts?

It was a mindboggling concept. And an incredibly sexy
one, thought Josh, biting his lip and wishing Julia would
hurry. How the hell did they do it? Make people dream . . .
Make them believe . . .

The info code was hip but cryptic.

EVER WANTED TO STEP OUT OF YOUR OWN SEX LIFE AND

4

INTO SOMEBODY ELSE'S? EVER WANTED TO MAKE YOUR
FANTASIES REAL? TRY THINGS YOU NEVER DARED? DO
THINGS YOUR PARTNER WON'T? TAKE RISKS? EVER
WANTED TO DO ALL THESE THINGS BUT NOT DONE THEM
BECAUSE YOU'VE GOT MORE SENSE?

IN THAT CASE WELCOME TO PLEASUREZONE INC. WE
CAN GIVE YOU ANYTHING AND EVERYTHING IN ABSOLUTE
SAFETY. THE ONLY RISK IS TO YOUR BANK BALANCE!

SO WHY NOT SPOIL YOURSELF? DO YOURSELF THE BIG-
GEST FAVOUR OF YOUR LIFE AND RUN WILD IN THE
WORLD OF SENSUAL FANTASY! THERE'S A FULL REFUND
AFTER THE FIRST SESSION IF YOU CAN'T STAND THE PACE,
BUT WE DARE YOU TO TAKE US ON . . . AND PUSH YOUR-
SELF TO THE LIMIT – AND BEYOND!

ACCESS CODE 0000000###000#01A/P FOR DETAILS
OF OUR FEES AND HOW TO PAY THEM. AND DON'T
FORGET . . . WE CHALLENGE *YOU* TO CHALLENGE *US* AND
EXPERIENCE THE MAGIC OF PLEASUREZONE INC!!!!

Don't do this, Josh, he told himself then, even as he reached
out to press the appropriate keys. Don't do it, it's a con.

Don't be a cretin, man, he murmured as the information
flicked into view.

You must be joking, he thought. Preposterous figures
pulsed green on black, yet the very mind-numbing outrage-
ousness of the price hardened him as he read.

To satisfy his as-yet formless fantasies, Pleasurezone Inc.
would require most of the money he'd worked so bloody
hard for on Phobos. He'd be back to square one. He'd have
to sign up again straight away.

And yet . . .

'This is it, old son,' he said aloud, laying his hand lightly
over his bulging groin. Then he laughed. He'd gone
bananas but he knew beyond doubt that he'd always torment himself if he didn't answer this ludicrous electronic
advert.

Commonsense fought to be heard, but couldn't fight the
throbbing clamour in his prick. One-handedly he keyed in
the 'commit and pay' code. His felt his flesh leap as the

final digit appeared and the screen went into 'credit check'. Within seconds verification appeared; his account could handle Pleasurezone's exorbitant charges. He moaned when the 'transaction complete, stand by for further instructions' message flashed up – not so much from his pathetically depleted bank balance, but because he'd never been harder or randier in his life.

It was at that moment, either mercifully or unfortunately – because he'd no time to cancel what he'd done – that Julia had arrived.

Not your fault, babe, he thought now, reaching for her hand and placing it on his newly hardened prick. She stirred slightly, her fingers curling instinctively around him like a sleepy child with a favourite toy.

He'd an aching stiffy again already, he noted, half pleased, half troubled, knowing that even though his body just wanted to sleep off the long journey from Phobos, his hyperactive tool was demanding more action.

This temporary extreme priapism was perfectly normal at the moment, though. Coming off Libidox stone cold – after taking the synthetic bromide for eight months to make a womanless job more bearable – was bound to put sparks in his sex drive.

He'd got eight whole months' worth of spunk backed up – no wonder he was crazy to fuck.

But he wanted more than just fucking, and even as he shook Julia gently by the shoulder, then tried a more effective method of waking her – flipping her slowly over and starting to suck her breast – he knew that Pleasurezone Inc., the destroyer of his new solvency, was the answer to his more complicated and as yet indefinable needs . . .

LA SELENE. FRIDAY 20.00 HOURS.

Bloody thing, Josh thought frustratedly as he twirled the cryptic plastic slip in his fingers. It was 19.30 hours and it was Friday, and he was about to set out for La Selene, the bar in question. The last twenty-four hours had been extremely peculiar and very frustrating, and he couldn't count the times he'd wished his rash deed undone. Starting the moment he'd seen this slip.

Julia had just left, with a yawn, a thanks-for-the-fuck grin and a drowsy 'See you around', and Josh had decided to find out exactly what he'd committed himself to. Punching in the command for hard copy, he'd expected a descriptive brochure at least and been both angry and puzzled to receive so little enlightenment.

What were they playing at? He'd spent all that money, and all he'd got was a place, a day and a time. Recognising a cynical curiosity-building ploy, he'd rekeyed in all the relevant codes – and got precisely nothing.

Tricky buggers, he'd thought, staring powerlessly at the screen. They'd pulled an immediate data drop-out and left him with no option but turn up at the appointed time and place.

Which was almost now.

Within quarter of an hour the City's rapid transport system had him at the portal of La Selene – and as he stood in its mirrored foyer, one of the most striking, famous and notorious on the planet – he almost turned tail and ran.

What have I got myself into? he wondered, hovering. They'd told him nothing. There was no guarantee he'd even get a fuck tonight.

'Your fantasies realised in perfect safety' they'd said. But how? How did they work it? Sexual amateur theatrics or somebody playing around with his mind? He didn't know which rattled him most . . . or which felt most exciting.

Gambling on his feeling that there *would* be a woman involved, he'd dressed in his best stone-killer style, and lingering in front of the long silvery mirrors, he gave himself a last once-over.

He saw a tallish figure, long-limbed, rangily built and broodingly male; a man dark of skin and hair and dressed in a pale silk-worsted designer-tailored suit.

He gave himself a little ego-boost and tried out his wide white smile. He shifted his weight, rocking lightly on the balls of his feet and enjoying the feel of his clothes. Indulging what he suspected was a low-grade fetish, he was wearing silk from the skin out. The smooth, sensuous fabric

7

seemed to kiss his whole body and made it tingle with wellbeing, especially where his close-fitting briefs caressed his cock. Aroused by this secret pleasure, and not a bit ashamed of his dandyish tendencies, Josh smoothed a hand over his fragrant, freshly washed hair.

On Phobos, where one had to wear a helmet most of the day, there were only two practical hairstyles for men: either cropped to a few millimetres, or worn long and tied back. Josh, always proud of his glossy black curls, naturally sported the latter style, and tonight had bound his 'tail' with a soft fabric tie, easily undone, of course, when the situation demanded it.

Women, in Josh's experience, were extremely susceptible to his long silky hair, and most couldn't keep their fingers out of it. He'd been told again and again how sexy it felt, especially when it brushed his partner's belly or breasts, or lay across her thighs as he sucked her.

This is it then, he thought. He made a discreet thumbs-up sign to his reflection, then pushed open the swing doors to the opulent bar. This is either the biggest night of your life, Josh, or the rip-off to end all rip-offs, he told himself. It could even end up being both.

The remarkable La Selene was subtly lit, and at this comparatively early hour, almost empty. Not more than a dozen couples and a handful of singletons were scattered around the sumptuous yet understated room. The whole place whispered of secrets and screamed of sex, and Josh looked around with a keen curiosity. Was everything true? The things that were said and heard . . .

La Selene, with its spectacular views over the City of Night and the main landing field, had a systemwide and ambiguous reputation. Not only was it a sophisticated and fashionable venue, frequented by glitterati from a variety of milieux, it was also an accepted stomping ground for whores of both sexes: dedicated professionals and enthusiastic part-timers alike. If Pleasurezone wanted to play at cloak and dagger silly buggers, at least they'd chosen the right place.

So . . . he was here and the time was ripe – where were

'they'? And how would they contact him? Sod this for a lark, thought Josh, suddenly angry with his unknown manipulators. I've had enough of all this shot-in-the-dark stuff.

Squaring his shoulders he walked straight to the bar, slid on to a stool and signalled for service. When the barman – a slim youth with a blond crew-cut and disturbingly sharp blue eyes – sidled up, Josh didn't wait to be asked.

'I'm supposed to meet someone here at eight. I don't know if it's a man or a woman, but they sent me this.' He held out the plastic slip with the entwined PL face up.

'Ah yes,' murmured the blond, his handsome face unrevealing, 'you must be Mr Mortimer. You're expected. Someone will be here for you in a moment. May I fix you a drink?'

'Er, yes, okay,' Josh answered, feeling both troubled and faintly aroused by the fact that his identity was known. 'Scotch, please. Make that a double.'

'If I could make a suggestion, sir,' the barman replied unexpectedly, 'you might find a glass of wine more suitable. Your . . . er . . . treatment will be more effective with a clear head. Hard liquor doesn't mix too well with the therapy.'

'Okay then, whatever you say.' Though he couldn't fault the man's discreet manner, Josh felt profoundly shaken. 'I'll have a glass of house white,' he muttered. 'Whatever you've got that's good.'

Hard liquor doesn't mix too well with the therapy . . . What were they going to do to him? As he settled on his seat, his prick jolted to sudden, fierce erection. Caused by fear? Yeah, it had to be. He'd got a stiff on again – an absolute stonker – because he was scared more shitless than he'd ever been in his life.

When the wine arrived, Josh sipped at it gratefully. If he hadn't been warned to the contrary, he'd have drained it down in one and signalled for another. Pleasurezone were going to have a ball with him if he got off on terror. And for some unknown reason, all his usual fantasies had conveniently blanked themselves out, leaving only this diffuse idea of being intimidated – a scenario that was making him harder by the second. He moved uneasily on his stool, tensioning the silk briefs across his cock and secretly masturbating.

Cool it, he admonished himself, realising what his subconscious was up to. Save yourself for the main event, man; you've paid enough. Checking the cubelike, stainless steel chronometer behind the bar, he saw there were still ten minutes to go. Shifting in his seat again, he cut his cock some slack and swivelled round to check out the room behind him.

La Selene consisted of two distinct sections: a long, mirror-backed, L-shaped bar which was bright, glittering and convivial, and a spacious, atmospherically lit area beyond that contained smallish tables for two and intimate, snugly upholstered booths.

Well then, Ms Pleasurezone, are you here yet? he wondered, panning his gaze across the various women in the room – women alone, with men, or with other women. Women sipping cocktails and talking in that low, seductive way that only women could. His mind reminded him that it wasn't forced to be a woman he was meeting, then his balls and soul told him resoundingly it was. But was she here yet? Was she sitting somewhere in the dark or light, biding her time and watching him squirm?

He fixed his eyes on a possible candidate at the other end of the bar. Foxy lady or what? Josh wished to God the sumptuous redhead in question really was the one.

She wasn't young, and she wasn't the sort of woman he would normally have fancied, but after one glimpse he couldn't take his eyes off her. She wore glamour and beauty like an ermine cloak and – he decided suddenly – she was almost certainly a whore. Slender yet magnificently full-breasted, she was draped over her stool like a bolt of silk and sipping diffidently at something rose-pink and icy. Her vaguely preoccupied expression made Josh long to do something that would shake her up, and when she reached for a pistachio nut from one of the many small bowls scattered along the bar, his cock leapt screaming to red alert and his balls jostled in their stretch-silk container.

Josh hadn't wolfwhistled since he was a green kid, but now he only just stopped himself. The unknown woman was wearing a tubular dress of some black sequined stuff, and its straight, strapless top bisected her spectacular bosom at several microns above nipple-height. In stretching for the savoury titbit, she'd nearly caused the gorgeous creamy spheres to tumble out of their precarious confinement, and made Josh, in his hypersexed state, clench his free hand into a fist. It was either that or grab his aching genitals.

This was not, obviously, a common or garden callgirl. With those looks – jade green eyes, lush crimson mouth, near-perfect features and a great mane of pure red curls – she could well be worth the enormous sum that Pleasure-zone were charging him. She was like a lioness who roared of wild, ecstatic and mind-blowing sex, yet she had a classy touch-me-not aura that Josh found irresistibly tantalising. Her gaze flicked idly in his direction, and he couldn't stop himself from smiling at her. The woman nodded almost imperceptibly, but made no move.

Josh Mortimer, you're a berk, he told himself, taking a swig of wine as the gorgeous whore turned away. If she was the one who'd been waiting for him, she'd have come over by now; especially as she seemed to be on good terms with the barman, who was obviously in cahoots with Pleasurezone.

Nope, I won't be enjoying that particular lady tonight, Josh reflected wistfully. But that didn't stop his fantasy muscle from flexing at last. A woman like that would get on top, he decided dreamily, taking a swig of his wine. Mouth, cunt, hands; she'd really *make* a man have it. He'd buy her, expecting a slave, but he'd get a goddess instead – a true-blue dominatrix who'd call all the shots.

Come on, little man, he imagined her saying, let's see it. Let's see you shoot. His fingers itched either to grab his crotch or pick up his glass and toss back the lot regardless of warnings, as she shuffled erotically on her stool, then crossed and recrossed her superb long legs. Slim, delicate ankles, circled by diamante, gave way to strong sleek calves, which in turn were crowned by smooth, biteable knees

11

encased in ultra-sheer nylon. Josh saw those knees now, still stocking-clad but braced against a fur bedspread, on either side of his own brown thighs. *Her* thighs rose in a wide-spread vee above him, crowned by a soft, downy bush of hair of the same almost fluorescent colour that crowned her lovely head. A dripping dew graced those scarlet curls . . . lovejuice that'd oozed spontaneously from a warm naked cunt.

She wanted him; she was a time-hardened whore and yet she wanted him – he, Josh, was the one who'd finally turned her on, made her desire him, and made her glorious quim run river. He saw muscles ripple minutely beneath the fine black mesh that covered her thighs, as slowly, oh, so slowly, that magnificent sex lowered to meet the equally magnificent cock that reared up in tribute.

'Joshua Mortimer?' enquired a soft voice, and Josh knocked over his empty glass in his tumble back to earth. His eyes were still only part-focused, but when he turned, he couldn't stop himself moaning aloud. Not sure whether he was disappointed, confused or scared, he saw that his new companion was *not* the woman his mind had been about to fuck. No, the sequin-clad stunner was still at the far end of the bar, lost in a reverie and munching pistachios. Sitting on the stool next to Josh was an entirely different woman. But a woman who was – if anything – even more alluring, despite the fact she was faceless.

No. Correction. She did have a face, but its beauty – or lack of it – was mostly hidden by a heavy veil of slate-grey lace. This filigree mask was attached to a small felt hat of the same colour which was perched, well forward and pertly angled, on the newcomer's quizzically tilted head.

'Are you okay?' she enquired, and Josh had to admit the voice fitted too. Low and husky, it wasn't hard but had a distinct ring of power. The words were unmuffled; the veil, though effectively obscuring the upper part of the face, left a small but suggestively curved mouth, the lips tinted a clear almost luminous rose, open to his view. Even so, Josh wondered how much she could see.

'Yeah, I'm fine, thanks,' he answered, reaching out to right the glass, which luckily was empty. 'I just got back to Earth. Yesterday.' The qualifier was necessary; he'd been so obviously miles away. 'I'm still getting used to civilisation.' He favoured the veiled woman with a shy smile, and felt a bit more back in himself when she returned it as warmly as her covered face would allow. He wondered what she looked like. Her mouth, on closer inspection, was utterly delectable, with soft dainty lips that would perfectly enclose a good-sized cock like his.

Josh's rambling mind stopped short. She'd addressed him by name . . . *She* was the one he was here to meet.

'You! You're from Pleasurezone,' he accused, appalled, in a detached sort of way, by his own abruptness.

'Yes,' she replied, apparently unruffled, although her face of course revealed little. 'I'm sorry if I've kept you waiting.'

'I . . . I didn't . . . ' He felt unnerved by the continued presence of the veil, 'I thought . . .' His eyes flicked towards the end of the bar, where the lush redhead was now talking softly and earnestly to a new arrival – a slim, hard-faced individual in a startlingly white suit and a matching and rather natty fedora hat. Her pimp?

'Oh, you thought it was Tricksie!' The veiled woman laughed delightfully, and the husky sound seemed to trickle down Josh's spine and pool around his balls. Oh God, this place was just heaving with sexy women! For the moment he abandoned all thought of the quaintly named whore in the distance, and focused on the closer and as yet un-named charmer in front of him.

Though not as pneumatically spectacular as Tricksie, Ms Pleasurezone was equally easy on the eye. Josh's interest, and sexual excitement, jumped a few notches when he realised she was wearing leather. Quite a lot of it. In fact, apart from her whimsical hat, she was dressed entirely in the stuff. A well-cut suit, in a buttersoft hide just a few shades lighter than her veil, skimmed rather than gripped what appeared to be a trimly shaped figure. Though not overtly busty, she had a nice full curve to her leather-covered chest, and a neat nip-in at her waist. The suit-skirt was straightish, hinted at slim but defined hips, and tapered to reveal the second set of exceptionally cute knees he'd seen in ten minutes.

'I'm sure you'd have had a very, shall we say, *pleasant* evening with her,' his companion said, dragging Josh's attention back to deep pink lips and the even white teeth they framed. 'She's not called Tricksie for nothing. But it's my expertise you've paid for.' An even pinker tongue flicked impishly at the rosy lips, and the whole delicious mouth formed into one of the most sensual smiles Josh had ever seen.

Lord, that naughty tonguetip, that soft, moist pinkness! Josh swallowed and shifted on his stool again. He tried to get a grip on himself.

'Come along, Josh. It is Josh, isn't it?' his enigmatic partner enquired. Then, as if reading his mind, she went on: 'We'll get a drink, grab a booth, and I'll tell you what's in store for you.'

'Is that wise? The drink I mean. He – ' Josh nodded in the direction of the blond doyen of the bar. 'He said I shouldn't have too much booze.'

'Wine's okay. Quite beneficial in fact,' the woman replied, signalling for the beverage in question. 'It's only hard spirits that are a problem. They impair the mental function rather too much for our purpose.' With the wine ordered, she extended a hand – gloved in pearl-grey leather, Josh noted with a genital throb – towards a nearby but secluded booth. 'We'll sit there, shall we?'

Josh was suspended between two realities as he followed her away from the bar. Half his attention was on the grey-clad bottom, which was moving like a well-oiled machine just a couple of yards in front of him. She had a beautiful walk, gently syncopated but not obvious, her easy sensuality facilitated by elegant but not over-high heels. He noticed, too, that she was fairly tall and had strange but rather lovely hair. It cascaded in a long thick sheaf down her back, its colour a brindle of auburn, rich brown, and subtle shades of muted blonde. These details he observed with the part of him that wasn't yowling with the need to jump her immediately.

It was those gloves. His prick was twitching, and he

could almost feel the kiss of that superfine hide on his stiff, sensitised shaft. Pushing both hands into his pockets, he tented the silk cloth of his trousers as much as he was able, and prayed that that, and the firm stretchy cling of his underpants, would keep him decent. It was a good job the booth area was fairly dark.

He let out his held breath inaudibly as he slid into the booth and faced his leather-clad enigma. 'Well, lady, you know my name. Who the hell are you?'

'Isis,' she answered, her smile open as she held out her gloved hand in formal greeting.

Josh accepted her hand gingerly, glad of the table to hide the leather's effect on his prick. 'Nobody could be called Isis. What is it? Some kind of code name?'

'No,' she replied blithely. 'I really am called Isis. My mother was something of an egyptophile . . . If I'd been a boy I'd be Rameses.'

The wine was served. 'Okay, then, I'll buy that. But what's your surname?'

Isis grinned and supplied her second name. It was so unlikely that Josh laughed out loud and shook his head.

She nodded, still grinning.

'All right, I believe you,' Josh replied, still shaking his head, but enjoying the new relaxation between them. 'But I'll just call you Isis, if that's okay by you?'

She nodded again, and suddenly, urgently, Josh had to see her face. Telepathy worked again and Isis raised her gloved hands to the swathe of grey lace. Almost in slo-mo, the delicately scalloped edge was lifted.

'Oh Christ!' Josh gasped before judgement could stop him. 'Oh Christ, I'm sorry . . .' He looked away for a second, felt remorse for doing so, then faced her again, reaching compulsively for his glass.

'No, it's me who should be sorry,' Isis said soberly. 'I tend to have this effect on people. I should have warned you.'

Isis was a startlingly beautiful woman. In part . . .

On the right side of her face she had an immaculate ivory complexion, an exquisite high-sweeping cheekbone and a

15

huge, long-lashed sable-gold eye. The left side of her face had the same underlying structure, and indeed was perfectly symmetrical with the right . . . But it was also half covered with a large, sprawling wine-coloured scar which extended from her delicately arched brow to the soft dimple that bracketed her mouth. The whole disfigurement had a vaguely floral shape – like an orchid, Josh's stunned brain suggested, or maybe even a cunt? – and in the socket it encircled was an eye of muddy red-streaked brown.

'I was in a laboratory accident. Years ago, when I was in Uni – ' Isis had softly anticipated his questions. 'I'll pop the veil down again if it bothers you. But I don't know which is worse, trying to talk to someone who can see this,' she touched leather to scar-tissue, 'or someone who can't. I'm used to it, of course, but that first oh-God-she's-a-monster moment still gets to me sometimes . . .' Her slim, gloved fingers rose towards her hat, ready to tweak the veil back into place.

'No,' Josh said firmly, and before he'd realised what he was doing, he'd gripped her wrist and gently brought her hand back down again. It dawned on him that he'd like to keep hold of that hand. She's ripping twenty thousand credits off you! he told himself. Carefully, he let her go.

'Are you sure?' she asked doubtfully, disbelief in her peculiar non-matching eyes.

'Yeah.' Josh nodded emphatically, 'It's not really so bad, you know . . . Not when you look at it properly. It reminds me of – ' He blushed pre-pubescently. 'Of something,' he finished lamely.

Isis threw back her head, her hair tossing luxuriantly, and laughed. It was a rich, sexy gurgle that made her bizarre face crinkle enchantingly and sent a frisson of pleasure through Josh's still-tense cock.

'Don't worry,' she said, still smirking, 'You're not the first to notice that rather interesting resemblance. And some of my closer friends have told me it's actually quite a good likeness.'

Josh's flesh pulsed in his pants. It was true. Isis was outrageously desirable. Apart from her scar – even because

16

of it – she was thrilling and luscious in all the ways he liked best. As she'd just pointed out, when viewed by the enlightened, her stigma was enough to rouse even the most jaded sexual palate.

As if fielding some unheard cue, Isis set down her glass with an attention-grabbing tap and looked Josh squarely in the eyes.

'Okay then, Josh,' she said. The change was only just perceptible, but the new power and confidence of her voice played a tune along Josh's aroused shaft and made the juices simmer in his balls. He sat motionless and rapt, his hormones in turmoil.

'Now that we've got my face out of the way, and what may, or may not, be etched upon it, I think it's time to talk Pleasurezone.'

'Pleasurezone?'

'The reason you're here!' Lights danced in her eyes: like flecks of gold the normal one, a muzzy, muted radiance in the flawed orb.

'You must have questions.' She reached for her wineglass and took a small sip. A droplet hovered on her rosy lower lip, and that sweet little tongue darted out to catch it. All Josh wanted at this moment – in spite of the cash he'd outlaid for his 'something different' – was to go somewhere and make it with this strange, scarred woman. He wanted to peel away the leather and explore the promise within, part those long, shapely thighs and discover if her cunt was as pink as her nimble tongue, if the folds there were as pronounced and flowerlike as the schematic on her left cheek suggested.

'Josh! If this is a fantasy, let's hear it,' she said sharply, as if recognising a fugue when she saw one. 'It could be a useful opener for us.'

'No, it wasn't,' he lied, wanting her, wanting to submit to her, yet resisting the very same urge. Still fighting both her and the compulsion, he blurted out the first stupid thing that came into his head. 'I was just wondering if I'll actually get laid tonight?'

Isis's soft laugh twinkled in the air. 'Now that's a tricky

question. You may well believe you're getting laid . . .'
Her smile broadened in relation to the puzzlement that
crimped Josh's brow. 'And you can have straight sex via
Pleasurezone, as yourself, if that's what you want. But
don't you think it'd be a waste? A handsome guy like you,'
her eyes flicked all-encompassingly over him, 'can get a
simple fuck without spending a cent . . . And if it was the
concept of "buying" that turned you on, you could have
the night of your life with friend Tricksie over there. For
a fraction of what you're paying us. Although – ' Isis
shrugged, 'straight sex is probably the last thing she'd
expect you to ask *her* for.'

Josh's mind was reeling. He felt like a gauche schoolboy,
pathetically randy in the face of this strange woman before
him – a woman who'd been tempered by suffering and
made as fine and steely as her cool grey suit. He glanced
towards the end of the bar, and the other woman. He'd
probably be safer with the whore.

'What do you mean by "believe I'll get laid" . . . and
"as myself"?' He already half knew the answer.

'Hah! I just knew it was in you,' Isis replied, lacing her
gloved fingers and studying him obliquely, sound cheek
leading. 'Only the brave, the bold, the curious, and the
astronomically horny would answer such a preposterous
advert as ours. To have committed yourself already proves
you want far more than straightforward sexual gratification.'

'What do you mean?'

'Well, with us you can have straight sex, or indeed any
other kind of sex, but the interesting thing about Pleasurezone is – ' she paused, tweaking out the tension, 'you can
have it as someone else. Think about it,' she went on. 'You
can step outside your own mind, your own bias, your own
inhibitions. You can be turned on by other turn-ons, need
other needs. You can understand the divine and the bizarre.
Be somebody else, Josh, and feel *their* pleasure. Do you
think you can handle that?'

2 Into the Pleasurezone

Well, could he?

Twenty minutes and another glass of wine later, Josh still wasn't sure. The only thing he did know was that the prospect of even *trying* to 'handle it' was making him randier than ever. That and the fact he'd do just about anything to get closer to Isis. Everything about her was driving him crazy, to the extent he was prepared to trust his living psyche into her slender leather-gloved hands – not to mention his horny male body, if he got half a chance.

And he still didn't understand what she was going to do to him . . .

Without being immodest, Josh was proud of his high IQ. But he also knew that as a mining engineer, his intelligence was of necessity the practical variety. He was a nuts-and-bolts man, an expert with machine tolerances and on-line troubleshooting. So, in spite of his reading, when Isis started throwing 'brain architecture' 'neural resonance' and 'enforced perception shifts' at him, he had to admit she'd lost him. He understood her moist, rosy mouth quite perfectly, but the incomprehensible psychotechnical jargon that came out of it? No way!

'Okay, I'm obviously not as smart as either of us thinks I am.' He shrugged hopelessly. 'I'll have the idiot's version, please.'

'You're no fool, Josh,' Isis replied, her voice light but serious, 'but the bottom line – '

Suddenly she stopped, pressed her gloved fingers to her lips and smothered an almost schoolgirlish giggle. 'The

19

bottom line is . . . with the sensory re-creator we can make your fantasies real.'

'So it's just a kind of glorified dream machine?'

'Oh no, Josh, it's more than that. As far as you're concerned, it'll all *happen*. Your brain will receive the same messages, both physical and emotional, that it would if the event were actually occurring . . . And you have the choice of three different modes. Either selecting and inducing your own fantasies, living through a pre-programmed, pre-recorded scenario, or what we call an "F & F" . . . which is where we provide the framework but your subconscious directs the action with free choice.' She was warming to her theme now, her voice sparkling, a slight blush rising in the unmarked side of her face. Josh was almost certain she was aroused. 'The last one is the most popular, but whichever you choose, Josh, to you it'll be real.'

'Okay then, let's do it.' Josh sighed. Decision at last. He'd been enjoying Isis's subtle domination of him – *and* the flexing of her obviously prodigious intellect – but it was time for things to get physical. How physical he wasn't sure . . . but his cock hoped very!

'So what happens to my body while my grey cells are getting their rocks off?' he asked casually as they rose, and once again, Isis led the way, 'I suppose I just lie there in a trance.' The prospect offered little comfort to Josh's aching prick, and in spite of his attempts to cool it, the sex-fiend inside the civilised man was still clamouring to get his end away.

'I suppose you could say that,' she said huskily. Her grin was what could only be described as evil, and its effect on her scar was devastating, given what that scar reminded him of. 'You'll certainly have to lie back and think of something.' She laughed that soft foreboding laugh again and Josh felt scareder and stiffer in about equal proportions.

'Let's not hang about then,' he snapped, embarrassed by Isis's slow perusal of his groin.

'Don't worry, Joshua,' she went on, investing his full Christian name with a heavy sensual emphasis, 'you won't be disappointed. In any department. That I can promise you.' Josh felt himself drowning, adrift on the waves of sex pouring out of her. 'Come on. This way,' she commanded, swirling again and leading Josh towards the far end of the room.

To boldly go! he thought half hysterically as Isis pushed open a door concealed in the red baize back wall of the spacious room. Had Captain Kirk ever got this hard being ordered around by women? Josh doubted it. And he doubted too whether the characters in that classic series had ever had an adventure as weird and wonderful as he was about to have . . .

Once through the secret door, they entered an austere white-painted corridor with a second door at its far end – stainless steel this time with only a digital lock to relieve its shiny featurelessness.

Acutely conscious of his aching cock, Josh tried to watch two things at once: Isis's deft manipulation of the control panel, and her sultry swaying bottom in its grey leather casing. She seemed to be one of those people who had a head full of music all the time, and her feet were tapping the floor as her fingers tapped out the entry code.

Josh had a sudden overwhelming urge to see her body, a stronger need by far than anything he'd felt since coming home. He'd been wracked by lust for women as a sex since the moment he'd touched down, but right now the whole boiling lot of it focused on this slim, grey-clad doctor with her strange scarred face and her sensually delectable shape.

Was she physically involved with the process ahead? Would she touch him? Would he touch her? The steel door sprang open and Isis gestured for him to follow her.

Inside was a vestibule as bland as the corridor, apart from a row of coloured prints on the wall. Josh registered that they were both erotic and oriental; Shunga most likely, the explicitly sexual ancient Japanese art. He would've liked to have lingered and studied them – to check out the back-breakingly gymnastic positions – but Isis was already half-way through another door.

'Wait in here a moment, please,' she said briskly, and ushered him into a luxuriously appointed room that seemed

21

part lounge and part library – all furnished in creams, browns and beiges.

'Make yourself comfortable and I'll bring you something to relax you. Dip into anything that takes your fancy. There's books, magazines, prints, holovids. A lot of clients find that when they actually get here their fantasy inspirations desert them, so we keep a selection of erotica as triggers.'

As she spoke, Isis reached behind her head and pulled out the pins that held her hat. Her thick, vari-coloured waves tumbled forward over her shoulders, and Josh shuddered violently, his prick hardening to iron. His bedmates weren't the only ones turned on by long hair against their skin.

'I won't be a second.' She smiled faintly and left him alone in the strange and sumptuous waiting room. Josh flopped down on to the nearest settee and stared blindly at the heap of leather-covered volumes on the coffee table in front of him.

'She's all different,' he murmured to himself. It'd been like watching a slow, subtle metamorphosis, from the cautious victim who'd been scared to lift her veil to a seasoned sexual professional in total command of her own exotic domain. She's fabulous, he thought, picking up the nearest volume on the table. Who needs mucky books? I've found *my* fantasy.

Nevertheless, the connoisseur inside him was intrigued by what seemed to be a heavy hide-backed photograph album – a ridiculous collector's anachronism in an age of electronic images. The book's cover was unmarked but inside was a series of prints depicting lesbian lovemaking: the first few quite gentle and innocuous, but getting gradually more explicit as the pages passed.

The artwork was superb and detailed, and Josh caught his breath at the sight of a beautiful oriental girl draped over a chaise longue, her slim olive thighs widely apart as a Junoesque blonde licked delicately at her glistening cunt. The genital detail was exquisite, but Josh found himself even more stirred by the ecstatic expressions on the women's faces. They were totally out of it, completely absorbed in the pleasure they were sharing, and not for the first time, Josh wondered what it was like to be a woman who wanted a woman. In his mind he saw Isis's small, elfin tongue probe Tricksie's crimson bush . . .

'Beautiful, aren't they?' said Isis, and Josh nearly jumped through the roof. He'd never heard her return.

'Er . . . yes,' he muttered, snapping the book shut and focusing on Isis and what she was holding out to him: an inch of amber-coloured fluid in a small cut-glass goblet.

'I thought I wasn't supposed to have spirits,' Josh said, more interested in her hand, suddenly, than the glass it held. At first he'd thought she was wearing pink lace gloves, but as he looked more closely he saw that the network of whorls and lines was actually on her skin.

'Another leftover from my accident,' she commented crisply, 'but there's not much more. My hands and face caught the worst of it. Now come on, drink up. You're the one that wants to get on with it.'

'What is it?' he asked, taking the goblet and swirling its contents. The tawny fluid clung ominously to the glass.

'An inhibition-buster,' she answered with a grin. 'And don't worry, it's made from all natural ingredients. It's to help you take the brakes off.'

'Are you licensed to dish out drugs?' Josh was worried now. Nothing was turning out quite as he'd expected.

'Don't worry.' She touched her fingers suddenly to his cheek. The skin of her hands was soft, warm and smooth; there was no tactile evidence of the scarring. 'You can trust me, I'm a doctor.'

'Oh, for crying out loud!'

'No, seriously, I am,' Isis protested. 'I'm an MD. I majored in psychosexual medicine.'

He believed her, although it didn't ease his suspicions about the gungy-looking drink. The first sip was thick and herby tasting, slightly bitter but not unpleasant. It warmed his gullet as he tossed it down, and though he was probably imagining things, he immediately felt less uptight. Handing the glass back, he returned Isis's smile.

'Okay then, I want you to relax and get into the mood,' she said, and Josh could've sworn she was flirting. 'Take off your jacket and tie, choose something to look at or watch, and lie on the settee. Let the ideas come, but don't force anything. Just take it easy, absorb the images, masturbate if you want to. But if you can't fix on a specific act or event, don't worry. That's what usually happens the first time. It's a good thing really. With no particular requirements from you, we can start you with one of our set pieces. Something that'll *really* show you what we can do.'

'What do you mean?' Josh wondered why he'd stopped being worried. He felt no alarm whatsoever now, just a loose, mellow glow.

'You'll see,' she said quietly. 'Now get in the groove while I set things up.'

With that she left him to it. He'd have considered following her but he'd heard the faint click of a lock.

Licking his lips he thought about the potion she'd given him. Was it an aphrodisiac? It'd certainly had some kind of effect on him. He felt curious about what awaited him, but in a gentle, spaced-out sort of way. There was no way to gauge if it'd made him any randier . . . he'd been rock hard since the moment he'd set eyes on Isis.

Masturbate, she'd said. The cheeky cow! At least she could've stayed around and done it for him. He imagined the feel of those lace-patterned hands on his cock. They were slender, elegant hands; they looked as if she could take a man to heaven and back with them. His flesh twitched at the very thought of it. Would she be rough or gentle with him? Would she tease him for hours with featherlight touches? Work the whole surface of his tool into a state of agonising sensitivity? Or would she be swift and clinical, bring him straight to ejaculation with ruthless scientific precision? Assess the number of spurts against a carefully researched norm? Measure the volume and consistency of his spunk . . . Oh God, he really didn't care, just as long as she touched him . . . For the first time in his life, Josh was ready to beg a woman to make him come.

He thought about orgasm . . .

Christ, he really needed to have one. But if he was locked in some kind of trance, what the hell would it be like? A glorious three-dee, electronic wet dream with spunk all over the ceiling? Or would he wake up at the point of climax and maybe shoot into Isis's waiting hand? Whichever it was, the need was getting desperate; his prick was so stiff now it was really hurting. He looked down and saw the mass of it bulging behind his zip.

Comfortable as he could be, Josh reached out for one of the leather-covered books and flipped it open.

Bondage.

It hit him in a series of stark, high-definition images of bodies in torment. A woman, obscenely spread-eagled and gagged, was held immobile in an array of leather and steel. A man was remorsely forcing a giant prosthetic phallus into her rectum and simultaneously frigging her clitoris. Juices glinted wetly on every detail of her shaven cunt: her clit enormous, knoblike and protruding, her anus stretched open several unbelievable inches. Shocked in spite of himself, Josh wriggled in his seat. There was something both repellent and captivating in the image, and he had an urgent need to understand it, to know the minds of both the man and woman. Her eyes were wide with humiliation and fear, yet her quim was dripping; his face was cool, remote, disinterested. For whose benefit was the scene being played?

He flipped through a few similar prints and the ache in his prick got both better and worse. He flung the book aside in favour of another. His prick was a jumping, steaming rod now, dancing in his pants. Isis's damned jungle juice was driving him crazy. Either that or he was a closet bondage freak . . . .

The next selection was more romantic, a selection of classic, stylised themes. A man and woman fucking naked in a forest glade; a samurai warrior parting the robe of an exquisite geisha; a dangerous liaison between a courtier and a half-disrobed queen.

Was this a book for female clients, Josh wondered suddenly. Did Pleasurezone *have* any female clients? Most of the women he'd known were like Julia. They liked the sexual shallows, the here and now of safe, straight positions and manageable thrills. There must be women who went in at the erotic deep end, but surely they were a minority? As a sex they were generally too practical and realistic to need or want a magical mystery tour.

Now here's an oldie but goodie, he thought, turning the page. The picture showed another well-loved fantasy. 'The Seraglio', at a guess. A young woman lay on a brocade-covered divan, almost swooning from the caresses of two other women, who were sliding aside her diaphanous robes and preparing her, it seemed, for the attentions of a prince of some kind. This bearded lord stood to one side, hand on cock, clearly getting off on the sight of the innocent young girl being primed for him. Who wouldn't? thought Josh with feeling. And the girl was in raptures too, her breast being suckled by a giant negress and her cuntlips carefully parted by a slender, naked houri with brightly hennaed hair.

'Layla and the Prince. Do you like it?' said a soft voice beside him, and Josh realised that once again, Isis had snuck in and caught him unawares.

'Yes, I do,' said Josh decisively. He loved it. He'd always fancied a harem. But when he looked up at Isis, he wondered if another of his long-time fantasies was coming true. It was, after all, every man's perennial yen to have it off with a nurse . . .

Isis had shed her leather suit and now wore a white overall in classic medical white. A doctor's garb, he realised, not a nurse's; and although it was just a simple tunic style, careful darting made the thin white cloth skim faithfully over what Josh suspected was a perfect figure. Slim but curvy; long legs; fine waist; high, rounded, but not too enormous breasts. The plain but prick-teasing garment had a tiny tab collar and ended just above the knee; and on her feet, Isis wore a pair of white canvas flatties. Her thick, brindled hair was tied back in a loose ponytail, and perched right on the end of her nose was a pair of metal-rimmed half spectacles.

Josh blinked, then stared. She was Frankenstein's naughty night nurse, the mad professor, and utterly gorgeous. He'd never wanted a woman more.

'This is an artist's impression of one of our "set pieces",' she said, taking the book from Josh and studying it as if she'd never seen it before. 'Care to try it? It's an excellent example, a *tour de force*, though I say it myself.'

'Why not?' Josh replied, leaping lightly to his feet, revitalised and eager to get stuck in. Isis could be the handmaiden to his prince. 'Any chance of having you in this sex dream of mine?' he said huskily, reaching towards her. Good God, he thought, that stuff was dynamite! He could've thrown her against the wall and shagged her where she stood. Isis evaded him nimbly and said nothing.

Did she have panties on under that cute little smock? Josh did a quick survey. There were no lines showing through, no evidence of lingerie. It'd be a simple matter to slide up the hem, glide his hand up her thigh, slip it into her crotch . . .

'Naughty, naughty!' she admonished, dancing out of his reach as he lunged forward, *'I'm* not what you're here for. I'm just the technician. And to answer your question, Josh – ' She rubbed her hands in a businesslike manner, and Josh suddenly realised she was wearing a pair of fine rubber gloves. Something inside him went 'flip', and if his cock had had a voice it would've whimpered. Oh God, not rubber as well!

Oblivious, Isis went on, 'It's too disruptive for clients to have me in their fantasies. They have to have faith in my expertise, put themselves in my hands, literally. To picture me in some . . . some possibly subjugated situation would undermine my authority and destroy their trust. Surely you see that?'

'Not really,' said Josh, advancing again. 'And anyway,

how do you stop me dreaming you up in one of these so-called free-choice scenarios?'

'Because, as I've already told you – although you obviously weren't listening – in the Pleasurezone, you're not actually dreaming. You're perceiving an induced reality. The re-creator reads your brain patterns and creates the scenario from the data it receives, and it's programmed to lock out any images of me. So there!'

'You're a mean cow, Isis.' He plunged forward and made a grab at her. Caught unawares, she couldn't stop him. He ran a rapid, exploring hand down her body and gleaned a crumb of sexual comfort. Her breast was firm and proud to the touch, with a nipple, he realised triumphantly, that was hard as a nut. She did fancy him after all!

'Get off, you idiot,' she said sharply, dashing away his fondling hand. 'Look, shall we get on with what you came here for? Or are you only interested in groping? If you don't want the treatment, we'll quit now and I'll have your money transferred back to you.'

Chastened, but still wanting her, Josh stepped back. 'Yes, ma'am,' he said facetiously. 'I'll behave myself.'

'Good. Now, do you see that door over there?' She pointed to one of several doors that opened off the lounge area. 'Behind it you'll find a bathroom. Go in, strip off all your clothes from the waist down and empty your bladder and bowels. When you've done, go through the other door beyond and I'll be waiting for you.'

'I beg your pardon?' Josh was flabbergasted. What the hell was going on? She'd vetoed any kind of sexplay between them, and now she was telling him she wanted to see his dick hanging out! And what the hell was all that about emptying his bladder and bowels?

'You heard what I said,' she replied, her voice like tensile steel.

'Okay. But why do I need to . . . to strip and . . . and everything? I thought the action was all up here.' He tapped a finger to his sweating brow.

'Some of it is,' Isis said, coming close again now he'd ceded control to her, 'but for the experience to be complete,

28

there has to be action down here too.' She reached out and closed her slim fingers on his cock, delicately testing its width and solidity through the cloth of his trousers. Josh groaned and she gave him an old-fashioned look over the top of her glasses, mischief bright in both her good eye and bad.

'Don't worry, Josh,' she murmured seductively. 'It'll all be worth it, I promise. Now let's get to it, shall we?'

She gave his shaft one last squeeze – quite lovingly, he thought through his daze – then let him go and left him to it.

The bathroom was also beautifully appointed, but as Josh followed Isis's instructions he was too befuddled to appreciate it. At first his erection made it difficult to piss, but eventually he calmed down enough to get a stream. He'd no problem with his bowels, but wondered, as he sat staring at his own bare feet, why the hell it was all necessary.

She's going to handle me somehow, he decided, loving the idea. He thought of those long fingers touching him – his bare skin this time, not through layers of silk – and smiled. Then, scrupulously, he washed himself both fore and aft, with his penis back at attention almost before he'd begun . . .

'You might change your mind, lady, when you see this,' he observed smugly to himself as he dried his smooth velvety shaft. It looked red and fierce as he held it against the fluffy white towelling: like a weapon, a tool, a rampant pussy-stuffing club. It was no use being modest. He'd a good sound cock on him; every woman he'd ever been with had praised it and he knew they were right. There was no way the good doctor could ignore its charm.

He gave himself an extra little rub, although he knew he was just about as stiff as a man could ever be; then, feeling a burst of ridiculously juvenile braggadocio, he stepped forward and opened the door.

The room beyond was smaller and more intimate than he'd expected, and seemed almost filled by a long, white, leather-upholstered couch.

The cradle of fantasy, thought Josh whimsically as he took in its single thick central pedestal and, behind and to the side of where the client – victim? – laid his head, a small bank of electronic gadgetry. He saw monitors, digital readouts, a disk drive of some sort, and – at both the head of the couch and underneath – coils of fine wiring. Isis was sitting on a tall stool, tapping busily at a keyboard, but at the sound of his arrival, she turned around.

She didn't say anything immediately, but took a long look at his swaying erection.

'Good,' she said with a slight smile.

Good? Was that all? Josh's ego deflated, but oddly his prick grew even stiffer. Of course, I forgot, he thought wryly. I get off on humiliation, don't I? He'd learnt more about his sexual psyche in the last hour than in the whole of the rest of his life.

'Okay, hop on the couch,' Isis said briskly. 'Are you feeling comfortable?'

Josh took a moment before replying. The couch had lowered to the perfect height for him to get on it, and as he did so, he noticed that its shape was moulded slightly, and that while the upper part was made in one whole piece, the lower half – from approximately where the base of the spine would rest – was made of two separate but presently flush panels. Unease coiled in Josh's belly as he lay down on the warm leather, and the whole structure rose again, purring almost inaudibly to a height that was ominously convenient for Isis's reach.

'I feel great, thank you,' he murmured airily. 'I've got a stiffy on that's killing me, but apart from that I've never felt better.'

'Fine,' Isis replied, ignoring the sarcasm, 'but what I meant was, have you emptied yourself?'

'Yes, ma'am, I'm a vacuum. What's the problem? Am I going to have so much fun I'll shit myself?'

'I suppose you could,' said Isis consideringly, dropping from her stool to stand beside him, 'but it's simply that we don't want any minor discomforts to spoil things, do we? Shuffle down a bit, please.' Josh complied, and as he did

30

so, Isis took him firmly by the hips, and carefully eased his buttocks into the soft leather indentations. She seemed oblivious to the pulsing erection so close to her rubber-clad hands; but Josh couldn't take his eyes off it. He watched it bobbing obscenely as Isis unbuttoned his shirt and folded it back on either side of his body. Easing the spare material from under his arse, she tucked it neatly beneath the small of his back. The leather couch seemed to kiss the cheeks of his bottom and he could feel the divide beneath his anus. His disquiet grew.

Machinery whirred again, and padded armrests rose up beside the body of the couch. Isis took Josh's wrists – first one, then the other – and placed them on the rests as if he were a rag-doll.

'Now then,' she said in a soft, authoritative voice, 'I'm going to position the sensory transceivers on your body, and as they're very precise and delicate, it's best that I strap you in position too. Whoah! Don't go ballistic.' She pushed down on Josh's chest as he started to rise, 'It's for your own good. You want to get the best out of this, don't you?'

'Yes, yes, I do,' cried Josh, not knowing whether to be angry or excited. He opted for both. 'I've paid good money for this, and I didn't bargain for being strapped in a glorified dentist's chair.'

'Easy, easy,' crooned Isis, coaxing his arms back on to the rests, stroking his wrists and forearms, making soothing little patterns on his hot skin, then suddenly and shockingly clipping on the restraints with a speed that left him breathless. The cuffs were steel, Josh noted in wondering horror, though lined with a feather-soft felt; and as he absorbed the impact of this first set of bonds, Isis ran her latex-clad fingers the entire length of his torso – chest, waist, hips – then on and down his leg to his right ankle. Before he had time to protest again, the foot was locked firmly in place, and, that one dealt with, she walked quickly around the couch and secured the other.

Josh closed his eyes, but behind them, shockingly, was the image he'd seen earlier – the spread-eagled woman in erotic bondage – and several clues slotted neatly and

31

awesomely into place. Empty your bowels, she'd said. No discomfort to spoil the experience. And notice how meticulously she'd folded his shirt out of the way . . . The division in the lower part of the couch assumed a dreadful significance.

'Omigod! What're you going to do to me?' He was appalled by the high whining note in his own voice. Where was the suave sophisticated Josh Mortimer now? The criminally smooth ladykiller who always took control? His eyes flew open but Isis was busy with her computer array and pretending, he suspected, not to have heard him.

'Are you listening? What're you going to do to me?'

'I think you've probably worked that out by now, Joshua,' she replied, turning away from her mystic calculations. 'Or at least some of it.'

'Maybe I have,' Josh replied, surly with confusion and fear, 'but I think I've paid enough for you to tell me.'

'Quite true,' she remarked amiably. 'So here it is. The next step is to position the transceivers on your body, the sensors that both receive information and transmit stimulation. Pleasurable stimulation, Josh, and for maximum sensation we go right to your pleasure centres to apply it. The brain, of course, is the primary sex organ and the main message goes there. But we'll also be working elsewhere. You being a man, we'll be applying direct stimulation to your prostate gland and the head of your penis.'

'Oh God.'

'I shouldn't worry, Josh. You could well end up believing you're God,' she murmured, turning back to her keyboard and punching in a code. The couch's mechanisms whirred again and Josh felt the lower half of his body tilting upwards and curving inwards. His prick seemed to dance before his eyes, stiffer and redder than it'd ever been, a little moisture already oozing from the tip. Isis still seemed unimpressed by its rigid magnificence, though, as she pressed one gloved hand flat on his belly to force his bottom right into the snugly shaped hollows of the leather seat.

'Relax, Josh,' she whispered in his ear, then reached out with her free hand to key in another command.

Josh moaned, then bit his lip as the cradling leather seemed to grip his arse-cheeks, then slowly but firmly eased them apart. The machine's soft purr and his own gasping breath were the loudest sounds in the universe. The couch's inexorable division seemed to go on and on until his legs and his thighs were widely splayed and the twin mounds of his bottom were almost unbelievably stretched apart.

'Relax, Josh,' she repeated, the words whispering in the cool empty air beneath his trembling anus. Josh closed his eyes tightly, trying to deny what was happening and shut out the sensations invading him. He'd never felt more vulnerable, yet the stark exposure was both exhilarating and voluptuous. And even though he knew now what was going to happen, he still jumped with shock as Isis touched a soft cool gel to his arsehole. He twitched, bit even deeper into his lower lip, and tossed his head as she slathered on more of the slippery scented substance, and worked a large dollop of it right inside him.

'Easy now, easy now,' she whispered, her lips close to his ear and mercifully masking the other small sounds. 'Relax again. More . . . Let yourself go, Josh . . . Open, sweetheart . . . Let yourself open up . . . That's it, my Josh, let it in . . .'

Something firm, smooth and rounded was pressing itself into Josh's rectum. Pressing, pressing, pressing; not cruel yet not kind, it moved remorselessly through the muscle-ring, stretching and opening. It felt huge, gigantic, shockingly good as it pushed in and in, filling him and distending the whole of his consciousness.

'Oh God, oh God, oh God,' he whispered through parched lips. This penetration suddenly seemed as if it were the whole of his life, the only thing that'd ever happened, ever mattered. He wanted to weep, and welcome the intruder in his bottom, while the same muscles that embraced it sought – automatically – to expel it.

'Oh Christ, I'm going to shit . . .'

'No, you're not,' said Isis firmly from somewhere behind his head. She'd done with coaxing him now, it seemed, and Josh felt suddenly and ridiculously frightened. 'It's just your nerve ends telling lies. And I don't know why you're making such a fuss. Surely you've felt anal penetration before?'

'Just what the hell do you think I am?' he demanded, twisting to try and see her, then thinking better of it. Every slight movement reminded him of the phallic object lodged in his bowel, and of the unacceptably delicious sensation of being stretched and invaded in the most intimate and demeaning way.

'What I think you are, Josh,' she said with slight impatience as if talking to a stubborn child, 'is a sexy and imaginative man. A man who's done everything and had everything done to him . . . Why else would you be here?' She moved around into his field of view, adjusting the probe with a gentle impersonal touch that made him feel more exposed than ever and set his prick pulsating unbearably.

He moved uneasily, hating himself for enjoying the sensations it brought. He wanted desperately to touch himself, but his bonds prevented it. He wished that she'd touch him. But she'd turned away to monitor the equipment, as if indifferent to his hugely straining erection. Moving again, and biting down on the resulting moan, Josh wished he could be indifferent to it; but strapped as he was, it reared up at him – in the centre of his field of view – and he couldn't seem to look anywhere else.

'There was once . . .'

Astounded, he heard his own hoarse voice, 'I was just a kid. I didn't want to . . . But I just couldn't seem to help myself . . .'

'What was it?' she asked, coming close again, standing by his head, smoothing back a lock of sweaty hair with infinite gentleness. He was reminded irresistibly of a nurse again, or a priestess, or a mother. To his horror, he felt he might burst into tears. 'What did you have inside you, Josh? A dildo or a man?'

'A man . . .' he whispered brokenly, remembering an experience quite unlike this controlled, clinical penetration. It'd hurt, it'd been a rough buggering and later he'd bled. But . . .

34

'Did you enjoy him?' she persisted quietly.

'Yes,' he croaked, feeling utterly weak and unmanned in spite of the monumental hard-on swaying before his eyes, 'Yes, goddam you. He tore my arse and fucked me and I loved every minute of it.'

'Well then.' Her voice was no-nonsense; the gentle confessional moment was over. 'If you'll just relax into the feeling, you'll enjoy the probe.'

'How the hell would you know?'

'Tut tut, Josh. What kind of therapist would I be if I hadn't tried the treatment myself?' she asked, slanting a sideways glance at him as she fiddled with a small wire-clad gadget attached to the console at the side of the couch. 'Of course I've had a transceiver in my arse. And one in my vagina at the same time. Now will you stop complaining?'

Josh closed his eyes, his prick leaping again as he saw Isis strapped to this same couch, nude, legs wide open, thighs twitching, dildoes protruding from both orifices . . . Wires trailed obscenely, and he could almost see fluid glistening on her clitoris and labia . . .

'Holy shit,' he shouted, feeling her fingers enclose the tip of his penis. Bare fingers this time. Though he hadn't heard the action, she must've shed her gloves now she'd finished handling his backside. His body rose involuntarily, only to fall back and lodge the probe more deeply in his rectum. The sensations were incredible! The wicked thing seemed to swell inside him, stretching his anus exquisitely. His balls pulsed, rose . . . His prick was on fire, a rod of iron waving and throbbing . . .

'I think I'm going to come,' he moaned, feeling pathetic and completely out of control.

'No problem,' said Isis, easing what seemed to be a small stretchy cuff over the circumcised knob of his penis. He hissed between his teeth, feeling the pleasure roil, then subside as the delicate grip controlled his impending orgasm. 'You'll probably come several times before this is over,' she murmured conversationally, 'and the majority of clients come at least once before they go under.'

Go under? thought Josh dazedly, then remembered that

this fabulous trial was simply a means to an end. Lying semi-naked with wires attached to his prick and a gigantic prod rammed up his backside seemed like hysterically good value already. He turned slowly towards Isis, and his languor dispelled when he saw her priming a small hypodermic.

'What the hell's that?' he demanded, and troubled by the idea of more drugs, he pressed himself down on to the probe in a bizarre yearning for comfort. It jostled gently inside him and he sighed with relief.

'You do like that, don't you?' Isis commented as she applied an antiseptic swab to his forearm, peering at him over the rim of her glasses.

'Of course I do, you sadist,' he snarled. 'But I still want to know what's in that needle. I don't like to think I'm being pumped full of junk I don't know about.'

'Tsk tsk, don't fret. It's just a mild hallucinogen. It helps with the visuals.' The needle went in, hurt minutely, then was gone as she dabbed again with antiseptic. 'You really don't have to worry, Josh. I've told you before. You're perfectly safe with me, I'm a doctor. Would you like to see my diploma?'

'I'd rather see your snatch,' Josh said. It'd be nice to just lie here, exposed and stimulated, and see Isis's cunt. She'd be beautiful down there, he decided dreamily. All red and moist and puffy . . . Then, maybe, she could kneel astride his face and let him lick and taste her . . . And as she came all over his mouth, she could throw one of her clever little switches and make him spunk on that sexy white coat of hers.

'Now don't be silly,' she admonished, giving Josh a flash of the stern schoolma'am, something else he found himself liking. 'You've paid for something far more esoteric than little old me.'

'But don't you fancy me?' he persisted. There was nothing to lose anymore: dignity, power, and control of his body were all in the scarred hands of this woman he'd met less than an hour ago. She'd even taken his voice; his words were coming out more and more slurred as the drug took hold. 'Don't lie to me, Isis,' he mumbled, then nodded towards his prick, so stiff and twitchy in the pleasure-giving cuff. 'You fancy some of that, don't you? I'd feel great up your twat. Why don't you climb on board?'

She gave him a long look. A considering look. And to Josh's addled brain it seemed almost as if she might succumb. His hopes – and then his penis – jumped as she slipped off her wire-framed specs, placed them to one side, and reached out to touch his lightly restrained flesh. Her fingers felt cool, and the touch of them was heartbreakingly delicate . . . but sadly, only momentary.

'You have a wonderful body, Josh, and a truly exceptional cock,' she said softly, with a genuine note of admiration. Abandoning his groin, she brought her blighted face close to his. Her voice was level and honest, and her odd eyes seemed to reach right through the narcotic mist and touch Josh's soul. 'If this weren't a professional relationship, I might be tempted. Really. But you must see it's impossible.'

All Josh could see was the most intriguing and desirable woman he'd met in years, but his consciousness was floating now and it was difficult to tell her that. He felt her soft hands slide behind his head, loosen his ponytail and fan his hair out over the shaped leather rest. He didn't protest when she fastened a soft felt-lined strap across his brow, but simply sighed and eased himself deeper on to the probe. You love it, you fairy, he told himself, not quite sure if he'd spoken out loud or not.

Almost on the brink, he felt Isis attach sensors to his temples and his wrists, then after the sound of tapping keys, the real world began a slow, gentle slide beyond his reach. More tapping, and his body came alive in a strange, almost multi-dimensional way. His prick tingled slightly, seemed to swell . . . and deep in the core of him, a soft warm glow was the most delectable sensation he'd ever felt. Looking around him he saw the whole scene was slightly out of phase, distorted yet strangely unalarming. Isis's scarred face had acquired a bright beatific beauty, and her voice, when she spoke, was alien music.

'I'm going to put a mask over your eyes now, Josh, and

I want you to close them as I do,' she whispered. Josh obeyed, lamblike, and felt the soft velvet-lined visor caress his brow and cheek.

'It's time now, Josh. When you open your eyes again you'll be in another world.' He felt the stroking touch of her fingers on his face, so soothing, so much like a lover. 'It's time now, my Josh, time. Time to dream . . .'

3   The Prince's Comforter

'It's time, Layla! Time to wake up. We must get you ready for the Prince.'

Rising from the deepest layers of sleep, Layla felt a gentle hand stroking her face. Momentarily disorientated, she brushed it away and pressed her fists to her eyes. She hardly dared open them and look around. The last few days had been so strange and beautiful, and in her half-awake state she was scared they'd just been a dream.

But when she dropped her slim fingers from her face, and opened her eyes to Raiza's kindly smile, Layla realised that *this* was the real world, and the other dream, the peculiar one she couldn't quite remember, was just the product of over-excitement and a wild sensual anticipation.

'That's better, little one,' said Raiza gently, 'we've got a lot to do yet. Tonight the Prince will make a woman of you. And for that, Safira and I must make you even more beautiful than you already are.'

Safira and Raiza were the Prince's two most trusted and experienced bondswomen, and they'd been taking care of Layla for the past two days, preparing her for her role as a 'comforter'.

The Prince's comforter . . . the one who, according to custom, would share his bed on the night before he went to war, the freshly deflowered virgin who would comfort him, and give him memories of sweetness and pleasure to sustain him through the horrors of battle. To become the Prince's comforter was one of the greatest honours in the land, the pinnacle of a loyal girl's aspirations; and Layla had had to do nothing at all – so far – to achieve it. The

Prince had seen her from a distance, walking in her father's garden, and decreed that it was she who would sustain him through the greatest test of his warriorhood. Her fresh young body would be his solace on the eve of a holy war.

Layla shuddered; wracked by the delight of newly born sensations, she savoured the heavy yearning ache she felt in her loins whenever she thought of Prince Suleiman and the pure unfettered desire she felt for this legend of strength and male beauty.

Until two days ago, and before the tutelage of Safira and Raiza, Layla had been ashamed of her feelings, confused by the physicality of them; but now that she understood their nature, and how right and natural they were, she welcomed them with a happy heart. Almost without thinking, she slid her fingers beneath her sleeping robe and began to stroke her cunt.

'Yes, that's right, little one,' Safira encouraged, joining her friend at Layla's bedside. 'Don't feel ashamed of your pleasure. The Prince will glory in it. He loves eagerness and sensuality. The law decrees you must be untried, but my Lord likes a comforter who welcomes the sex act gladly. He doesn't like girls who cringe and grizzle, and he adores women who make their own pleasure.

'Relax, Layla, enjoy your body. It's very beautiful,' Safira said softly, kissing her charge's cheek, then easing the loosely tied robe off Layla's shoulders. She smiled at the sight of firm young breasts and small stiff nipples. 'Bring the mirror, Raiza,' she told the younger bondswoman, then returned her attentions to Layla, lifting the delicate gauzy skirt of her robe and uncovering her slim thighs, soft gold-brown curls and the slender hand that moved amongst them.

Layla turned languorously towards the polished metal mirror they'd wheeled to the side of her couch. She'd watched herself masturbate many times in the past few days, and in the name of erotic education, been shown how to improve her technique.

And Layla herself was the first to admit she'd needed teaching. The subjects she'd studied in her nineteen years had all been bookish and highly academic. She was pre-cociously gifted in literature, art, mathematics, astronomy and the various sciences, and she'd even covered the theory of human biology; but until Safira and Raiza had gently explained things to her, she'd been abysmally ignorant about sexuality. Nevertheless, being a quick study in every-thing she'd ever turned her hand to, Layla had taken to sexual pleasure with a hungry and full-blooded enthusiasm: she loved all the wild new sensations she was experiencing, whether induced by her own fingers or by the hands and mouths of her two teachers. All she lacked now was what the Prince would teach her tonight . . . the penetration of her eager young cunt by the hard flesh of a man.

She tried to imagine it as she gazed into the mirror at her reflection: a slim, lovely girl with her sex and breasts wantonly displayed. And on either side of her, two older, darker women whose eyes twinkled with experience as they watched her frenzied contortions. Inflamed by the sight of her fingers paddling in her own juices, Layla rubbed furi-ously at her clitoris and pumped her hips in time to the strokes.

'Easy, sweetheart, easy,' whispered Safira, reaching down to slow the rapidly frigging fingers. 'Work yourself more slowly, savour the pleasure. I swear I've never met a virgin as randy as you are, little one. It's hard to believe you've never made love. And yet – ' She reached gently between Layla's thighs, down past her still-moving fingers, and tested her own finger against the slippery mouth of her vagina, 'you are a virgin.' She pushed against the revealing membrane and Layla whimpered. It wasn't the pain that bothered her, just the desperate craving to be penetrated.

Sweet heaven, how I want it, thought Layla wildly, jer-king her hips then groaning again as Safira removed her hand. In the last two days, this exquisite joy – rubbing herself to orgasm – had become almost a drug to Layla, but much as she revelled in it and half-died each time her clitoris seemed to explode, backfire up her spine and con-nect directly with her brain, she was becoming desperate for more. She wanted to experience the ecstasy with a prick inside her. The prick of His Serene Highness Prince Suleiman Ariffa Ib'n Alu.

How beautiful you must be, my lord, she told him silently in her mind, as her cunt screamed with lust. Oh my Prince, my beautiful Prince, I want you so much! it seemed to wail, a voice of weeping desire that sang between her thighs.

She'd seen her lord quite often from the discreet secrecy of her window, and each time, he'd looked more handsome and virile than the last. But on one particular day, she'd learnt far more than she'd expected . . .

The desert wind had been blowing hard and fast, and Layla had winced empathically as an especially vicious gust had battered the Prince and moulded his robes to his lean powerful body. Then in an instant her fears had ceded to fierier feelings. She'd felt faint, with flaming cheeks and a racing pulse, at the sight of Prince Suleiman's thin silk pantaloons plastered almost translucently across his bulging loins. From her studies of anatomy, Layla had known exactly what that mass between his thighs was, yet she'd been shocked and thrilled by its majestic dimensions.

And now, as her intimate flesh began to burn and flutter, she superimposed a mental picture of that sovereign rod on to the sight of her own tortured cunt.

'Oh lord! My lord!,' she screamed hoarsely and driving pulsations ripped through her vulva. Her hips rose clear of the bed and gyrated helplessly in the air.

'That was wonderful, little darling,' cried Safira as Layla collapsed on to the coverlet in a sweating heap.

'Oh Layla, you're so beautiful when you frig yourself,' murmured Raiza, cradling her sobbing, half-naked charge. 'The Prince will adore you. You're so perfect he may even take you as his wife.'

Layla could hear her teacher's soft words, but so closely tuned was she to her own throbbing flesh that she could hardly make sense of them. She could hardly think further than tonight. Tonight she would ascend to the sweet heights so longed for by every woman in the land; she would lie beneath His Highness Prince Suleiman, and feel his sacred prick slide possessively into her cunt.

But for the moment, Layla must rest a little more, and conserve her energies for his pleasure. Safira – who was older and more senior than Raiza – rose gracefully from the couch and made a start on Layla's elaborate toilette: moving the mirror, she turned out chests and cupboards to select clothes and cosmetics, then sniffed her way through a selection of perfumes, looking for the scent that would most please His Highness. Raiza, who was closer to Layla's age and very tenderhearted, remained on the bed, cuddling her trembling charge and settling her after the tumults of orgasm.

It took quite a while.

Layla had been shocked by her own emerging sensuality, and even though she now knew that sexual pleasure was natural and beautiful, she was still shaken to the core by the power of her own climax. Safe in Raiza's cradling arms, she sent her consciousness winging through her body to absorb the effects of her sweet, self-induced delight.

The delicate fleshy groove between her legs – her cunt as she now liked to call it after Safira had taught her bedroom language instead of the coldly clinical textbook terms – was flooded with slippery juice. She'd learned recently that this silken moisture, far from being something to be ashamed of, was an extremely happy product and was exuded by the excited woman to welcome her lover's prick. Both Safira and Raiza had marvelled at how quickly Layla became juicy, and told her how much easier it would make things when the time came to take her virginity.

The Prince, they told her, had adopted a very civilised custom when it came to deflowering his comforters. He preferred that their maidenheads be dealt with first by the women who attended them. He considered it kinder for a girl to be broken by a gently wielded dildo in the hands of a sensitive woman, rather than subject her to the blind ramming force of a lustful man, even if that man were himself.

This revelation had, at first, surprised Layla very much.

Her scanty knowledge of sex had led her to believe that the Prince, like most men, would set great store by piercing the membrane himself. But on thinking more about his way of doing things, Layla found herself falling even deeper under his spell. How caring he was, how considerate of a timid untutored girl like herself! Prince Suleiman was everything a man should be. Magnificent in face and body, he was beautiful on the inside too – a hero to inspire the utmost devotion, and more.

A moment ago she'd achieved fulfilment by her own manipulations, but now she felt her body blooming again, glowing slick and turgid and ready for the Prince. Matters of state, and his imminent departure, all decreed that their coupling would be for one brief night only; but Layla swore to herself, as her young cunt began to swell and throb, that every second of their time together would count. When he pressed his hard flesh into her she would keep her eyes wide open. She would look into his handsome face as he fucked her, and print it in her soul forever. She would see his eyes lust-dark in her heart, even if he never came back.

'You're dreaming of the Prince, aren't you, my sweet?' Raiza murmured, cupping Layla's rounded breast and rolling the nipple between her fingers. 'Your body gives you away, little one.' She pinched gently, running her hand down the flat white plain of Layla's belly. Within seconds she'd parted the tawny curls below and was rubbing her charge's stiffened clitoris.

Layla moaned, rising instinctively to the tantalising pressure.

'Oh Layla, my beauty . . .' Raiza's voice was husky, and Layla sensed more than simple affection in it. Of her two teachers, Safira was more technically skilled in lovemaking, but Raiza displayed more genuine lust. Layla had sensed a personal rather than tuitional interest, and while she herself didn't mind at all, Safira was careful to restrain Raiza's excesses. The two bondswomen had a common purpose: they had to rouse Layla to sensuality in the universal sense, not to make her want only women.

'Oh Layla,' Raiza repeated, 'I'd love to make you come

right now.' She pressed harder on the fleshy little bud and Layla's pelvis rose towards the source of pleasure. 'I want to nibble your clitoris and lick all the juice that's drooling from your slit.' Layla tossed her head, as excited by Raiza's unexpected crudeness as she was by her attentions to her cunt.

'Raiza! Stop that!' Safira cried sharply, abandoning a silk robe and striding over to haul the two of them apart. In a turmoil of lust, Layla could do nothing but lie panting on the couch, her legs wide open and her quim all pink and tumescent. She saw Safira peer closely at it, and knew she could see how wet and aroused it was. Layla had never felt more lewd in her life, and almost wept for someone to relieve her stimulated flesh.

'But, Safira,' protested Raiza, 'look at Layla's cunt. See how swollen her clitty is, how puffed up her lips are . . . She needs to have a climax, Saffy, it's cruel to leave her like that.'

'No, it's not,' Safira said firmly, then looked Layla in the fierily blushing face. 'Just think how much more you'll enjoy the Prince, little Layla,' she whispered, 'if your cunt is so swollen and ready for him. Now come along, my sweet, we've got to bathe and prepare you. Every part of you must be immaculate for our lord's enjoyment.'

Accepting the wisdom of Safira's words, Layla struggled to rise, biting her lip at the delicious discomfort it caused. Her tender flesh was so engorged that it was difficult to walk without creating waves of intense and intimate sensation. As she walked between Safira and Raiza to the bath house she was hard pressed not to rub herself like an animal. And it was hopeless to expect her randy body to contain itself. Layla knew she'd climax again – long before Prince Suleiman set eyes on her – especially as many of the bathing rituals were so arousing.

Every nook and cranny, every chink and crevice of her body was first cleansed, then pampered and perfumed. And it was while one of the most private of all these cleanings was going on that Layla had her next orgasm.

After first pissing, then emptying her bowel in the normal

way, Safira made Layla crouch, bitch-fashion, over one of the bath house's fast-running pools. Ordered to relax, Layla laid her head on her arms and parted her thighs widely, then let out a little shriek of alarm when she felt a metal nozzle pushed into her exposed backside.

'Patience, little one,' Safira said soothingly. 'His Highness may wish to use this hole and you've got to be completely clean for him.' Layla whimpered in fear as the lukewarm water flowed into her rectum, but Raiza knelt down and stroked her hair reassuringly.

Within moments, the fear was replaced by an entirely different feeling, a beautiful feeling of fullness that seemed to caress Layla from the inside out. Her swelling bowel pressed hard on the base of her clitoris, and she couldn't stop herself swivelling her bottom around to intensify the forbidden stimulation.

'Aaagh!' she screamed out, climaxing violently as Raiza, in defiance of Safira's orders, reached between her charge's shaking thighs and frigged the aching bud of her sex.

Wracked by pleasure, Layla's wet body bucked wildly, but her two companions held fast, Safira taking particular care that the warm enematic flow continued. With no let-up in the pressure, Layla has several more orgasms, her hips pumping obscenely as the water gurgled softly inside her. Her spasms increased shockingly when she saw herself in the mirror, her slim buttocks jumping and the fine metal tube snaking out from the rosebud of her anus.

At last Safira gently withdrew the nozzle, and she and Raiza held Layla in the fast cleansing stream as the fluid gushed out of her bottom. The relief was so glorious that Layla came again, tears of shame pouring down her beautiful face.

'Don't be ashamed, my sweet. It's quite natural to be aroused by a purge,' Safira said soothingly as Layla came back to her senses. 'Lots of people find it pleasurable. The Prince himself enjoys been cleaned out this way, especially when there's a beautiful young woman to administer the enema.'

'Oh yes, Layla,' said Raiza in answer to Layla's astonished look, 'I'm sure it'll be you one day. So remember, he likes you to push your finger into him afterwards and fuck his freshly sluiced bottom.'

'Surely not!' Even as she protested, Layla imagined the scene, and to her confusion found it unbearably exciting.

'Oh yes, little one,' returned Raiza with an impish grin, 'the Prince is sensual throughout the whole of his body, not like most men, who are entirely obsessed with their pricks. Imagine it, Layla, the naughtiest of erotic sights . . .' The girl paused, and with glazed eyes, ran her tongue slowly over her lips, 'My lord Prince Suleiman all stretched out and naked on a couch, his limbs writhing helplessly as you push a huge dildo into his arse – '

'Raiza! Enough!' rapped Safira, 'Layla is young and untried. It's not right to describe such advanced pleasures to her. His Highness will suggest them in the fullness of time. For tonight, a simple fuck will be all that's required.'

Yet as the bathing continued, Layla mulled over the Prince's 'advanced' pleasures. With the enematic experience still fresh in her imagination, and the whole of her lower body still glowing from its benefits, she could well imagine that Prince Suleiman would enjoy having his bottom pleasured. For all her virgin state, Layla was gradually discovering her own lack of inhibitions. Surely no act or pleasure should be forbidden – as long as it didn't harm others? Why shouldn't men also enjoy being penetrated? Why should anyone be confined to purely conventional roads to pleasure?

I suppose I'm too modern, Layla reflected as Safira helped her into the perfumed and blissfully warm large bath. The idea of Lord Suleiman with a dildo into his bottom was extremely stimulating. For her, somehow, it did nothing to undermine his royal dignity. In fact it had a certain rightness to it. It seemed to her . . . appropriate? Familiar? Had she once dreamed of it, yet not consciously remembered the dream?

Consigning the thought to the back of her mind, yet hoping one day to make it reality, Layla applied herself to the here and now, and the task of scrupulous bathing, anointing and perfuming of every last inch of her skin.

Naked like herself, Safira and Raiza set about washing the whole of Layla's body with a gentle vegetable soap that enhanced the smoothness and softness of her skin. As her hair was so thick and long, they'd bound it on top of her head so it wouldn't get wet, but otherwise, every part of her was washed with the beneficial lather, then rinsed in the crystal-fresh water that flowed from the fountains. Especial care was taken with her breasts, armpits and groin; Raiza very craftily got the job of soaping her there.

And Safira had obviously changed her mind about Layla's having orgasms before going to the Prince. She was the one who slid her arm under her charge's bottom, lifting her up so her crotch was offered to Raiza's cleansing fingers. Layla relaxed back in Safira's strong arms – buoyed up in the water with her thighs wide apart and her vulva fully exposed. With her pretty face creased in concentration, Raiza applied herself to the task, working up a rich foam then slathering it thickly on to Layla's genitals. First the labia were gently pulled and pummelled, then all attention was focused on the clitoris.

Ablutions as such were forgotten as Raiza took the little nub firmly between her finger and thumb and worked it rhythmically up and down. Layla thrashed like a fury, drenching everybody, but Safira held her fast so the ministrations could continue. Within a few moments the victim was jerking in a violent climax, her lovely mouth drooling and distorted by the uncouth animal grunts that issued from it. And below, when the tumult was over, her cunt needed a second soaping to wash away all the freshly exuded juices.

Eventually Layla was led from the bath, perfectly purified, and ready to be painted and clothed in her sacrificial finery. The first stage was to make her skin even softer with an emollient made from the same smoothing ingredient as the soap. This was applied all over her face and body, then followed by a sweetly exotic perfume rubbed into her limbs and body hair: an essence of patchouli, musk and tuberose, a head combination that would rouse the most abstemious ascetic let alone the notoriously sensual Prince. Then, with her long hair dressed in soft, maidenly waves, and her eyes, lips and nipples painted with benign herbal dyes, Layla was ready to be dressed for her possession by Prince Suleiman.

Her clothes consisted of two simple garments topped by a densely obscuring floor-length veil – and for her feet, a pair of dainty embroidered slippers. The top half of her outfit was a short, sleeveless jacket made of blue and gold brocade, which fastened down the front with three easily released buttons. On her lower half, Layla wore a deceptive and ingenious pair of silk gauze pantaloons held up by a wide sash that matched her jacket. The trick of her silky bloomers was that although the material, draped in luxuriant folds, kept her completely decent, the whole affair was made in two separate pieces that could be simply opened to allow access to her vulva. Anonymous modesty was assured by the thick but beautiful veil.

'But surely,' said Layla, puzzled, 'my lord will want me naked once we're in private?'

'That's possible, eventually,' said knowledgeable Safira. 'But Prince Suleiman is fond of ornamentation and beautiful clothes, both for himself and his women.' To illustrate this she put a dazzling beaten gold and lapis lazuli necklace around Layla's throat, then added a bracelet and dangling earrings to match. 'So don't worry if he asks you to remain partially dressed.'

'That's nice,' murmured Layla dreamily, taking pleasure in her own reflection in the mirror. The jewels glinted as she moved, and by a daring manipulation of her floating trousers, she could display her own living jewel: the delicate hair-shrouded folds of her cunt.

Prince Suleiman sounded more wonderful with every second that passed. All his preferences seemed to suit Layla too. It was almost as if some kind genie – some wise-eyed ancient with incredible powers beyond human comprehension – had created him especially to satisfy her fantasy, to fulfil her body's destiny and make real her wildest romantic dreams.

Dreams that would very soon come true.

'Come along,' said Safira, when she and Raiza had put their clothes on too, 'we mustn't keep the Prince waiting.' The two helpers wore garments similar to Layla's – though not quite as sumptuous – but because they were no longer virgins, their veils were merely token gestures that covered just the lower halves of their faces.

Layla was trembling with anticipation as they walked through the lamp-lit corridors of the palace, and was blind to everything but her own increasingly heated visions – visions of the Prince's naked body and how it would entwine – intimately – with her own silk-covered one. Her cunt trembled, and her legs could hardly carry her as the interior picture sharpened lewdly, and focused on Prince Suleiman's erect penis as it slid majestically into her well-moistened slit.

'The Lady Layla to see my Lord Prince Suleiman,' cried Safira with a good deal of pomp. Layla blinked behind her heavy veil; she'd been so lost in her erotic dreams that she hadn't noticed they'd arrived.

Fiercely armed guards protected the door, but as Layla and her two companions were obviously expected, they stood aside, bowing with their eyes downcast. Even if she was carefully veiled, it was still forbidden for them to look at a virgin destined for the Prince's bed.

Layla and her own 'honour guard' passed through a beautifully decorated anteroom into an even more spectacular inner chamber. Opulent hangings decorated the walls, all alight with precious metal threads; richly woven carpets were underfoot throughout. Several thickly upholstered couches of various heights were arranged about the room, along with various stools and low tables of exquisitely carved hardwood.

But the priceless furnishings – and indeed the other two men in the room – lost all meaning in the presence of the man reclining on the central couch. Unbidden, Layla flung herself face down on the carpet, assuming without instruction the pose that protocol demanded. Yet even with her veiled forehead pressed to the rug, an image burned before her dazzled eyes.

His Serene Highness the Lord Prince Suleiman – the sovereign of all Layla's young dreams and the most glorious human being she'd ever seen. Enraptured and hardly daring to breathe, she awaited his mercy.

'Rise, gentle Layla,' said the soft, harmonious voice she'd long waited to hear, 'and you too, my friends Safira and Raiza. Welcome, ladies, to my humble abode.' Despite her awe, Layla's lips twitched with a smile at the subtle humour in the Prince's sensuous tone. 'Matters of state oppress me even now; I would be grateful if you could all make yourselves at ease while I attend to my onerous duties.'

Following the example of Safira and Raiza, Layla sat down on the carpet a little distance away from the Prince and his two advisers, reflecting as she did that his sarcastically tinged words must be aimed at the officious clods who pestered him with documents and decisions when he had so few hours of serenity left to him. But at least their presence gave her a chance to study the object of all her newly forged desire.

Her heart started pounding and her cunt grew moist at the new wonders his informal clothes now revealed. It was the first time she'd seen him without his traditional head-dress and the lack of it gave Layla a thrilling and wonderful surprise. She'd expected him to be close-cropped – as all the men she'd ever seen bare-headed were – but to her intense delight, Prince Suleiman had long hair instead. Rich black waves tumbled to his shoulders and beyond and gleamed with an almost metallic sheen in the flickering torchlight. Immediately she imagined it a thick perfumed mass across her skin as he knelt to kiss her body . . .

The Prince kneel? What a preposterous thought. But Layla still prayed he'd let her touch his hair.

At this close range, and with her veil to conceal her curiosity, Layla could study him in every detail – and everything she saw made her desire burn hotter than ever.

A tall man of some thirty summers, it was obvious even to those who'd no idea of his origins that Suleiman Ariffa

Ib'n Alu was a Prince. His slightest movement betrayed an innate grace and power, and his long, lean limbs and slim but well-muscled physique hinted at his enormous strength and great endurance. All these qualities had served him well in the defence of his country, although they had not stopped him from getting his share of honourable battle scars. The most notable of these made Layla wince empathically. There must've been a lot of pain in the long, purple cicatrix that marred the sculpted perfection of his handsome face.

And Prince Suleiman was a most elegantly fine-featured man, so much so that, given his newly revealed long hair, he would have looked almost femininely beautiful if it hadn't been for the lurid scar and the neatly trimmed beard and moustache that graced the lower half of his face. The sight of that amazing face left Layla swooning, torn between adoration, and a desire to rain kisses along the livid line of his wound, the high curve of his cheekbone and his broad noble brow. All this . . . then she'd feast on the lusciousness of his full red lips until both he and she were desperate to join their bodies as one.

'How much more, gentlemen?' he demanded of his advisers, sighing at the huge pile of documents still set before him. 'Patience, ladies. I'm as eager as you to see the back of this, but alas . . .' He shrugged expressively and favoured Layla with a particularly sensual smile. The heat in his black velvet eyes made her innards melt and she was afraid her satin gauze trousers would be soiled with her own juices; and the sparkle of fine white teeth against rich swarthy skin was so wicked and promising that her vulva twitched and shivered in response.

'My lord,' she heard one of the statesmen protest. 'All these petitions must be read and considered. Who knows how long you will be away, Sire, and these matters must be resolved first, for the good of your people.'

The Prince smiled gravely, and in spite of her lust, Layla was moved by the serious expression on his perfect face. Lord Suleiman's concern for the welfare of his subjects was legendary. Many times he'd put their needs before his own, and their government before the satisfaction of his highly libidinous nature. It seemed that tonight was a particular instance.

But . . .

'Does the study and signing of these papers require your presence?' he enquired of the chamberlains.

'No, Sire,' answered the spokesman, 'all that is needed is a note of your decision on each one and they'll be put into effect in your absence.'

'In that case, gentlemen, you may leave and I'll work on the documents with only these fair ladies for company. Their beauty will make the job more pleasant.'

With that the advisers left the room, bowing as they did so. When the heavy door closed, Layla, Safira and Raiza were left alone with their liege lord.

'Forgive me, sweet Layla,' he murmured, rising from his couch to approach her. 'I would have liked to have been with you right from the beginning, but now it seems I've got state duties to perform, even while Safira and Raiza are preparing you.'

He stood before her, so tall and strong, his magnificent body clearly displayed by a loose robe of the same sheer gauze that she was wearing. Overcome, Layla threw herself again into face down obeisance. He was too much! Too handsome, too manly, far too much her own beloved Prince!

'No, no, no, precious one,' he admonished kindly, reaching down to help Layla to her feet. She gasped as with only one arm he lifted her whole weight momentarily off the carpet. 'No, gentle Layla, you mustn't kneel to me tonight. I'm the one who should abase myself before your beauty . . .'

As if at a signal, Safira and Raiza stepped forward and lifted the veil clear of Layla's face and body.

There was a long silent moment while Lord Suleiman's gaze wandered from the top of Layla's head to the tips of her toes and back again, repeatedly lingering and returning to certain portions of her anatomy: her blushing face, the

53

proud swell of her breasts, the shadowy juncture of her thighs.

'Lady, you are a jewel,' he said at last, his voice suddenly very deep and husky. 'When I first saw you in your father's garden, I knew you were the only one who could soothe me tonight . . . If only I had more time.' He paused, reached for her hand and drew it to his lips. Layla shuddered at the warmth of the touch, the gentle pressure and the slight tickle of his moustache on her skin. 'I should like to spend the whole night sheathed in your exquisite body,' he said, 'but I'm afraid that's not possible, beautiful one.' He nodded in the direction of the state papers. 'I'll promise you one thing, though. On my return we'll have our night. Many nights . . . and I'll make up for this shabby treatment.'

'My lord!' cried Layla, preparing to throw herself at his feet again.

But he wouldn't let her. He pressed one kiss to her warm face, then turned, with a heavy sigh, towards his duties. 'Begin, ladies,' he said simply when he'd taken his seat and picked up his first document.

Without a word, Safira and Raiza led Layla to a couch close to the Prince's. Large and lushly upholstered, it was made with a clever tilt so he had only to lift his eyes slightly to have a perfect view of everything that happened on it, everything that Layla did or had done to her, her every intimate response.

Guided by her companions, Layla reclined on the soft bed and arranged herself as gracefully and alluringly as she could. Scared, yet unbearably excited, she pinned her gaze on the Prince, but he was already deep in his documents.

Yet even though he seemed to be concentrating so hard, Layla sensed that at least some of his attention was still on her. With his sixth sense he 'knew' her, her face and body, her fears, her hopes and her innermost needs. Acutely aware of this subconscious link, Layla trembled as Safira unfastened her ornately embroidered waistcoat. At least, she thought it was Safira. In spite of her ever-growing desire, Layla suddenly felt embarrassed. She yearned for her royal master's touch, yet she'd automatically closed her eyes in mortification. Her body was too wanton, too obvious. Her rouged nipples were hard and swollen, twin pouting signals of a lust she couldn't control. And even though with her eyes tight shut she couldn't see him, her other senses were meshing with his. Prince Suleiman was as aware of her engorged breasts as she was.

Layla moved uneasily on the couch, and instantly Raiza soothed her with caresses: first to her blushing face, then to her breasts – in a slow, purposeful glide that inflamed the already sensitised curves. And when the stroking became pinching, and Raiza was tantalising her stiff, pink nipples without mercy, Layla began to gasp and moan. It felt as if a pair of fine silk cords were entwined around her clitoris, and the more that Raiza tweaked and pulled at Layla's nipples, the more that tiny organ swelled and pulsed and cried out for contact.

In the vivid world of Layla's mind, the Prince reached out to her and took hold of her clitoris, working the little bud in time to Raiza's inflammatory tugging. A seething mass of sensations, Layla wriggled on the soft divan, her buttocks moving compulsively against its padded velvet surface as her body cried out to the Prince for his attention. She groaned, low in her throat, as cool air hit the moist membranes of her cunt. Safira had pulled apart the wispy trousers to show Prince Suleiman his comfort.

As if from a great distance, Layla heard a harsh male gasp, then a muffled curse and the vicious scratch of a pen. If she hadn't been so wracked by lust, she could have pitied him. He was hot blooded and highly sexed; it must be pure torture to have a fresh, beautiful virgin half naked, wet and panting just inches away, and be forbidden – by duty – to touch her.

Being displayed like this was an exquisite frustration, and Layla wanted to scream; and scream and scream when Safira and Raiza started dragging her thighs apart.

Raiza whispered in her ear. 'Layla, my darling, play with your nipples the way I was doing. Go on, do it, sweetheart, frig your beautiful little titties while we prepare your sex for my lord.'

'I can't,' whimpered Layla.

'You must,' ordered Safira as Raiza guided Layla's hands to their task. She flinched at the heat in her own body. Her breasts were simmering . . . her cunt a boiling pot, her sex fluids churning in readiness for her princely lover. Tentatively, she moulded her fingers around herself, shaping the smooth globes, the pale resilient flesh. Surely she was bigger now? Her nipples felt unnaturally hard, like little pebbles that sent instant fiery messages to her naked slit. Experimentally she pinched them and felt such a blast of sensation between her legs that her bottom kicked up off the pillow beneath her.

'That's good, little one,' Safira murmured, sliding her fingers between Layla's slippery labia and bringing an agitated gasp to her charge's parched lips.

'Beautiful, beautiful,' came a soft male sound, a long exhalation, half moan, half sob. No prince now was he, but a simple lusting male who hungered for his virgin feast. Papers fluttered to the floor and the pen scratched on, more jerkily than ever.

Layla was jerking too. Like one in a fit, she bounced and struggled while Safira pulled insistently on her clitoris and Raiza fondled the soft inner cheeks of her bottom and tickled her exposed anus. Layla could feel the juices trickling into the cleft of her backside and coating her friend's probing fingers. The pressure, and the delicate pinching of her clitty, was both appalling and sublime. Layla could almost taste the orgasm as it rolled towards her from the other end of the universe. And as it hit, and the most delicate membranes of her body throbbed exquisitely, she felt intimately joined to the Prince – the man who was both yards and a whole world away.

'Devil take it,' he growled, pushing aside his papers as Layla moaned and sobbed. 'I'll make time before I leave. I can't wait. Make her ready!'

Layla's eyes flickered open and she saw the scene around her through a haze of pleasure. Her gaze, and her consciousness focused sharply as Prince Suleiman rose from his couch and, with a couple of lithe steps, drew close to her lewdly sprawled body.

'A few moments, gentle Layla,' he said softly, his handsome bearded face shockingly close, 'a few moments of pain and you'll be mine. I long for you, sweet one. I've never seen a virgin girl so responsive. You'll be perfect. I know it. Hurry, you two,' he said, grinning first at Safira, then at Raiza. 'Have mercy on your sovereign. See how he suffers.'

Layla gasped as the Prince sat back on his haunches, pulled open the luxurious folds of his silk-gauze robes . . . and his erection bounced into full magnificent life.

As a virgin of good family, whose father had foreseen this night, Layla had therefore never seen a fully naked man. But in spite of that she was a sensual girl, who'd studied her anatomical texts minutely and been entranced by the drawings of penises. But no pen and ink, however cleverly used, could have prepared her for the real thing, the vibrant beauty of Prince Suleiman's prick.

Generously formed, he had a long thick shaft crowned by a bulging plum-like glans; and from her slight knowledge, and the way the organ stood up stiffly, almost pointing the way to her virginity, Layla deduced that not only was her Prince a circumcised man, he was also intensely aroused and ready to enter a woman. To enter her . . .

She shuddered, thankful she would not be broken by the blind strength of that living rod; it had a little eye that wept a pearly drop, but she knew it could batter its way mercilessly through her tender tissues and hurt her far more than the carefully wielded ivory phallus that Safira was preparing to use.

'Don't be afraid, little dove,' the Prince said kindly, obviously attuned to her fears. Taking his prick in his long brown fingers, he worked it a little, then, as his breath became ragged, stopped again. 'This won't hurt you,' he wagged the blood-filled shaft in her direction, 'not once Safira has readied you. All I want is to please you, Layla. Give you the love your body was formed for.'

Dazed as she was, Layla gasped with shock when he

leant forward, bending over his own rigid penis, and bowed to her, reaching out to kiss her slim trembling foot. She gave a little moan as his warm lips touched her skin, not from fear or distress, but because the tiny salute seemed to travel straight up her leg and kiss her streaming cunt, to land on her shivering clitoris like a gentle, pleasure-giving butterfly.

'Soon,' whispered the Prince, then he nodded to Safira. 'Do it!'

Layla watched in numbed fascination as her friend held out the fat white dildo. It glistened in the flickering light, its surface coated with a soothing oil that would ease its passage into Layla's unsullied body. In the instant before Safira brought it to the entrance of Layla's vagina, Raiza trickled a few drops of the oil on to its target – Layla's already well-moistened cunt.

As Layla felt the nudge of the phallus, its intrusion was almost forgotten as Raiza started frigging her again. But even as the pleasure of this mounted and mounted, threatening to take Layla's mind again, she could still feel the Prince's soft mouth on her naked instep. She looked down at him as the dildo began to press and stretch, feeling its discomfort but finding it made bearable by the Prince's burning dark eyes – and the way they devoured the sight of her semi-impaled cunt. For a second, those eyes flared as the phallus went still deeper; then he looked up straight into Layla's mesmerised gaze. 'Courage, exquisite one,' he mouthed, his breath red-hot on the skin of her foot.

Tears sprang into Layla's eyes as the ivory rod bored deeper. Having enjoyed orgasms, and the physical stimulation of her own and her friends' fingers, she'd never expected *this* to hurt so much. At a nod from Prince Suleiman, Raiza began to work harder against the pain. Palpating Layla's clitoris in a delicate, persistent rhythm, she bent over her and began to suckle on a nipple too, thus entwining the pleasure of the breast with that of the besieged cunt. The Prince himself caressed the long smooth length of Layla's thigh.

Though she tried to stay still and bear her immolation

with grace, Layla couldn't stop herself wriggling about. The combination of lovingly applied stimulation, and the remorseless progress of the dildo, was driving her half mad, and it was difficult to tell where pain ended and pleasure began. All three were holding her down now, either soothing her or exciting her. Safira was draped across her, kissing and nuzzling at her victim's stomach, even as she continued to shove steadily with the dildo.

'She's very tight, my lord,' the bondswoman whispered.

'So sweet and pure . . .' replied the Prince distractedly, matching Layla's latest flinch with one of his own, then pressing his mouth to her thigh. 'Maybe we should stop – '

Hearing these words, Layla grabbed at a fragment of reason, and with a harsh cry, bucked her hips into the dildo's pressure. A white shard of pain sliced through her cunt, then, just as suddenly, was gone – leaving only the delight of Raiza's fingers and their tireless frigging. Layla's vulva fluttered in a slight orgasm, the pleasure sweet but indescribably strange for having the ivory rod lodged firmly inside her vagina.

'It's done, my lord,' Safira said quietly, drawing away, with Raiza, from Layla's newly opened body. They were presenting her; she was no longer a virgin and she was ready to receive Prince Suleiman . . . once the hard white phallus was removed. Four pairs of eyes were fixed on the object protruding from Layla's rose-pink cunt.

It seemed strange to her, that odd carved white thing sticking out amongst her russet curls; and yet it was very real and very solid in a deliciously stretching way. There was no pain now, just a novel feeling of fullness. But it was a static sensation, and Layla suddenly craved movement, a hand rocking the rod inside her body, or better still a living rod to replace the dead ivory one – Prince Suleiman's beautiful penis, throbbing and waving between the rich folds of his robe. Fearless now, Layla met his eyes, held them, then let her gaze drop to his erection. Lying there, his slave, bleeding and penetrated, she felt more regal and powerful than any princess that ever lived. His equal, she wafted her cunt to him in mute invitation.

59

'I will not need you any more tonight, ladies,' the Prince said, nodding to Safira and Raiza. 'Thank you for your gentleness and skill. I won't forget it. But I'd like to be alone with Layla now.'

'But shouldn't we cleanse her, my lord?' Raiza asked, surprise in her voice.

'Don't worry, gentle Raiza,' the Prince replied kindly, 'I'll take care of Layla. Now go. Rest. Amuse yourselves. You'll be well rewarded for your skills tonight.'

'Yes, my lord.'

'Yes, my lord.'

In a rustle of silk, the two helpers were gone, and with them went Layla's last shred of fear and inhibition. Lifting herself on one elbow, she put the other hand to her cunt and explored herself, conscious of the Prince's fiery brown gaze following her every movement. She ran a finger around the bulky white intruder then lifted it to observe the slick blend of pink-streaked juices that moistened the whole of her slit. Satisfied that the wetness was more arousal than injury, she smoothed a little fluid over her clitoris and began to rub herself. The dildo inside her made her feel lewd and hungry for satisfaction, as did the blazing desire in the Prince's eyes. Woman's instinct told Layla that he enjoyed watching displays like this, enjoyed them very much . . . and loved having the sex act teased out to the limit of his erotic endurance.

She frowned though, when he rose and walked quickly across the room, his penis bouncing stiffly as he moved; then she smiled again when he returned with a large free-standing mirror in a gold frame, which he set at an angle allowing Layla to see her own actions – and soon the sight of the Prince's cock sliding into her cunt.

'Thank you, my lord,' she murmured.

'Suleiman, sweet Layla,' he said, bending to kiss her foot again, 'not "Lord" or "Prince". Tonight, I'm Suleiman. Suleiman who wants you . . . and loves the sight and sound and glory of your pleasure. I'd like to watch you make yourself come before I take you . . . But only if it's what you want too.'

'It is, my – ' She stopped and smiled. 'It is, Suleiman, it is!'

'Then please. . . . Begin. I'm dying for the sight of it.' Settling himself beside the couch, his face just inches from Layla's wet flesh, Suleiman took hold of his prick and began a slow cautious rub. Layla could see both their bodies in the gold-framed mirror, and it was difficult to say which sight was most arousing: her own moist distended cunt with the ivory phallus obscenely protruding, or Suleiman's penis, so rigid and purple as his brown hand moved smoothly over it.

Within seconds Layla was coming, her body riding a great crest of pleasure that brought a soft, whimpering cry to her lips. Her eyes had closed – a reflex action – but even in the unseeing haze, she was aware of Suleiman's movements. As her vagina spasmed and pulsed, she felt him withdraw the cold ivory rod and replace it with his prick – a warm, living bar of flesh. She moaned even louder, and her fingers slid from her cunt. Nothing on earth must obstruct this man . . .

It was Suleiman, shafting slowly and smoothly, who pleasured her now – and Layla arched into his thrusts, lifting her pelvis to match his rhythm, pushing her crotch to meet his as her hands grabbed and kneaded his muscular, working buttocks. Orgasm stretched out into one long seamless sheet of bliss. Layla screamed with joy into his kissing mouth, and carved it – with her nails – into the silky skin of his back and arse. And when at last his control snapped, and he stabbed and fucked and pumped his semen into her, she heard and felt a great sobbing cry – Suleiman's wail of release – that matched and mated with her own. Tears streamed down her cheeks, but she knew he was weeping as hard as she was.

'My Layla,' he whispered, 'my sweet, precious, beautiful Layla.'

'My lord,' she answered, heedless of his desire for equality. 'Oh my lord, I love you so much . . .' Sleepy, she registered the absurdity of what she'd said, but was too relaxed and sated to worry about it.

'And I you, gentle Layla,' he replied, but just as she expected him to snuggle close, he drew away from her. Confused by this, and by the sudden realisation of what he'd said, she moaned softly.

'Hush, my sweet . . .'

And then he was close again – as close as when they'd been fucking – and he was folding a rich, soft blanket around their sweat-streaked bodies. Layla knew her thighs were smeared with semen, and her face stained with tears, but for the moment nothing mattered but Suleiman's strong arms around her, and his thrilling voice whispering in her ear.

'Rest now, Layla. When you wake up I'll be gone, but when I return we'll be together. You'll be my princess, sweet one. My princess . . .'

'Suleiman,' she whispered, knowing it was already a dream.

'Hush, my little one. Go to sleep. Go to sleep . . .'

Accepting the dream, Layla smiled and set herself adrift. The last things she remembered were warmth, peace and safety.

And a long, gentle hand slowly stroking her hair . . .

4 *Intermezzo I*

. . . a long, gentle hand slowly stroking his hair.

It felt nice, and very comforting; and enjoying the sensation of warmth and safety, Josh stirred slightly and stretched. He didn't open his eyes, but he sensed he was in a softly lit place, lying on a settee and wrapped in a large fluffy blanket. He moved again, savouring the friendly wool against his naked thighs and belly.

'How do you feel, Josh?' said a nearby, but somewhat disembodied voice. It was husky, but sounded wrong. Suleiman's voice was far deeper . . .

Suleiman?

Prince Suleiman!

'Holy shit.' Josh sat up like a shot, knocking away both the blanket and the stroking hand.

'Oh shit, oh shit, oh shit,' he moaned, covering his face with his hands. He couldn't keep out the fast-dawning truth . . .

'Take it easy, Josh. You're okay. You're back.'

That voice . . . Not the man he'd just made love with. Not Suleiman but a woman, a doctor . . . a tricky mind-twisting lady quack!

'You bitch!' he shouted, opening his eyes and glaring into the pale, scarred face that hovered over him.

'Charming.' Despite Josh's sullen struggles, Isis reached out, took his wrist and monitored his pulse. 'I give you the fantasy experience of a lifetime, and how do you thank me? You call me a bitch. I'm very disappointed in you, Josh Mortimer. I thought you had better manners.'

He shook her off and scowled.

'When I asked for a fantasy, I expected a man's fantasy. You made me a woman!'

'Almost, but not quite,' she replied. 'For a limited period of time, you experienced the mind, the body and the responses of a woman. Surely you must've wondered, Josh, imagined what it'd be like to cross over? Admit it, isn't that the greatest sexual adventure of all time? And doesn't it just show you how clever Pleasurezone really is?'

'Yes, I suppose it does.' And yes, he admitted grudgingly, she was right. It'd been the most bizarre and incredible experience of his life. It'd been *real*! He'd *been* Layla, felt her emotions, her pleasure, her orgasms . . .

Suddenly he felt scared. 'There won't be any after effects, will there?' He was feeling a wonderful sense of satisfied wellbeing, a feeling he'd never felt before. Was this how a woman felt after really great sex? 'I mean, I won't keep on thinking I'm a woman, will I? Start wanting to make it with men . . .'

'No,' Isis said decisively. 'You'll remember the experience, and I should imagine it'll make a great masturbation fantasy. But there's no way it can affect your fundamental sexuality.' Before he could stop her, she reached out and laid her fingers on his naked prick, holding it lightly and reverently. 'You're a man, Josh, and very much a heterosexual man. Examine your feelings, your body . . . You haven't changed, have you? Pleasurezone will expand your experience and understanding almost beyond belief, but we can't alter what you are.'

Josh's flesh leapt in her soft, pink-scarred hand. It was very much a woman's hand and that heterosexual man's body of his was responding to it. And more than just her hand . . . He was stiffening for her slim curves encased in that cool white smock. Her long, sleek legs. Most puzzling of all, he was excited by her blighted face and its crazy, lop-sided smile.

'Be honest, Josh,' she drawled, 'you enjoyed yourself, didn't you?'

'Yes,' he said softly, accepting the wonderful truth. 'Yes, I did.'

It'd been the most incredible sexual experience of his life and now he felt completely and utterly satisfied. He looked down at his prick, still cradled in her long elegant hand. 'Thank you, Isis. I don't know what to say. It was amazing. A blast. But . . .' A sudden thought occurred. He glanced down at his prick again. 'What happened to . . . Didn't I?'

'The semen?' She grinned, and Josh nodded, blushing beet-red like a schoolboy caught wanking.

'You spunked several times, Josh. In considerable quantities. I'm very impressed.' She let go of his penis then and covered him with the tails of his shirt. Putting temptation out of sight? 'Don't worry, I cleaned you up when I unhitched you.'

Unhitched? Oh God, yes! What'd happened before the fantasy was less real than the 'adventure' itself. But now it all came back. Being strapped half-naked to a white leather couch. The giant prod in his rectum. His erection, red and waving in the air . . .

'But how did I get here?' he asked uncertainly. That was in the treatment room, and now he was back in the 'lounge'.

'You walked. Under my guidance, though, because you were still actually under at the time.'

'That's wild. I don't remember it at all.'

'No, you won't. And that's perfectly normal.' She laid the back of her hand against his brow, testing for undue heat. It was a routine medical gesture, and yet strangely tender. Josh's cock started twitching, wanting her delicate fingers to touch him there again too.

'How do you feel now, Josh? Physically. Emotionally. Sexually. Tell me exactly how you feel; then I'll know if I got it right for you.' She grinned crookedly. 'And if you're getting your money's worth.'

Good God! He'd been so far out of it, he'd completely forgotten the money, forgotten that he'd virtually bartered his freedom for this, and gone broke to buy the ultimate in sexual fantasy.

'Josh?' she prompted.

'Er, yes.' He sank into himself, trying to assess the

unquantifiable. The state of his body and mind. 'I feel great,' he said after less than a second.

He did. He felt better than great. Back in his own head again, he realised just how well he *was* feeling. His limbs were heavy and relaxed, as if he'd just had a particularly satisfying workout, or a prolonged and strenuous fuck. Isis had said he'd come several times and he could well believe it. His balls felt warm and slack, and there wasn't a scrap of tension left in him. His cock felt especially good: quiescent now, all passion spent, but alive with possibilities, and ready – soon – to grow again. It pulsed suddenly, as if remembering its moments of glory or speculating on moments yet to come. He was flaccid, yet not entirely limp: his flesh felt peaceful yet promising and completely tuned in to the woman at his side.

In a word, he felt alive. And more so than he'd done in months.

But what about his mind?

Again, he felt great. With the initial disorientation over, he was thoroughly 'Josh' once more – yet with delicious memories of being Layla. And there was no gender confusion, even though he remembered coming as a woman . . .

As that thought resurfaced, he glanced sharply at Isis.

She winked with her bad eye, then grinned. She had read his mind!

'What do you think of it then?' she asked huskily.

'I think women get a pretty good deal. You can come as much as you like and as often . . . and you've no tool to let you down when you most need it.'

'I can't imagine yours ever letting you down, Josh,' Isis said after a moment. 'But on the whole I agree with you. Women are the luckier sex. I've tried being both – ' she nodded vaguely in the direction of the treatment room and her magic sex machine, 'but given a choice I'd climax as a woman.'

'It's . . . it's different,' Josh said thoughtfully, knowing the adjective was inadequate. He shuddered, feeling cool, yet more affected by memory than temperature. Isis, frighteningly aware of his responses, picked up the blanket and swaddled it around his shoulders.

'When I was Layla,' he continued, 'the orgasms were a sort of inward experience, not a bit like the ones I have as . . . as me. When I'm me the feelings are kind of outgoing, outpouring. The semen moves out, shoots – it travels. But a woman seems to "arrive" inside herself . . . "Come" is the wrong word. Women are already there. Their cunts fall in on themselves, they collapse into inner space. It's beautiful.' He paused and quirked his brow at his raptly listening companion. 'I'm not explaining all this very well, am I?'

'Oh, you are, Josh,' she said softly. 'You're explaining it very well. You're the first client to even try.'

Josh frowned, then on the point of replying, he found himself yawning hugely. God, he was bushed! Losing your virginity was a tiring business.

'Yes, it's pretty exhausting, isn't it?'

Uncannily, Isis seemed to have read his mind again. 'Look, why don't you lie down again? Sleep a while. I'll bring you your clothes and a drink when you're ready.'

'Sounds great,' Josh mumbled, fighting unsuccessfully to keep his eyes open. 'Just great.' Yawning again, he stopped fighting, lay down and let his eyelids droop. He felt Isis adjusting the blanket around him, and as he wished, muzzily, that she'd strip off and crawl beneath it with him, he suddenly realised who Suleiman had been.

'You said I couldn't dream about you,' he whispered from the edge of slumber.

'You can't, Josh.'

'Then how come Prince Suleiman had a bloody great scar on his cheek?'

He never heard the answer.

Back at his flat – some time later – Josh wasn't sure she even had answered.

He was alone now, in bed and naked, yet his thoughts were filled with the strange doctor-cum-sorceress who'd shown him the secrets of the female mind and handled his body with such devastating intimacy.

It oughtn't to have been such a big deal. Women had been touching him all his adult life. Lots of them. Yet when Isis had laid hands on him, the contact had had a million dimensions that were far beyond simple touching. For half an hour of real time, he'd entrusted his body and soul to her, and she'd cherished both with care and tenderness. Not to mention thrilling him with a tour de force of psychodramatic art.

The whole Layla scenario was the product of Isis's inventive, romantic, and wickedly sexy mind. She'd admitted that afterwards, while Josh was putting on his clothes again, even though she'd vehemently denied her presence in the fantasy itself.

But she had been there. It was undeniable. And Josh suspected he'd made something of a breakthrough. But Isis hadn't mentioned Prince Suleiman's scar, either when Josh confronted her about it, or afterwards, when he'd rested and he and she were sorting out the mundane business details. Signing over the bulk of his bank balance for a set of bizarre wet dreams, it'd been hard to believe that the brisk, methodical administrator beside him was the same creature who'd teased and threatened and touched him, who'd stuffed his arsehole and run her pink-scarred fingers tantalisingly up and down his cock.

The treatment itself seemed as much a dream as being Layla. And yet not so. Of Layla's vagina – that had been stretched by the ivory dildo and Prince Suleiman's substantial prick – there was no longer any trace. Josh could remember the sensations, but he couldn't actually 'feel' them any more. The dream, the 'adventure' as he liked to call it, now seemed as if it'd happened to somebody else.

But what'd happened in the run-up to the adventure had happened to *him* – and to his all-too-real body. He reached beneath the sheets and touched his bare bum. Yes, what'd happened there was real enough . . .

Resting on his hip, he drew up a knee and with one hand prised apart the cheeks of his bottom. With the other he delicately explored his opening. Running his fingertip over the puckered rim, it felt no different. Yet from the inside, he felt slightly loose and stretched. He'd no idea how big the transceiver probe had been, but it had seemed gigantic at the time. He shuddered, still troubled by the pleasure he'd felt . . . and the memories it'd stirred up from his teens.

Am I bisexual? Josh pondered, reinforcing the question by prodding at the sensitive little hole. Or am I just more anal-erotic than I thought. His cock trembled in partial answer, and Josh augmented the question by trying to imagine a second naked man on the bed with him. He was relieved when his mind showed him Isis instead.

Old Scarface. The mad doctor. Boy did he want to fuck her! Drowsy now, aroused yet far too sleepy to do anything about it, he summoned the image of his erstwhile torment-ress, faintly astounded by its incredible almost four-dimen-sional clarity.

Sweet dreams are made of this . . . of grey leather suits and lush curves within. He'd always liked ladies in hides, and Isis – in this frighteningly hyperreal fantasy – looked better in hers than any woman he'd ever met.

But luscious as it looked, he wanted the leather off. In his mind, he flicked his way down the popper buttons and revealed lace underneath – shimmering, steel-grey lace to match the suit; lace so sheer it displayed the flesh beneath rather than concealed it. Isis's breasts rose and fell as she panted with desire.

'Isis,' he hissed, seeing the mirror of his own lust in those odd un-matching eyes. Her long fingers – beautifully manicured in spite of the scars – were unfastening tiny buttons and drawing back the dainty panels of her camisole like the wings of a blue-grey dragonfly. Her breasts were larger than he'd expected, not huge but rounded and orb-like with a perfect magical evenness that her poor sorry face would never have. Dreaming, Josh bent to kiss the rose-tipped nipples, and savoured the warm, creamy flavour of the ultimate woman. He sucked, and taking the illusion one step further, she tasted of milk and became his maternal nurturing goddess. Far out, thought the real analytical man in Josh's meandering mind.

Then suddenly, with the unquestionable pseudologic of fantasies, the leather and lace were gone and he was peeling her, nude, from the unbuttoned white coat. Her skin was as pale as the smock, yet warm-toned. The whole surface of her breasts, belly and thighs seemed to pulse with life. The brindled hair at her groin was a living flame, a match for the luxuriant mass that streamed over her shoulders. Her scarred face grew soft and sensually smiling, and as she shifted the slim columns of her thighs, her cunt-lips peeked pink and endearing through her pretty pubic thatch. They were shining and juicy; she wanted him.

'Josh . . . oh, Josh!' That soft husky voice murmuring through his dreams – he heard it as clearly as he saw her face, and saw the succulent flesh it mirrored. The scar, and the offered cunt below, were utterly alike, identical save for the wet gleam of her arousal. Instinctively, Josh smacked his lips, relishing the tasty fragrance that rose up from her oozing slit.

I'll eat you, lady! I swear it! One day I'll eat that beautiful cunt of yours. He felt really tired now, and as he hovered on the edge of sleep, he smiled at his own fuddled and randy silliness.

'Isis . . . Isis . . . Isis . . .'

The name beat the air in a soft, almost religious sibilation. He wanted to hear it while he fell asleep, so he could dream of her. And then, because it was his own dream this time, he could have it all his own way and fuck her.

Three nights later, back in La Selene, he still wanted to fuck her.

And in his new and bizarrely enhanced fantasies, he'd already done so. Not to mention sucked her, groped her and taken every other liberty he could think of, including some divinely dirty ones he'd never imagined doing with a woman before.

It was as if Pleasurezone had spilled over into his every-day sex fantasies. With a breathtaking sensation of immediacy and involvement, he'd smacked her bottom, pushed dildoes into her delicious holes, and teased and abused her until she lost her clinically clever air and sobbed and grovelled before him. Then he'd made it all better by bringing the lady herself to endless screaming orgasms, and finished off by handing his quivering carcass over to her for precisely the same thing.

Steady on, he told himself, sipping the obligatory white wine and scanning his glittering surroundings. He was already rigid inside his black jeans, and the resulting pleasant discomfort made him want to wriggle on his stool like an excited juvenile. It took a massive effort to keep still, but he did it. Writhing about to ease an obvious hard-on was simply not too cool. Especially in a place like La Selene.

Josh had dressed with extra care again tonight, because looking good was now even more crucial than ever. Isis had already seen him in a pale outfit – not to mention stark bollock naked from the waist down – so he'd chosen a easy winner this time. Drama-black from head to toe: leather jeans, loose cotton jacket and fine silk polo-neck top. Not that he'd be seeing too much of his real-world appearance. Before the end of the night, his psyche might be in anything: tutu, toga, crinoline, you name it.

But no. He'd not wear a frock tonight, he decided. He'd have a say in his adventure this time, seeing as he was paying so much. It was beginning to look, though, as if he'd have to give Isis a fairly free rein again, because at the moment he hadn't a single real-world fantasy that didn't include her. Glancing around the bar, he searched for some stimulus that didn't have a cunt-shaped scar and an eye the colour of blood-stained mud. The tricky whore with the vermilion hair might've done, but that lushly voluptuous stimulus was nowhere to be seen.

Probably entertaining a customer, thought Josh with a grin, rather fancying the chance to sample her wares. He'd seen her only briefly, but in a respite from Isis, he pictured her now, flat on her back, her thighs lewdly splayed as a well-hung man slammed rhythmically into her dribbling cunt. Suddenly the fantasy took flight, as they seemed to so often now, and both whore and punter began to buck spasmodically. With sound engaged as well as sight, Josh heard guttural groans, and the prostitute cursing a blue streak as the client's prick squelched obscenely in her climaxing slit . . .

The pressure in his groin began to nag again. It was like having a customised porno holoflick running right inside his own head. He took another sip of his wine, and mercifully managed to switch the movie off. If he went on like this, he'd be coming even before Isis arrived.

Raised voices suddenly came distractingly to his aid. A couple at a nearby table were arguing, and as Josh swivelled for a discreet look, he realised to his surprise that he recognised them.

La Selene was a notorious haunt for the famous, and the squabbling pair were well known, to say the least: a red-hot pop star and his equally celebrated journalist wife – Kenny Jayston and Rio da Ville were perhaps the media love story of the year, but right now they seemed to be involved in the mother and father of all rows.

They were just too far away for Josh to hear their actual words, but the antagonism poured off them in waves, and it was easy to follow the ebb and flow of the conflict by facial expression alone. Rio was blonde, and delicate yet determined looking, while the famous Kenny was dark and flamboyant, and also, judging by the gist of the exchange, currently in the deepest of deep shit.

Temporarily forgetting his mad dreams and the resulting genital torment, Josh found himself intrigued by possible causes of this high-profile domestic war.

Sex probably, he thought, and his stiff cock reasserted itself with an excruciating stab. Rio was a pretty woman with small but quite delightful breasts and long, slim legs. Her pale skin and platinum curls would look superb against her adversary's olive complexion and dark sable-brown hair. Their fucking bodies would make a fabulous contrast!

A germ of an idea formed . . .

Who'd win this fight? Josh mused. How would it be resolved? What retribution would be demanded of the loser? If the penance were as erotic as the sparks flying now, he had the basis of a mind-blowing fantasy.

'Well, who'd have thought it?' said a soft, creamily familiar voice at his side. 'Aren't they supposed to be the lovey-doveyest couple in the business?'

Isis.

'They don't seem very devoted at the moment,' Josh said. The effort of sounding casual made him tremble as 'the mad doctor' slid gracefully onto the stool beside him and signalled for a drink. Josh gave her what he hoped wasn't a dopey sex-struck grin and turned back toward the Jaystons to hide his confusion. Oh God, if he was like this in a public bar with her, how the hell would he cope when she got his pants off him?

But as a distraction the rowing couple rose magnificently to the occasion.

'Get fucked, you bastard!' shouted Rio, belying her dainty appearance. Then, with an acid scowl, she sprang to her feet. 'Don't you bloody well condescend to me, Kenny Jayston! People were reading my articles before they bought your crummy music!'

'Aw, honey, don't take on! I'm sorry!' The 'bastard' seemed, now, to be admitting his fault, although this had little effect on his enraged wife.

'Don't you "honey" me!' she flung over her shoulder, stalking away. 'You'll pay for this, I'm telling you! You won't know what's hit you!' Disappearing in the direction of the exit, her whole body was a column of righteous fury, and Josh couldn't help but admire the swing of her trim buttocks as she stomped away from him. Women were gorgeous in a temper, he reflected. And that applied especially to parts encased in skin-tight stretch jersey.

The condemned man rose too, and made to follow his wife. 'I guess I've been a bad boy again,' he said, addressing his attentive fellow drinkers with a shrug and the engaging grin that made teenage girls swoon before walking off with a surprisingly eager stride to take his punishment.

'He doesn't seem too bothered, does he?' Josh observed, turning back towards Isis and suddenly feeling far less interested in the fate of Kenny Jayston. If a scarred woman could look lovely, the good doctor surely did tonight.

'Of course he's not bothered,' she murmured, an arch smile curving across her face. 'The whole thing's a set-up, Josh, a game they play. Hadn't you realised that?'

Josh shook his head, although the light had already dawned.

'Aw come on, Josh! You're not that naive, are you? The row's a part of a little sex drama they're acting out. He pretends to be "bad" and she has to punish him. The shouting match is just to add spice. It's an appetiser. You can't get into a domination trip stone cold, Josh. It's got to be part of a scenario. You've been around, haven't you? Surely you know these things?'

'Kind of,' he demurred, 'but I think I need to learn a little more – ' he paused for effect, slanting a sharp glance her way, 'if you get my drift?'

She did.

'Ah, so that's the way the wind's blowing, is it?'

'Could be.' Now it was his turn to be oblique. Let Isis ponder for a change.

Josh admitted, however, as he took another sip of wine, that he'd already settled on tonight's adventure. He only wished the real Isis could be in it and use her real gift. She was a true-born sexual dominatrix, he was sure of it. Beside her, Rio Jayston da Ville would be a rank amateur. And if the way Isis behaved in the treatment room was a guide, she'd be awesome if she ever really cracked the whip!

Not that she wasn't awesome now. Josh stole the chance to observe her as – deep in thought, and obviously planning *his* fate – she swirled a long leather-covered finger around the base of her glass. It was an unconscious gesture that'd always turned him on and tonight was no exception. He remembered those nimble fingers handling his cock, touching his body, both directly and through thinnest latex, and wanted it again, and more . . . and immediately.

Isis wore no veil or hat tonight, although her scarred hands were hidden by a pair of rust-red kidskin gloves that exactly matched the colour of her dress. The dress itself was deceptively demure, with a high neck and long close-fitting sleeves, but to those who looked with more care, its softly-clinging velour fabric revealed far more than it concealed . . .

Josh had never looked at anything or anybody more carefully in his life. He studied the erotically draped dress and the tantalising body beneath it as if his next breath depended on it. Stirring uncomfortably on his stool, he used the rigidly stitched seam of his jeans to rub his prick – and decided that for him Isis's shape was the acme of female perfection.

Her breasts weren't huge, but had a high round firmness that spoke directly to his hands and mouth. The naughty velour of her dress hinted that her nipples might be hard; and her thighs, and the gentle hollow of her crotch – both excitingly defined by the rich velvet cloth – sang an inflaming siren song to Josh's loins. And while he struggled to sit still and disguise his acute discomfort, Isis sat on her stool with an easy grace, the confident I-am-woman sensuality of one who had a luscious wet fanny sizzling away beneath the modest opacity of her skirt.

Josh swallowed convulsively, his mouth full of saliva at the thought of her juices. His vivid hyped-up imagination put the taste of her directly onto his tongue, and the sight of her, red and dripping with pouting lips and stiff, swollen clit, right in the centre of his bedazzled vision. And what made it even easier to picture was the purple cuntscape etched on her face, peeking so coyly from behind the heavy fall of her silky, autumn-coloured hair.

'Look, Isis, can't we forget all the technology and just go somewhere and fuck?' he heard a voice say. Astoundingly, it was his.

Shit! Why did he keep giving himself away? Talk about dominance . . . She could make him into a shambling adolescent, and strip away his last ounce of sexual savoire-faire, just by the simple act of sitting down beside him.

She laughed: deeply, richly and irresistibly. 'I've told you, Josh, you've paid for far more than just a simple lay.

You've paid for Pleasurezone Inc., not poor old battle-scarred Isis.'

'Stuff Pleasurezone.'

'You do realise that now you've had the taster and signed the agreement, they're aren't any refunds?'

He did, and though it didn't seem to matter at this moment, Josh realised that he might kick himself to kingdom come and back when he was away from this crazy-making woman and her sensational effect on his bollocks.

'All right already,' he said grudgingly and tossed down the last of his wine.

'Now now, Joshua, don't be so sulky. You're going to have one helluva time tonight. I promise you.' She grinned, the livid scar making her look positively demonic. 'To quote the lady, you won't know what's hit you.' She finished her own drink, set down the glass and rose elegantly to her feet. 'Come along, Mr Mortimer, sir, it's adventure time. Let's get moving, shall we?'

Moving?

Get moving, she'd said. But strapped to the treatment couch once more, Josh didn't care to think too much about moving. Every slight muscle-shift, even the necessary process of breathing, reminded him of his aching vulnerability, and forced him to face the fact that he liked being vulnerable. The fact that he actually got off on it.

He *liked* being strapped half naked to a leather couch with a fat plastic dildo wedged in his bottom and his prick wagging in a helpless erection. If this was reality, the idea of what would happen when the adventure itself started didn't bear contemplating. He'd already climaxed once as Isis was easing in the plug . . .

Ashamed of his loss of control, Josh had closed his eyes tightly while Isis was gently cleaning the spunk from his thighs, but not before he'd caught a single glimpse of an arrangement of almost Japanese purity: the reddened, softening flesh of his prick, his black pubic hair and tanned belly, and Isis's long, graceful fingers dealing efficiently with a sticky white mess.

And no power in the world could shut out the sense of touch, the delicate ministrations of those skilled fingers, the gentle stroking of his sweaty brow – then her robust, uncompromising handwork as she wanked him back to hardness.

It hadn't taken long, and now he was left with little to do but observe his rigid prick and feel its insistent throb as Isis busied herself with the console. He had to grin, though. She was humming a little tune to herself as she tapped away – one of Kenny Jayston's hits, appropriately enough – just like a witch chanting over a spell.

Reluctantly, yet with a sneaky sense of pride, Josh turned his attention back to his penis. He was as hard now as if he'd never shot, and the head looked fat and swollen as it protruded cheekily through the transceiver cuff. In fact the whole view downwards was fairly obscene . . .

As before, he'd followed Isis's instructions and stripped only from the waist down, and to see his naked hips, thighs and genitals, then pan up to the neatly stitched edge of his conservative black silk sweater, as it bisected his flat brown belly, was oddly piquant. It was a far ruder display than if he'd been totally nude.

Suddenly he jerked into the air, his cock-head tingling violently, then landed back on the dildo with an eye-watering jolt.

'Be careful!' he croaked when his ability to speak came back.

'Sorry about that,' she said airily, 'just a teensy little power surge. Nothing to worry about . . .'

'Look, it's my prick you nearly fried! Are you sure you know what you're doing?' Was he imagining things, or was the fear making him stiffer than ever?

'Yes, Joshua, I know it's your prick,' she answered, returning to his side, the controls presumably stabilised, 'and a very delectable one it is too.' She reached out and lightly flicked the member in question. Josh moaned softly. 'And yes, I do know what I'm doing. I designed all this, remember?' Her broad gesture encompassed the computer, the couch and himself, the recipient of her genius.

'You've got a warped mind, Isis,' Josh said, making no attempt to hide a genuine rush of old-fashioned affection. She was one helluva woman to get tough, fearless Josh Mortimer into a pickle as deep as this.

He was still feeling quite fond of her when she carefully pushed up the sleeve of his sweater and injected the hallucinogen.

'Hey, lady scientist, answer me one question,' he mumbled as the drug took effect and things started getting swimmy. 'I'm not going to be a girlie again, am I?'

'No, Josh my sweetheart,' she answered, positioning the velvet-lined mask over his eyes, 'you're not going to be a girlie.'

''S probably worse . . .' The dream was starting to take a hold now and it was hard to frame words.

'Just remember this.' Her words were faint now: sweet and kind, yet deliciously threatening, 'You've been a bad boy again, Josh. A bad boy. A bad bad bad . . .'

5   Bad

❧

'. . . Bad boy,' murmured Kenny, then sat up with a jolt.

How in hell could he have nodded off with what Rio had
in store for him? The treat ahead that he didn't deserve,
because, to be honest, he'd been hard and thoughtless
towards her. He'd no right to talk down to her, not now,
not ever; and yet he'd done it. He'd patronised a woman
who was as bright a star in her own firmament as he was
in his. His only defence was the business's disastrous effect
on the ego.

Rio.

Jesus, how he loved that woman! He'd do anything for
her. Which was probably why they'd started this little game
of theirs. He couldn't bear to upset or hurt her, and when
he'd first done it – a trivial row over something now forgotten – he'd suddenly found himself begging her to punish
him.

And she had.

But not in the way he'd expected. Not at all. Because
Rio loved him – bless every gorgeous sexy divine hair on her
marvellous head! – the punishment had been so delicious it
was more reward than retribution.

'Okay, you bastard, it's time.'

Her voice alone got him going. It was so husky, sexy,
and perfectly modulated that when its blonde, imperious
owner strode into the room, Kenny jumped nervously to
his feet, his prick already a pole in his pants.

'I'm sorry, honey,' he murmured, his voice small and
respectful as he slid into the ritual. 'I've been a shit. I need
to be punished. Do what you want with me.'

'I will do, mister. You'd better believe it.' Rio's huge blue eyes sparkled like river sapphires and her full mouth twitched in a knowing smile. 'And I'll have less of the bad language, if you don't mind. Pretty soon you won't know what you're saying, but until then I want some respect.'

'Yes, my lady,' said Kenny, accepting his role as a thrill surged through his groin. With eyes submissively lowered, he studied the gleaming nut-brown toes of his mistress's dainty, highly polished riding boots. He couldn't see Rio's eyes now but he knew exactly where they were looking.

'You've got an erection, haven't you, you disgusting little pig?'

'Yes, my lady.'

'And I suppose you'd like to rub it, wouldn't you? Get it out of your pants and play with it?'

He nodded.

'Answer me, pig!'

'Yes, my lady, I'd like to masturbate.'

'Masturbate, eh? How prim. That's not what you usually call it, is it?' Sweet, gentle Rio was light years away now, her voice was steel: hard, cold and beautiful. 'You're a dirty brute, aren't you Kenny? You want to wank yourself, toss off, finger that fat meat of yours, pull your rod till you spunk uncontrollably. That's what you want, isn't it?'

'Yes, my lady, I'd like to touch my penis.'

' "Touch my penis",' she mocked, her voice rich with enjoyment. 'Well, that's as may be. But on this occasion I don't allow it. You may, however, look at me.'

Kenny complied: loving, adoring and worshipping the woman he was permitted sight of. Rio was perfect to his eyes: tall, slender and curvaceous in her boots, her skin-tight leggings and her lush white shirt; exquisitely beautiful in face and body, with a great mane of shimmering platinum hair that swept nobly back from her broad intelligent brow. Her dark blue eyes impaled him.

'See it and weep, little man! You won't be getting any of this tonight . . .' With a deliberately lewd gesture, she cupped her crotch and wafted her hips in a parody of fucking.

Kenny suppressed a groan, almost feeling those glorious thighs wrapping around him, that strong pelvis surging up to meet his, that soft fiery cunt engulfing his hungry tool. She made sex, she made love, she turned the insubstantial world into paradise. And every time she satisfied him utterly, he wanted her more than ever.

'Rio,' he whispered in an agony of need.

'Shut up!'

He clamped his lips together but couldn't tear his eyes from that slim, taut, energy-filled body.

'Come here,' she commanded, pointing with one long, red-gloved finger to a spot a few feet in front of her. Kenny moved quickly to comply, looking down again, trying to hide the fact he was studying the exquisite vee at her crotch. He'd just stripped her to the soft bush of gold-white curls he knew nestled there when he felt the glide of leather against his cheek and jaw. The insistent pressure of her fingers forced up his face.

'Poor little Kenny,' she murmured, her blue eyes almost kind. 'Poor little Kenny,' she repeated, stroking his face with one gloved hand as the other reached down to his groin to assess the weight of his need.

Even through layers of leather, denim and silk, her touch was electrifying. First a hold, ineffably light, then a slow, delicate exploration with elegant fingers that traced the hard bar of his erection. 'Poor little Kenny . . .' She continued her soft chant into his ear, even though he felt himself huge and pulsating in the cradle of her grip. As she squeezed ever so slightly, he felt her painted lips against his cheek, and then the moist flick of her tongue as she licked the corner of his trembling mouth.

He wanted to cry. This was only the beginning and yet already he was her helpless, palpitating slave. She blew soft, wine-scented breath against the hot skin of his face, then brushed wayward strands of hair out of his eyes. 'Come along, little Kenny, present your crotch for me. Push that nasty bulge forward. Show me what you've got.'

It was another part of the ceremony, another way to demean him. Bending his knees, dipping slightly, Kenny tilted his pelvis forward and pushed his swollen body into her hand. His own hands hung at his side, fingers flexing as he balanced his weight. A single tear trickled from beneath his closed lids.

'Thrust,' she ordered softly, and Kenny began a slow undulation, trying to obey as smoothly and as gracefully as he could. It was hopeless. He was without power; he felt crude, rude, obscene, and the debasement had barely started.

'Open your mouth.'

His lips parted on a sob and immediately Rio jammed her mouth on his and began thrusting her tongue into him in time to his pelvic movements. The game denied his tongue permission to thrust back; his mouth was simply an orifice for violation, a symbol of his utter submission.

And as Rio raped his mouth and set her bruising seal on him, Kenny hardened in her hand. Oh my lovely woman, I love you, he cried inside his mind. Use me, my darling, I'm yours. I want it. I want you. I want anything, everything . . .

His jaw ached from the force of her kiss, and he marvelled anew at the pure strength of a creature so feminine. She was fine and hard and potent, a living force who could bend his spirit like a bow.

'Enough of this,' she said, depriving him of both hand and mouth. 'I'm too soft with you, bad boy. It's time to get down to business. Isn't it, Kenny?'

He nodded, silently thrilling to her purposeful tone.

'My case, if you please?' She tossed her spun-silver mop despotically, and nodded towards a slim black case that lay in a chair. Heart pounding, Kenny brought the simple but menacing object to her, then stood, holding it out, his head bowed respectfully.

'On the table.'

He placed it on the small mahogany table, its customary resting place.

'Open it and take out the cuffs.'

Flipping the locks, Kenny raised the lid, then winced with familiar joyous fear at the sight of the items within.

Restraints. Gags. Prods and bungs of unbelievable girth. Small electronic devices of luscious obscenity.

'Come, little man, the cuffs. Chop, chop!'

He lifted them out: silvery cruel, yet kind in the soft velvety lining that would surround his straining wrists.

Her next order was another slight nod, and Kenny walked over to the wall and stood in front of its tapestry hanging – an ornament that was suspended from a forged steel rail bedded deep into the brickwork. The tapestry was richly embroidered, and luxuriously thick and heavy . . . but the rail was designed to bear a significantly greater weight, and resist forces no inanimate antique wall hanging would exert. Rio grinned in arch wickedness, and at a second nod, Kenny tossed the glittering handcuffs over the rail and let them dangle there in silent threat.

'Well?' she queried, eyeing the cuffs, then smoothing the ruddy-rose leather that encased her own hands. Positioning himself with care, Kenny faced-front before the tapestry and raised his hands above his head. His wrists hovered at the precise level of the cuffs, but they shook uncontrollably as Rio advanced towards him.

'What's this? The dying swan?' she taunted, then reached effortlessly to secure him. She was as tall as he was, and hardly had to stretch, yet as she shot the catches, her arms and body in parallel to his, Kenny pressed forward and smeared his chest against her firm, resilient breasts.

Seconds later, his face stung like fury from a hard leather-coated slap, delivered with the full weight and force of a powerful superbly fit woman.

'Don't you touch me,' she hissed. 'Do you hear? You don't put your miserable disgusting body anywhere near me, do you understand?'

Kenny nodded, then felt his left cheek flame even more viciously as she landed a second crack.

'I'm not hearing an answer, Kenny.'

'I'm sorry, my lady.' He blinked the moisture from his eyes, loath to have the vision before him blurred, even though it was her white-clad back and the sleek, tight, jersey-covered curves of her magnificent arse. There was no wrinkle in the stretchy fabric, yet he hardly dare speculate on her possible lack of panties. At times like this Rio was a mind-reader.

Hardly daring to breathe, the focus of Kenny's body sank inevitably to his groin. He didn't need to read minds to anticipate Rio's next, and most magnanimous move. Her hands were at work in front of her, and though he couldn't yet see the revelation, he knew his wife was unbuttoning her shirt. His prick throbbed and leapt as he imagined the sight – Rio's full, yet exquisite body, the silky, milky curves and the stiff, rosy bud-like peaks of her nipples. He bit his lip, struggling against hope for some control. If he wasn't able to pace himself, she'd laugh. And she'd despise him. There'd be no silver lining to this cloud of punishment. He wouldn't be worthy of her.

Pivoting slowly on her booted heel, she displayed herself. So beautiful . . . The silken wings of her voluminous shirt flanked flesh that was almost as pale, and the high proud swell of her breasts was more exposed than concealed by a sheer camisole of snow-white lace.

'Like them?' Rio enquired, her smile a siren temptress's. Red seemed to scream against white as she cupped her titties in her gloved hands and pressed their fullness up and in.

Kenny tasted blood. A memory fragment – from a few nights ago – had made him bite down harder. Himself, astride Rio's slim body, his prick gliding in the sweaty channel between those lushly swollen mounds. Then the supreme bliss of ejaculation, and the semen falling on her flawless face, her soft, sweet mouth. All this, of course, before he'd hurt her with thoughtless words.

'Oh Rio,' he groaned, awaiting retribution.

Her long, blonde-tipped lashes drifted down, the tiny movement slow and languorous as she pinched her own teats and her hips described a slight, involuntary undulation. For Kenny the torment only grew; there was nothing more inflaming than this woman alive with her own lust.

'Mmmm . . .' The sound was a low, feline rumble in her throat as her pelvis flicked explicitly. Kenny jerked in his bonds. She was too much, too fabulous for any man to resist.

The rattling cuffs broke the spell, and Rio dropped her hands to her side, regarding him through narrowed eyes.

'I think perhaps I'll overlook that,' she said silkily. 'I'm starting to feel sexy, Kenny. Very sexy indeed. I think I may be kind to you.' She walked slowly towards him and halted within touching distance. 'Not too much, though. Just a teeny little bit.' In a blur of red and white, she ripped open the front of his shirt and sent black pearl buttons skittering across the room. Carefully, meticulously, she folded back his black shirt in a mirror of her own white one, then stared speculatively at the expanse of chest she'd revealed. Unwillingly, Kenny followed her look.

Perspiration lay slick on his skin; his brown flesh gleamed and his nipples were dark and tightly puckered. They looked feeble, though, beside those stiff rosy nubs still half concealed by Rio's lace bodice. His gaze tracked lower, as hers did, to the heavy bulge in his jeans, and the little spiralling curls of black hair that peeked out above his belt.

'Nice,' she said, reaching out and laying her hand flat on his chest. The red leather felt deliciously cooling against his skin. 'Nice . . . but let's even things up a bit, shall we?' In a series of tiny neat manipulations she unfastened the ribbons down the front of her camisole.

But before Kenny could glimpse the complete beauty of her, she pressed her body hard against him, and found his mouth again, searing it with another voracious kiss. His arm muscles screamed with the urge to grab hold of her, crush that gorgeous flesh to his, grind nipple to nipple, belly to belly, groin to groin. The punishment was over now, he realised, the knowledge flowing into him through Rio's rubbing skin and devouring mouth. She'd play her game with him a while yet – in a drama that could last hours – but the heat in her breasts and the sweet savage power of her mouth told Kenny he was already forgiven.

He moaned again when she broke free, already missing the textures of her body and lips. Her mouth was like her breasts: aggressive yet yielding, soft and yet defiantly firm.

To Kenny his own mouth felt meaningless without his wife's kiss; redundant when not filled with her moist pointed tongue. Tonight, as ever during these interludes, Rio was full of attack. Primally female, so by definition penisless, she used her whole body on him like a cock, an organ to dominate and possess him.

'Nice . . . Nice . . .' She darted forward again, running her mouth down his jaw and throat, nipping at his collarbone, licking a wet path down his sternum, across the dense cushion of chest muscle and ending at his left nipple. This she rolled menacingly between her perfect white teeth, and Kenny bucked and heaved as the sensation transferred directly to the very tip of his cock.

'Oh God, Rio, please.' He pushed his crotch at her breasts as she nibbled his teat.

'Please what, bad boy?' she purred, her grin impish. Smacking her lips with relish, she dipped quickly down to suck the other nipple. The pull was so fierce that Kenny's nerve snapped.

'Touch my cock.'

'Such insolence,' she remarked, straightening up again. There was a hard sparkle in her eyes and it made him tremble. Had he screwed up? The bitterest punishment of all would be for Rio to unfasten him and walk away.

Instead, to his relief, she pinched his nipple, feathering her fingers across his cheek as she did so. 'That was very rude and naughty of you, Kenny. For that you'll have to wait a while.' She kissed his cheek, his eyes and the lobe of his left ear, then poked her tongue inside the ear itself and teased him by fucking it. 'You'll appreciate that, though, you know you will . . . You don't want to come too quickly and disappoint me, do you?'

He shook his head.

'No, of course you don't. Now, let's have a look at the offending item, shall we?'

He nodded this time.

'But we're only going to look.' She gave a small, decisive nod of her own. 'No touching. No rubbing.' She smoothed her hands together, gliding her leather-clad fingers over each other, circling one forefinger in a slow wickedly suggestive gesture. Thrills shot up and down his shaft as if she were really wanking him. 'No caressing. No fondling. Not yet.'

Looking him directly in the eye, she unfastened his heavy belt by touch alone, unbuttoned his waistband, then pulled tantalisingly on the zipper tag. Unholy tension was at work on those small metal teeth. Kenny begged her with his eyes, begged her to release the throbbing rod that adored her.

Slowly, she opened his jeans and looked down. Fine white cloth tented obscenely; his shorts, marked with a spreading stain of wetness, bulged out between the flanking black denim.

'Oh my.' Rio revealed her delight in her husband's body. 'Oh my,' she reiterated, tossing back the spun-silver mass of her hair so she could see better. Then, with almost surgical precision, she pushed down the white cotton and lifted out his prick and testicles. Letting the elastic slide underneath and lift, she arranged his meat for her inspection. He almost begged aloud that she taste him.

'That's a fine specimen,' she said in a pseudo-clinical voice. 'Really quite spectacular. Don't you think so?'

Kenny couldn't speak. At that moment his prick existed solely to honour the woman before him. He could hardly breathe. He was going to die if she didn't touch or kiss his flesh. Enfold it with her own . . . In torment, he closed his eyes.

'Kenny!' She was softly imperious. 'Look at your penis.'

Shaking with mortification, he looked down at the bobbing stiffness of his own body. The head was lividly red atop the paler, veiny shaft; the glans was stretched and feverish, the eye quite large and glistening with a steady flow of pre-come. Even as he watched, a drop of it grew too heavy to hang there, and dribbled like a slow, silken string to the carpet below.

'So juicy . . .'

Kenny looked up sharply and caught his wife licking her lips. Her slender red-clad hand was reaching out. He bumped his hips towards it, but she whirled away, far too quick for him.

'Not so fast!' Standing well out of range, she set her hands determinedly on her hips. 'We've a way to go yet, horny boy, and I'd like to please myself a little first.' Glancing around the room, she lit on her favourite chair, then dragged it over and set it facing him but out of reach. Flinging herself languidly into its upholstered depths, she settled her body with fastidious care and proceeded to drape one long, perfectly toned thigh over one of the padded arms. Eyes steadily on Kenny's, she unfastened the heavy brown leather belt she wore around her waist.

'There, that's better,' she murmured sensuously. 'I look almost as nice as you do.' Her gaze dropped to his swaying prick, and Kenny watched in a kind of agonised anguish as she wriggled her bottom deeper into the chair. She laid her hand lightly over her crotch and his prick leapt as if he'd been electrocuted.

'Yes,' she whispered, flexing her middle finger experimentally, then looking up directly at her husband's rampant body. Although already exposed, Kenny felt as if she'd just bared him all over again.

This was a humiliating experience any normal man should've hated, yet Kenny was almost deliriously happy. Standing there, shackled and with his prick pointing out in front of him, he was completely at home in his world. His body was a ferment of lust and aching tension, yet he felt utterly peaceful as his beautiful wife prepared to wank.

There was grace in those long leather-covered hands, a magic dexterity that let her paint, sew and use a keyboard with effortless ease. But of all Rio's manual skills, the most accomplished was masturbation. Even gloved and clothed, her fingers flew straight to the most effective spot, and her jersey-covered hips lifted slightly to meet the pressure.

Was she wearing panties? Or was the fine tan-coloured cloth being pressed directly onto her clitoris? Either way, the sorceress was working her spell, on herself and on Kenny. He seemed to feel that delicate rolling action throughout the whole of his cock, those short merciless stabs in the very quick of his own sex. It would've been easier for him not to look. Rio's mounting pleasure and the accelerating jerk of her supple pelvis were torture in the extreme. Need, and the denial of it, were tearing his guts apart.

Rio was grunting now, the deep guttural sound that she made when he was shafting her to the hilt. Eyes closed, her blonde head thrown back, she was humping her own hand, and seemed oblivious of her imprisoned watcher. Her lithe body was lifting inches out of the chair, her breasts bouncing and her throat working as she gulped in air. She scrabbled wildly at her cunt now, the millimetre accuracy lost in her desperate thrash towards orgasm.

Suddenly she shoved her whole hand inelegantly inside her leggings to frig herself without the hindrance of fabric.

Kenny's eyes bugged, and his own crotch boiled at the sight of that moving bulge in his wife's tight trousers. Some small demon animal was feeding on her snatch, wriggling and burrowing in its unashamed greed. Rio's beautiful face was contorted into a snarling rictus of lust, her lush red lips drawn back from the white gleam of her teeth. He saw spittle at the corner of her mouth as her working bottom first pounded the chair, then bounced her obscenely mounded groin high into the air again. He imagined that cherry-red cunt inflamed by those stiff, hard-frigging fingers. He saw the rich juices bubbling, the pulsing twitch of impending climax.

'Kenny!' she cried again and again; it was a growl, then a shout, then a scream as Rio's slim body became an epileptic blur, her every muscle jerking in spasmodic motion.

She seemed to come for a thousand years, and seemed in danger of wrenching herself limb from limb in the process; yet eventually, with a long, falling croon, she relaxed back into the depths of the chair.

Kenny kept his own body perfectly still. He took small, shallow breaths. Any movement now and he'd spunk helplessly into nothingness. His cock had only to sway and he'd have an orgasm.

'Oh, my. Oh my oh my oh my . . . ' Rio seemed to be

rising out of a coma just as Kenny felt safe to leave his own self-induced stasis. She stirred and stretched in her chair, pulling her hand out of her trousers and adjusting the cloth at her crotch. Businesslike again, she sprang to her feet, her belt flapping in its loops. With an impatient flick, she unshipped its length and dropped it into the chair. 'Your turn now, I think.' She turned glittering eyes towards her trembling husband.

My goddess, he thought as she approached him. She moved like fate, her glove stained dark with her own juices, the air around her thick with the miasma of sex. My goddess, he thought again as she stood just inches from him, staring straight into his eyes.

'This is it, Kenny,' she said, making him flinch as she reach up to brush the platinum tresses clear of her brow. Flight and fight had said she was going to touch him. 'Can you take it, my angel?'

He nodded, not sure whether he could, or even exactly what 'it' might be. Anything with Rio, he thought. Anything *for* her. He'd endure and adore anything and everything that sprang from her creatively fertile mind.

'I'm going to have to be very careful, though, I think.' Her gaze had dropped to his cock. It was still rodlike and pointing at her naked breasts, the tip red and slick. He'd come down from the hair-trigger state now, but with Rio so close and so scented with lust, and her beautiful body still half on show, he felt danger mass in his balls again.

He watched nervously as she assessed the swaying organ, then pulled her gloves on more snugly. The red leather on her right-hand fingers – fore, middle and ring – was dark to the first joint, and irresistibly he glanced at her crotch. She was the juiciest woman he'd ever known and he suspected she was nude under her leggings. Sure enough, a damp patch was crawling out of the vee.

'A G-string, you dirty boy.' She gave a rich chuckle. 'The question was all over your face. You don't seriously think I'd go out without panties, do you?'

'I dunno . . . I couldn't see a line,' he muttered, imagining the delicate scrap of sodden lace now lodged between his wife's legs. What colour? he wondered, even as his mind made it red. Red and completely saturated with the most delicious nectar in the universe, the same elixir that'd spoiled an expensive pair of gloves.

As if in slow motion, she reached out towards his cock, then paused, her fingertips just millimetres away. 'Ever so careful,' she chanted to herself, then took the tip between finger and thumb.

Kenny jerked and felt the rush begin, then die away, as Rio squeezed with killing accuracy. Using this exquisitely precise grip she could keep him simmering for hours, bring him to the brink a dozen times, extend his pleasure, and extend it again and again and again till he feared for his sanity.

His prick subsided ever so slightly, yet remained bouncingly erect. Rio dropped down, still holding him, her long haunches flexing in the tight jersey leggings. He could feel her warm breath on the moist membrane of his glans. The whole of his consciousness gathered in that purplish, plumlike knob, and a silent voice screamed for her to suck it; then, knowing the instantaneous consequences, begged her not to.

'Hmmm,' she murmured assessingly, then gave another little squeeze. She was a connoisseuse of cocks and the acknowledged expert on his. She tipped her blonde head on one side, as if listening to his churning juices. A third tiny pressuring and she stood again and released him. 'Okay, we've tamed the beast. But what're we going to do with his master?'

Kenny had no idea, but a lot of mind-blowing speculations. He didn't care what this woman did to him; for these few hours he was her willing slave, a subjugated male body she could touch, inspect and manipulate to her heart and her cunt's content.

Evidently Rio now knew what she was doing, because she took his hips in her two hands and forced him to turn and face the wall.

Oh no. Oh God, yes. My arse . . . Oh, yes yes yes. Do my arse, please!

The voice in his head was vociferous again. Kenny pressed his hot face to the tapestry as his bottom came alive in readiness. He gasped as he felt a series of small deft movements that led to the cold air on his backside. She'd pulled his shorts and jeans down to his knees in one thick bunch, then lifted his shirt and knotted it at waist level. He was glad there was no mirror nearby; he didn't think he could bear the sight of himself like this. The ignominious exposure.

'Move your feet away from the wall. I don't want you frigging yourself on the tapestry.'

He obeyed, and felt humiliation grow as his cock swayed heavily between his body and the wall. The position was difficult to hold; his thighs were twitching with tension and there was barely enough play in the cuff-chain. He could rest his hands on the wall, but only just.

Suddenly he shot forward like a rocket. Rio's gloved hands were cupping the cheeks of his arse.

'God, you've got a beautiful tush.' She backed up her praise by kneading the hard muscular mounds, first squashing them together, then pulling them as far apart as the stretched skin would allow. Kenny felt his arsehole flutter like a trembling mouth. He was open and utterly and completely exposed, his eyes filled with tears of mortified joy. Strong hands went on pushing and shaping his flesh.

After what seemed a lifetime of shame, Rio kissed his silk-covered shoulder and released her hold on his bottom. 'I love your arse,' she whispered against his ear, 'I'm going to do incredible things to it, sweetheart. You won't know what's hit you.' Sliding her hand around to his cock, she reapplied the tempering pinch. His throbbing tool was momentarily pacified but the pressure on it seemed to transfer elsewhere.

Kenny moaned softly as his anus pulsed and pouted. He felt as if his own body was betraying him; when Rio squeezed a little harder, his hips waggled automatically, coquettishly inviting her attention. I've gone crazy, he thought, as his bottom wafted as lewdly as a bitch's.

'You want it, don't you?' Rio's free hand flirted up the

crease, loitering at the hole itself, dipping in with a teasing little prod, then scooting on to circle the upper curve of his buttock. 'Yes, my sweet, of course, you do,' she answered on his behalf.

It was the sweet demeaning truth.

'Some lubrication, I think,' she announced matter-of-factly.

Kenny ground his forehead into the tapestry. For pity's sake, what was she going to use? Something slick and gooey that came in a tube? Or something more human? Something warm and freshly exuded . . . There was a rustling, then a sigh and a vulgar squelching sound, and when the lubricant finally touched him it was warm. He pushed his bottom towards the anointing, thrilled to feel both her gloved fingers and her newly drawn juices upon him. Her middle finger poked inside a little way, its entry frictionless with such a slippery coating. The fingertip wiggled and he danced; he was a puppet governed by the minutest pressure on and in his anus.

'Is that nice?' she asked, prodding harder. Kenny nodded, staring down at the juice dripping from the end of his prick, and the red-gloved hand that some of it was trickling on to.

'I asked you if this is nice?' The finger pushed again, the movement rougher this time, not exactly hurting but causing a delicious discomfort.

'Yes. It's nice.' It was starting to be sublime, he thought, grateful too for the clever pinching fingers that were taming his cock-tip. Without them, he would've come by now, but Rio was intent, as he'd known she would be, on extending his pleasure as long as she humanly could.

'What would you like me to do next?' The probing finger slid out, then described delicate little circles in the area between his arsehole and his sack.

'I . . . I don't know . . . Oh God, anything! Anything!'

'Oh no no no,' she purred. 'You must tell me what you want. Describe it. I want to hear the words, the details. I want to hear it from your own mouth. I want you to ask me for it. Ask me to push my fingers into your bottom and fuck you until you come.' With her fingers enclosing his testicles, she placed her thumb teasingly over his anus. She had him in both hands now, and she swirled his genitals in a slow rocking movement, exerting her dominion over the most intimate portions of his body, commanding, with her grip, her closeness and her perfume, that he speak the lewdest of words.

And a grown man of thirty-four was suddenly stuttering like a mortified adolescent. 'Please, my lady, I . . .' He closed his eyes, fighting for composure as she feathered his arsehole and perineum, 'Please, Rio, will you put your fingers into . . . into my bottom? Please, my love, I want you to fuck my bottom until I come . . .' His prick trembled as he said it, jumping at the word 'bottom' yet being effortlessly controlled by Rio's magic touch.

'Of course, my darling, whatever you want.' She paused, refocused her attentions, then made a small sound of irritation as the muscle ring resisted her. 'More lubrication, I think.'

Kenny gasped as his arse and his crotch were suddenly his own again, and there were sounds of Rio searching in her case for things. He smiled dreamily, knowing what those things might be.

Then she was back again, close, and he could sense her neatly laying out what she'd chosen. Almost voluptuously anxious, he resisted the urge to look.

A gob of something cool and runny was slapped into the groove of his arse, then worked up and down and in. Rio paused for a moment, then cupping one cheek, pulled it sideways to open the crack a little. Kenny jumped as another enormous dollop of jelly was applied and spread, followed by another and another. Each time she worked it in a little further, the last application being applied only to the hole itself.

'Isn't this nice?' she asked softly. 'I'm going to fill your bum right up with jelly, then it won't hurt a bit.' She reached away for a second – getting another tube? – then Kenny felt something small and metallic touch his arsehole. It stayed there doing nothing, as Rio took careful hold of his cock-tip, then slowly and inexorably he felt the lubricant start oozing into his rectum. Cool, soft and slippery, it nevertheless took up space. Within moments, he started to feel full up, stuffed, and in dangerous need of shitting himself. It's only a reflex, his mind told him, even as his straining, swimming bottom screamed exactly the opposite.

The diabolical filling stopped for a moment, and as Rio reached away again, he snicked his arse-cheeks together to hold in the load. Seconds later a third tube touched his anus, and she started packing him again.

When tears were streaming down his cheeks, and his prick was hard as iron, Rio dropped the tube and plugged his hole with her fingertip.

'There, nice and full, eh?' Her voice was gentle and maternal. 'Wriggle your hips a bit. Feel it all gloop about.'

Plumbing the depths of shame, he obeyed, nearly fainting from the sensations inside, the jelly's heavy drag as it pushed and pulled on the root of his cock.

'Come on, you can do better than that,' coaxed Rio, as her forefinger rode his waggling bum.

He tried. He really did. He made his bursting bottom dance and sway, and almost gnawed the tapestry in his attempt to stave off a humiliating orgasm.

'I . . . Agh . . . I think I'm going to come!'

'No, you're not. Not yet.' The controlling pressure on his cock-tip increased, and completely subjugated, Kenny continued his delicious demeaning display.

It was purgatory, it seemed to go on for hours, and he'd never been more excited in his life. His wife was a she-devil and he adored her so much, he'd suffer any debasement she cared to dream up.

'Still now, darling,' she said suddenly, and a soft note in her voice made Kenny almost sob with relief. She was going to put him out of his misery. 'You can relax your bottom. I'm going to penetrate you . . .'

Planting his feet as firmly as he could, Kenny let his arse go slack and fall back on the intruding finger. Jelly oozed out of his anus as Rio displaced it. The pressure inside him didn't ease though; the rigid, relentless digit was pushing in faster than the lubricant could get out. With a harsh groan, he jammed himself back on to his wife's hand.

'Good, eh, sweetheart?' she murmured, pulling back an inch or two then shoving in harder than ever. Kenny felt as if his cock, his arse and his head were going to explode simultaneously, and his whimpers and squeals seemed only to spur his tormentress on.

She was genuinely fucking his bottom now, pushing in first two fingers, then three, sending jelly drooling and slurping out all over the place. His balls and thighs were coated in the stuff, and his cock and rectum were one gorgeous fiery mass of pleasure. His own juices were bubbling out of his glans, and streaming out over Rio's leather-covered fingers to pour down his shaft.

Kenny's world was a maelstrom. Erotic sound and movement surrounded him inside and out. He heard obscene slurpings and sloshings, felt their shockwaves searing the whole of his bouncing loins. As his pelvis jerked back and forth, suspended between two red-gloved poles of ecstasy, he heard two voices chanting and hardly knew which was which. One was a screaming, shouting, slavering madman; one was a coaxing, soothing, cajoling woman . . . who he knew was just as mad.

'You're going to come now, my love,' she gasped. And deliriously Kenny let her position him for the *coup de grâce*.

She spun him on the chain so he was backed against the tapestry; her hand was between him and the wall, cradling his bottom, her forefinger lodged as deep in his rectum as it would go. Quickly and urgently she brought her free hand to his lips. 'The glove, Kenny, take off my glove!'

Struggling out of the erotic stupor, he understood. He took the tip of one red leather finger between his teeth and felt Rio pull her hand out of the glove, then grasp the thing from his mouth and fling it across the room. She turned his tear-stained face to hers, took his mouth in a kiss, and then took his pulsing cock in her naked fingers.

Two swift exquisite strokes burst his dam. Bliss bathed him from the waist down and love filled his heart and his brain. Rio released his mouth, and as the semen stormed up from his balls and shot out of his cock's tormented tip, they both watched it fly in a high majestic arc that ended many feet away on the carpet. Again and again the creamy stuff jetted out, as if she'd been goading him for a year instead of for barely quarter of an hour.

The spasms were so intense, and the release so complete, that within seconds Kenny was soaked in lethargy, his prick resting wilted and spent in Rio's gentle hold. As he slumped against the wall, he felt her finger slip out of his behind and then her whole hand stroke his arse very tenderly. 'Oh Kenny, I love you so much,' she whispered, patting his cock and then reaching up to release him from his bonds.

Exhausted, he almost fell, but her strong arms were around him immediately, helping to lie down on the soft carpet just a few feet from the sight of his erotic martyrdom. Pulling off her second glove, she lay down beside him, snuggling close so she could massage his freed wrists. The caress was so gentle, so kind that he felt great waves of peace and contentment washing through his whole body from the point where her fingers touched him.

Drifting, he let himself be soothed for a while, then presently, he took her caressing hands to his mouth. Kissing them he tasted himself on the one that'd wanked his cock, all overlaid by the warm afterscent of fine leather. The salutation over, he took her into his arms, enjoying the feel of her bare breasts against his chest and the sensation of his sated prick resting against her cloth-covered thigh. He knew that in a while they'd make simple, elegant, and perfectly orthodox love, but for the moment, they both needed to rest.

'I love you,' she murmured again. 'I wasn't too unkind to you, was I?'

'No, my sweet, you were wonderful.' He reached up to touch her lovely, worried face. 'I upset you before, I admit it. And instead of being punished, you . . . you do a thing like that for me. I could get addicted to being a bad boy, you know.'

'And I could get addicted to it myself,' she whispered,

kissing his fingers. 'I love you, Kenny,' she said as he drowsily pulled her closer.

'And I love you, my lovely lady.' His voice slurred, as sleep took a hold, 'You're so beautiful, so clever . . . So beautiful, beautiful, beautiful, beautiful . . .'

6 Intermezzo II

'. . . beautiful. You're beautiful, beautiful, beautiful,' Josh murmured dreamily, rubbing his face against the gentle hand that caressed him.

'No, I'm not,' said a voice that was firm, yet kind and indulgent. 'I'm probably the ugliest woman you'll ever meet, so come on, Josh, open those sleepy eyes of yours. Face the awful truth.'

'What . . . whadoya mean?' Josh mumbled, reluctant to face that or any truth. And particularly the truth that this time, within seconds, he was fully and completely 'back'. The adventure was over, he wasn't Kenny, and a holy terror with platinum hair was no longer a part of his life.

Isis, however, was still a part of it, and after a few moments of reorientation, Josh opened his bleary eyes to look at her.

'Okay now?' she enquired, her good eye full of concern.

'Yeah, I think so.' Josh blinked a few times, then looked beyond Isis and around the room. There was something else different about this awakening, he realised, taking in his surroundings. This time he'd woken up sooner. He was still in the treatment room and lying on the white leather couch. Sitting up without thinking, he flinched as his head started spinning. With a groan, he flopped back down again, covering his dazzled eyes with his hand . . .

His hand?

Cautiously, Josh tested the mobility of both his limbs and his body, then drew some conclusions. There weren't any wires and restraints on him any more, and his arse was completely his own. Wriggling his bare bottom against the indented leather, he realised that the lower half of the couch was now one undivided piece and the probe, like wonderful tormenting Rio, had gone.

Risking a peek between his fingers, he found that Isis had thoughtfully dimmed the main lights; and when he glanced down at his body, he discovered just how very recently his adventure had ended. His thighs and belly were splattered with silky globules of semen and his cock-head still glistened with a silvery ooze. He was flaccid, but his entire sex felt gorgeous; in fact the whole of his body from the waist down seemed to be bathed in a golden sexual glow. He was totally sated – completely at peace – and though his spunk-smeared skin felt slightly icky, he was too tired, too dreamy, and too deliciously shagged out to care.

Closing his eyes, Josh lay for a few minutes and listened to the small sounds of Isis moving about the room. Total lethargy stopped him wondering what she was up to and he was too spaced out even to analyse his adventure.

He'd been submissive to a woman. Utterly so. As Kenny, he'd let her torment and demean him, and at the same time inflict a pleasure so brilliant and intense that he'd almost lost his mind. Moving himself luxuriously against the soft hide of the couch, he decided that his rear end had a lot to answer for. Lying here drifting, he liked what had 'happened' to him – in fact, the memories were almost too exquisite to bear – but he'd a sneaky feeling that once he was fully awake and firing on all cylinders, he might have a cause for concern.

Frowning slightly, he suddenly detected a new odour in the room. Until now the smells had been predominantly semen and his genital sweat, with an underlay of the citrus cologne he'd applied earlier, and – when she was close – the delicately seductive rose-musk that Isis always wore.

But now there was another smell around, a stronger one, a fresh, bright tang so delectably clean and piney that Josh sighed with appreciation.

He opened his eyes again, and Isis was bending over him, a moist cloth in her hand.

'It's okay. Relax. I'm just going to clean you up a bit.' The lovely odour rose up like a great wave and Josh sighed again as Isis touched the cloth to his sweaty spunk-daubed thigh.

Josh did as he'd been told. He relaxed. He'd no secrets left now, he supposed, so there was nothing to do but enjoy the attention. The cloth was damp, fragrant and surprisingly warm against his skin, and Isis cleaned him with a series of precise but gentle swipes that soon had his thighs and belly pristine.

And it felt fabulous. Half in his dreams, Josh imagined Layla doing this for her Prince, then grinned, remembering belatedly that *he'd* been Layla. Would Rio perform such a service for Kenny? After she'd taken him right to the sexual edge and almost blown every nerve-end in his body?

In the real world, Josh realised, it was probably only Isis who would take care of him so intimately. The whore, Tricksie, looked too proud and haughty to do something so menial, and none of Josh's previous girlfriends had ever had cause to. He'd had a life full of sex, women, and more sex, but never anything so different and so freaky as this.

'Roll onto your side, please, Josh,' said Isis, pressing lightly his naked hip. Starting to tremble slightly, he complied, baring the tight rounds of his buttocks for her inspection. Pressing his face to the soft leather of the couch, he stifled a moan as she took a fresh cloth to his naked bottom.

Even though he'd just had several orgasms and, presumably, disarmed his sexuality for the time being, this meticulous cleansing of his anus and testicles was indescribably pleasurable. Isis's touch was light as thistledown, and the moist cloth so blissfully refreshing to his hot sweaty flesh, that Josh couldn't stop himself crooning with delight.

'Good?' she questioned softly.

'Beautiful,' murmured Josh in reply, lifting his arse to meet her gentle stokes. 'Feels so nice and clean.'

She made a few more delicate passes, then set Josh to gnawing his lip as she probed the puckered hole itself. He was still shaking, his head bowed and pressing against the leather, when the washcloth was replaced by a soft fluffy

101

towel which she dabbed gently over the whole area. 'Okay, pop yourself on to your back and I'll do the rest of you,' she said matter-of-factly.

Josh was grateful for Isis's professional tone. What he'd felt during that intimate and sensitive cleansing – both erotically and for Isis herself – had brought him dangerously close to doing something very very silly. He didn't know quite what it was, but Isis's briskness had saved him from it; helped him face the fact that she was now going to clean his penis.

Flat on his back again, Josh ventured a glance downwards.

He wasn't erect but he was getting there. His flesh had perceptibly thickened, and his shaft had the characteristic meaty look to it that usually preceded a hard-on. It was only because he'd already come so many times, he thought shakily, that he wasn't a screaming rampant pole by now. After what Isis had just done to his behind . . . His tool gave a tiny but visible throb and he looked up immediately into her pale, scarred face.

She'd been watching his rod as attentively as he had, but now she met his eyes. Josh tried to hold her gaze but couldn't; his eyelids fluttered closed. It'd been pointless, anyway, because like a mystic, one-eyed sphinx, Isis was completely unreadable.

But as he lay there, locked in the interminable seconds-long wait for her touch, Josh set his highly coloured imagination on 'hypothesise'. How did she really respond to his nakedness and vulnerability – to his spunk, his prick and his orgasms?

Did she get off on having men at her mercy? And specifically, and closest to Josh's heart . . . did she get off on him?

What was it she'd said? That she was tempted. Could she really be indifferent to him when he was strapped to a table in front of her: half-nude, with a huge erection and a dildo rammed inside his bottom. She was a sensual, highly imaginative woman; surely a sight like that would turn her on?

'Isis – ,' he began, then stopped on a half-drawn breath as she began to wipe the moist cloth over his prick.

'Yes?' she enquired, taking him very delicately by his cock-tip and lifting him up so she could pass the soft material along the throbbing underside of his tool.

'Nothing,' he gasped through gritted teeth. 'It's nothing.'

'Sure?'

'Sure.'

'Okay,' she said blandly, then ever so gently tilted his cock from side to side to wipe its now considerable circumference.

I'm going to die, thought Josh, knowing that he was now fully erect. Isis's painstaking ablutions were both agony and ecstasy, and his hips bounced when she cleaned the hypersensitive ridge beneath his glans.

'Would you like me to bring you off?'

Her voice sounded cool, clear and bell-like, and its very detachment calmed Josh's whirling brain.

'Yes, please,' he replied, emulating her tone, 'I'd be grateful . . .' He paused, then managed to look her unblinkingly in her equally unblinking eyes, 'But, please. No frills. Just make me ejaculate, that's all.' He closed his eyes again, proud of his clinical choice of words.

For the next few moments he made his face a mask and his body a statue, and concentrated the whole of his consciousness on his aching prick. He tried to ignore the fact that it was Isis who was wanking him off, that it was her expert fist gliding so superbly over his tool. He told himself that one pair of hands was much like another, and that even though these hands were slim and scarred, and so inventive and accomplished that they made him want to weep like a child, this was really no different at all to any average, everyday tossing off.

But it *was* different. And better. And utterly and completely glorious.

In a series of smooth, precisely pressured strokes, Isis slid the skin of his prick over its solid, blood-filled core. The action was millimetre perfect in both speed and drag-length.

And there were no frills. It was a pure masturbation, elegant: hand and prick in magic synchronicity. And when, after approximately a minute, he came and screamed her name, his soul shot out of his loins and was neatly caught in a small square of moist, perfumed cloth.

Dimly, an indeterminate time later, a half-dreaming Josh felt Isis clean him up again, then drape his sexed-out body with a thick, soft blanket.

'Get some sleep, Josh,' she said quietly, stroking his brow as she had when he'd first woken. 'You weren't really ready to wake up yet. You're imagining things. You don't know what you're talking about.'

But I do, thought Josh. I came, and I screamed your name when I did. I didn't imagine it, lady, did you? He grinned then, and fell asleep, cuddled in his blanket and vaguely aware that he might just have been speaking out aloud . . .

'Well?'

'Well what?'

'What did you think of it?' Isis enquired when they were back in La Selene.

Josh was himself again now, dressed and nursing a much-needed double scotch. 'Oh, you mean the hand job?' he replied, wondering why he was being so obtuse. 'It was first class, Isis. I've never had better. And if that was the "no frills" version, God help me if I ever get the de-luxe.'

'Idiot,' she hissed, then took a rather large pull at her drink – the large whisky she'd surprised Josh by accepting.

Josh sipped his own drink, feeling both niggled and aroused that Isis was being as evasive as he was. Why wouldn't she admit she'd just given him the most beautiful wank he'd ever had? And why had her scarred face suddenly become a convenient mask? She was acting as if they were total strangers when not half an hour ago she'd had his prick in her long elegant fingers.

'You still haven't answered me,' she said after a few moments. 'What did you think of your first self-generated fantasy?'

'Self-generated?'

'Yes.' She turned to him, her good eye glinting, 'I thought you realised. Tonight's adventure had nothing to do with me, or Kenny and Rio for that matter. They probably went home and played Scrabble. It was your scenario, Josh. What you wanted.'

'Holy shit.' She'd knocked him sideways. Again. With a quick, nervous gesture Josh summoned another round of whiskies.

'What's wrong, Josh?' asked Isis after the fresh drinks had arrived. 'You got exactly what you wanted. You tailored your own fantasy tonight, at least your subconscious did. And there's nothing wrong with wanting to be submissive.'

'I don't . . . I didn't . . .' Josh faltered as a truly horrendous suspicion formed. He'd never really taken much notice of Isis's computer hardware, but now he got a clear picture of a fine-wire head set, a touch-contact pad . . . And . . . Oh God, what if that monitor of hers didn't always show incomprehensible strings of figures?

'Isis, you know when I'm . . . when I'm under?'

She was watching him very closely now . . .

'When I'm having an "adventure", can you actually see what's happening?' He whipped out his hand, caught her leather-clad one, and squeezed it hard, 'Look, Isis, tell me. Do you see all that crazy shit? Tell me. I want to know!'

'Keep your hair on, Josh. And stop hurting me,' she ordered, shaking off his grip with surprising ease. 'It *is* possible to represent the experience visually and for me to watch it.'

Josh gasped, but Isis went on quickly, 'However, I choose *not* to watch. It doesn't seem ethical. I'd only switch to visual if you seemed to be in distress.'

'Thank Christ for that.'

'And besides, I don't need to view,' she announced blithely. 'I can interpret neural wave forms as clearly as holovid . . . I know what's going on without having to see it.' She paused for wicked effect. 'And of course, you *tell* me what's happening. I get a running commentary. Not all clients are vocal when they're under, but you certainly are. You're a one-man band, Josh, a three-ring circus. I've never been so right royally entertained in my life!'

Josh – the one who'd screamed and groaned and whimpered – was suddenly struck dumb, beyond horror or embarrassment. He couldn't think of a single thing to say. The thought of Isis listening to his ecstatic outpourings was . . . was . . . His mind became a complete blank. He lifted his glass towards his lips then halted it halfway, just staring.

'Josh,' she said softly, placing her gloved hand on his arm.

'What can I say that I haven't howled or babbled or grunted already?' he replied, his sense of the absurd rushing in to save him. He took a quick swig of whisky. 'Do you hear everything?'

'No, Josh, not everything. I was exaggerating a bit there. Sorry,' she said with a slightly sheepish look, 'it's just fragments actually. Real time and dream time aren't contiguous. What you experience is too compressed for a running commentary as such . . .'

'Thank God. You must think I'm a raving loony.'

'Josh, look at me,' said Isis with a steady seriousness that, ludicrously, made Josh's prick leap and throb. 'You don't think this diminishes you, do you?'

'I don't know,' he said, both confused and intensely turned on by the grave expression on that odd, lop-sided face.

'You've a beautiful voice, Josh. However you use it,' her hand tightened on his cloth-covered forearm, 'you're magical, special. When you cry out in orgasm it . . . it touches the soul, Josh, it's thrilling. Your cock stands up like a great spear, your spunk shoots out . . . Oh God,' she paused, as if she knew she'd said too much, given herself away just as he did when he was 'under'. 'It's . . . you're awesome, Josh, quite unique . . .' Her voice fizzled out awkwardly.

Josh's heart was pounding and his mouth dry. She *did*

want him! His arousal, his fantasies, his climaxes: they all turned her on . . .

'Come back to my flat, Isis,' he gasped without stopping to think. 'Please! I want you, you want me. We'd be fabulous together.'

Isis was silent for about a minute. A minute in which Josh almost forgot to breathe. A minute in which his cock seemed to vibrate in his pants. A minute in which the most important thing in the whole of his thirty-odd years of life was to take this woman to bed and come deeply and violently in her cunt. He wanted to spew his very soul into her gash, to live in her and die in her, and to make her live and die in him.

'You know it's impossible, don't you?' she said at last, in a voice that didn't sound quite steady; and when she slanted him a cautious glance, Josh saw more expression in that half a face than he'd ever seen in anyone else's whole one. 'Thanks for the drink, Josh, but I think I ought to be going now.'

Josh felt torn in two. The stud in him – the successful fucker of Julia and a hundred others like her – wanted to tell Isis to go to hell. Who did she think she was, turning him down like this?

Then, perhaps a nanosecond later, the real Josh – the nice guy who didn't like hurting people – told Mr Hardcase-Legover to take a running jump. Isis had her reasons for avoiding involvement, and he could accept them – even if his erection *was* killing him.

'I'm sorry, Isis, I was out of line,' he said, smiling what he hoped was a winning smile. 'Why don't you stay a while? I promise not to come on to you.'

'Okay,' she said quietly, smiling her own bizarre version of a smile, 'but not for long, though. And don't try and make things complicated.'

'You got it,' he said, almost laughing with relief. 'I'll behave myself. Cross my heart.'

It was easier said than done.

As they sat and chatted, Josh's hard-on showed no sign

whatsoever of subsiding; in fact, if anything, it got even stiffer.

Am I a masochist on top of everything else? he wondered when it got to the point of actual pain and he found he was enjoying it. Surreptitiously, he edged forward in his seat and forced the aching flesh hard against the double-stitched seam of his leather jeans. The sensation almost made his eyes cross; and as he summoned a vision of Isis, nude and waiting for him, he suspected his cock was probably leaking its juice for her.

'So, what do you think of your fantasies so far then?' Isis enquired, obviously trying to steer matters towards their bona-fide relationship.

'Sensational,' he replied with feeling. 'But disturbing too.'

'In what way disturbing?'

'The sexual pleasure is mind-blowing.' He smiled briefly at the apt choice of word. 'But I'm learning about a whole new Josh Mortimer. I'm discovering a side of me I never knew existed.' He sipped speculatively at his drink, trying to ignore Isis's slim body just inches away, the haunting tang of her perfume, the fact that what went on in her brilliant mind was probably ten times as sexy as her supremely feminine body. 'I . . . I'm beginning to wonder about my sexuality,' he went on, 'the submission, the anal thing . . . I always thought I was strictly macho, strictly hetero, but now I'm not so sure.'

'Does it matter?' Isis asked softly. 'Heterosexual. Homosexual. Bisexual. What's the problem as long as you're *sexual*?'

'I suppose you're right.'

'I know I am. Now stop worrying and just go with the flow.'

Easy for her to say; she was a scientist, a sexologist, not a man discovering alarming new facets of himself. And not just when he was 'adventuring' either. 'Isis, these trips I have . . . They don't have any effect on my imagination in general, do they? It's just that everything I . . . er . . .

Well, what I mean is . . . My ordinary fantasies seem more real now as well.'

'Hmm. That's interesting,' she answered thoughtfully, and obviously half to herself. 'It has been predicted, but you're the first actual case I've encountered.'

'Case of what?' demanded Josh, mental alarm bells clanging wildly.

'Theoretically, the process of sensory re-creation should actually expand the network of neural paths, and quite literally augment a person's imagination and their ability to dream.' She turned to him, her good eye twinkling, 'That's what must've happened to you, Josh. I told you you were special, didn't I?'

Josh went hot and cold. 'Do you mean to say that my brain's actually changed?'

'Only for the better,' replied Isis archly. 'Imagination is one of humankind's greatest gifts.'

'If you say so,' Josh mumbled grudgingly. Right now *his* imagination was promoting severe discomfort in the groin area. He could not stop picturing Isis's naked body and wondering what it'd be like to be thrusting into it.

They lapsed into thoughtful silence for a while, Isis staring into her glass, her scarred face enigmatic; Josh slowly sipping his scotch, and resisting the urge to wriggle in order to relieve his throbbing erection.

'What about *your* imagination?' he demanded suddenly. It was no good just sitting here aching; the pictures in his head were getting too vivid . . . Wasn't it about time they looked at *her* pictures instead?

'What about it?' She eyed him warily.

'Well, is it boosted or whatever? You've had "adventures". Has your brain got extra networks and stuff?'

'Josh! What are you on about now?'

'I . . . I was trying to find out what your fantasies are,' he admitted shamefacedly, 'and whether you have the same incredible ones that I have.'

'Nice try, Mr Mortimer,' she said with a soft, throaty laugh, and Josh liked the sweet way her body shook in time to it. In fact he liked everything about that body – whether static or moving – although it had to be said that for some-one who protested that she only wanted a business relation-ship with him, her clothes seemed to indicate otherwise.

She'd changed her outfit since they were here earlier and now wore a sleek black ensemble – quite similar in a way, he noticed, to the one he was wearing. But her fine-knit sweater clung faithfully to a chest that wasn't at all similar to his. And the silky stuff it was woven from looked quite lewd in the way it defined a pair of obviously unfettered breasts. And her trousers were worse, if anything. No, they were better . . . Oh hell!

Did women know what jeans cut like that did to the men who looked at them? Did Isis know? Did she realise that the reinforced seam that ran between her thighs was almost as masturbatory as the one that ran between his?

That double-stitched line – worked in satin in her case – was so distinct, so come-and-get-it-it's-here, that Josh was having a very difficult time restraining an urge to reach out and run his fingers down it. Her cleft would be directly under that join . . . He imagined the heat and darkness; the pungent, humid furriness. Then, parting the thick puffy lips, the sticky yearning juiciness within . . . Oh, to get his hand in, his tongue in, or best of all, his needy twitching cock!

'Josh! What the hell planet are you on? You haven't spoken for at least a minute . . . Are you all right?'

'Er . . . Oh yes, I'm fine. I was just thinking . . .' Josh babbled, his augmented imagination putting the taste of her lovejuice on to his tongue with a startling and groin-wrenching reality. In that instant, his disorientated mind flung him back to Rio and her stretchy leggings, then threw him forward the next giddy, but logical step . . .

Did Isis masturbate? And what did she fantasise about whilst doing so?

'You were going to tell me about your fantasies,' he asked, knowing full well that such a childish trick had no chance of working.

'I was going to do no such thing!' Isis retorted, nearly killing Josh as she sat up straight, inhaled, and seemed to

110

offer her breasts even more blatantly to his gaze. 'And anyway, you'd be grossly disappointed.'

'No way.'

'Don't be so sure, Josh,' she replied, taking a sip from her glass. 'My fantasies are so average they'd sound boring after Pleasurezone . . .'

'Try me.'

'Okay,' she murmured, rubbing her finger provocatively around the rim of her glass, and bringing Josh almost to the point of ejaculation. 'Okay. What I fantasise about, Josh, is romance. All that mushy stuff – soft lights, candle-lit dinners, champagne from my slipper and all that jazz. Oh, I like to dream about a little screwing *after* that, but to me the hors d'oeuvres are as important as the main course. Disappointed?' She met his eye challengingly, something almost combative in her own good orb.

'No! Go on.'

'I dream about a man who's gentle and gentlemanly, who'd treat me like a lady, as if this didn't exist.' She touched her face, putting her red leather glove against the ruby-red cicatrix.

'But can't it be fixed?' Josh said, suddenly wondering why Isis had to *stay* scarred. Current surgical techniques were amazing.

'You don't understand, Josh, do you? This is "after", not "before". They've fixed me up as best they could. I had rejection problems. Grafts wouldn't take. I could've had sterile plastiskin put on it, I suppose; it looks almost real. But at least this is still *me*.' She patted the crumpled tissue beneath her muddy eye. 'This is the best it gets, Josh . . . For keeps.'

But it shouldn't matter, thought Josh, soaping his own unblemished face.

He was in the shower now, an hour and a half later, but he was still brooding about Isis, her dreams and her stigma, and the lack of men who'd look beyond a few square centimetres of burned skin and see the gloriously sexual woman

111

it belonged to. He couldn't be the only one to whom the scar didn't matter, could he?

I could give you the old-fashioned romance, Isis, he thought as he lathered his body and wondered what hers would feel like through a coating of fine, scented bubbles . . .

Closing his eyes, he wished her into the shower with him, and slid his hands over her soft, fresh skin. Growing instantly erect, he cupped the lovely globes of her breasts, then moved lower to ease his fingers between her thighs and explore the soft silky thatch and the even silkier slit within. Dipping deep, he took up some of her moisture on his fingertips, and brought it slick and savoury to his hungering mouth. What meal could taste more delicious?

And they would have wined and dined, of course. Caviare, smoked salmon, the finest delicacies . . . Candlelight, moonlight, music, the whole bit. But nothing, not even the finest vintage champagne, would compare to the flavour of Isis's beautiful cunt.

As the water poured down, he explored the interior of this extravagant fantasy, expanded and enhanced a pampering, old-fashioned indulgence that would blend inexorably into luxurious and mind-bending sex.

He'd drink his champagne from Isis's body: lick it from her breasts, lap it from her navel, slurp and slobber it from her juice-sodden quim. He'd get drunk on her, get high on her; gorge himself senseless on the luscious cocktail between her long sleek thighs . . .

But wait a minute. What else was on the menu?

Aha! The caviare. I'll give you caviare, you gorgeous woman! In the world behind his eyelids he looked down at his hand: a hand full of sticky shiny fish eggs – a thousand credits' worth – that he jammed, with enormous glee, straight into her equally glistening cunt. He saw her writhe in outrage, moan, then lick her lips and buck her body into his messy black-smeared grip. The liquor from the tiny crushed eggs blended with hers, and Josh's mouth was awash with saliva as he bent to taste the brew.

Oh yes, he murmured, sucking and swallowing down.

Too delicious! Salt on salt on musk . . . Womanflesh . . . Orgasm . . .

'Do you like caviare?' he asked her two nights later, when they were sitting at the bar in La Selene.

'Caviare? Just what the hell are you up to, Josh Mortimer?' Isis demanded, sounding tetchy and looking narrow-eyed. 'If you think you're going to get into my pants by offering me caviare, you can forget it.'

The delicious irony of her words set Josh laughing uncontrollably for almost a minute, and even though *he* couldn't stop chortling, he was aware that the frowning Isis was decidedly unamused.

'Sat on a feather, have we?' she enquired tartly, shifting on her seat as if in discomfort.

'No . . . no . . .' Josh managed when his mirth had subsided. 'It's just that what you said reminded me of a rather nifty little fantasy I've thought of . . . Can't do it with the old box of tricks, though, because you were in it.' He shot her a sidelong glance and surprised an expression of pain creasing the unmarked side of her face. 'Hey, Isis, are you okay?' Reaching out, he patted her hand, a hand clad tonight in the finest black kid leather.

'Yeah, I'm okay,' she answered rather wearily, then flashed him one of her skew-whiff smiles, 'and I'm sorry for snarling at you like that. It was uncalled for.'

'No harm done,' Josh replied, still concerned by her obvious unease. 'And that offer, caviare and stuff . . . it still stands. No strings attached.'

'That's kind, Josh. But I'll pass, if you don't mind.' She paused, thought, then grinned again. 'I'd love a glass of mineral water instead, though.'

'You got it.' Josh signalled the barman – the seemingly omnipresent blond – and ordered wine for himself and a bottle of Astrapure for Isis. 'Are you sure you won't have a real drink?' he asked as their order was being filled.

'No, thanks, Josh. I don't think it's wise.' And when the barman returned, she addressed him as he poured her water, 'Do you have any analgesic handy, Guido?'

113

The young man nodded, reached into a drawer behind his bar, then dropped a couple of green capsules into Isis's outstretched palm. With a grateful smile, she tossed them between her soft, rose-glossed lips and washed them down with a swig of her water.

'There,' she said more perkily, 'I'll soon feel better now.'

'What's wrong, Isis?' Josh peered at her worriedly. She looked as beautiful as ever on her good side, and the scar as always looked exotic and titillating, but studying her more closely, Josh discerned some changes: she looked paler, there were tiny lines of strain around her eyes . . . and though she still looked svelte and delectably slim, there was something vaguely ungainly about her. She looked – and it sounded barmy to Josh even as he thought it – ever so slightly too big for her skin. Everything about her seemed to bulge a little, like a fully ripe fruit; and although it was only to the minutest degree, her flesh looked puffy, her breasts swollen.

'Is it . . . Is it your injuries?' he persisted when she didn't answer.

'No, Josh,' she murmured, giving him a small wry smile. 'Nothing so radical . . .'

'What then?'

It was Isis's turn to laugh now, a short ironic chuckle. 'You'd think that in this day and age, when science can take us to other worlds and even *I* can create a gizmo like Pleasurezone . . . You'd think someone could invent an effective cure for period pains, wouldn't you?'

So that was it. Considering his reply, Josh studied his companion carefully, then felt a sudden and quite astounding response. For some reason he couldn't explain, the idea that Isis might be bleeding brought an intense stab of arousal. He had a sudden flash vision of her vulva agleam with blood – and his prick replied with a sudden, painful leap.

'I . . . I'm sorry if you're hurting,' he muttered, ashamed of his rather weird reaction. 'If you don't feel like . . . Well, if you'd rather go home and put your feet up or something, it's okay by me. Another night will do just fine.'

114

'No, it's okay, Josh. I'll struggle on bravely. I wouldn't dream of denying you your jollies.' She toasted him with her blandly innocent tipple. 'But thanks.' She hesitated, vaguely embarrassed. 'Thanks for caring.'

But I do care, he wanted to shout. I more than care. I'm falling under your spell, Doctor Isis, and I'm falling so fast I'm frightened by it.

'I'll be fine in a minute anyway,' she went on, oblivious of Josh's silent passion. 'That junk of Guido's usually does the trick.'

'Are they dangerous?'

'Hell no!' Isis laughed. 'And anyway I'm taking them under medical supervision, aren't I? I may be somewhat "fringe" now, but I've never actually been struck off.'

'I was just worried about you.'

'Well, thanks again, Josh,' she replied, already visibly brighter. 'But it's your welfare we're concerned with, isn't it? Any thoughts for tonight?'

'Not really,' he lied, his mind full of Isis's cunt. In a series of freeze-frames he covered it in caviare again, then semen . . . and kisses. He had a million outrageous fantasies to live with this woman, and yet, by her decree, none of them could be re-created by Pleasurezone.

'I can't make you out, Josh,' she cried, tapping her black-clad fingers exasperatedly. 'You strike me as such an imaginative guy – especially now – and when you've got the chance of a lifetime to use that imagination, you strike out.' Turning from him, she glanced sharply across the room. 'Never mind . . . here comes somebody who might help. Two somebodies, in fact.'

Following her gaze, he saw that Tricksie had just entered the bar, closely followed by the same steely-eyed character she'd been with on Josh's first visit to La Selene. The redhead, as before, looked magnificent, her curvaceous body enticingly displayed in a scarlet leather bustier and mini-skirt, with a bold broad-shouldered jacket in the same eye-catching hide. It wasn't a very subtle look, Josh had to admit, especially as her crimson hair was teased out into the archetypal hooker's mane; yet for all her screaming

115

sluttishness, the woman still had class. And so, in an equally unlikely way, did her companion, despite the fact that to Josh's mind the stranger looked just as sluttish as the call-girl beside him.

He's her pimp, decided Josh, his suspicions of last time confirmed by Tricksie's almost deferential demeanour. The impression was only strengthened by the man's equally archetypal choice of clothes . . .

In almost every movie and holovid, the evil, unscrupulous pimp wore a flashy white suit. Josh couldn't be sure that Tricksie's pimp was either evil or unscrupulous, but he certainly wore the uniform: a fluidly cut white ensemble in a fine lightweight linen that draped like a dream and seemed to float over its wearer's body as he almost danced across the room. Josh had never seen anyone move so sinuously and yet still look all male. The white-clad man sashayed forward like an albino panther, and to his utter amazement, Josh felt a faint reactive twinge in his loins.

Maybe I am bi after all, he thought, unable to look away from the stunning stranger, and feeling the hairs at the back of his neck stand on end. Flustered, he managed to wrench his glance from the pimp and turn to Isis.

Who was watching him closely . . .

'Diabolo has that effect on people,' she murmured knowingly as the couple seated themselves some distance away at the other end of the bar.

'What effect? What the fuck are you talking about?' Josh demanded, rounding on her.

'You know.' Her glance flicked to his groin, and Josh could've kicked himself when his eyes followed hers.

Actually there was nothing showing as such – his jeans and briefs were tight enough to contain any incriminating bulges – but Josh had an irrational suspicion that Isis had super powers, and in this specific case, x-ray vision.

'No, I don't,' he snapped, 'I was looking at them both. Hell, Isis, the guy's so obvious, anybody'd look at him. That suit is just too much.'

'Or too little.'

Isis's comment was cryptic until Josh followed her eyeline

116

straight to Diabolo's groin. Unlike Josh, the pimp was obviously *not* wearing underwear. His semi-erect cock was clearly visible through the pale summer-weight fabric of his trousers. Josh looked away quickly.

But not quickly enough. Out of the corner of his eye, Josh saw Diabolo glance narrowly across at him from under the brim of a snow-white fedora hat.

'He's clocked you, you know,' whispered Isis. 'That weasel has seven extra senses. He can sniff out sex from a thousand yards.'

'And how come you know so much about him?' Josh demanded, turning to her and choosing attack as his best – and only – form of defence.

'Because he's a colleague of mine,' she replied smoothly.

Josh's jaw dropped at the implications, and for a full ten seconds his mind went blank. Then came the questions.

'Are you a procuress on the side then?' he sniped. 'Do you run a brothel as well as a fantasy machine? I wish I'd have known. It might have been cheaper for you to get me a few whores instead of frying my willy and scrambling my mind. You could fix me up with Tricksie for a start.'

'I'm sure it could be arranged,' Isis said coolly. 'Although I'm not a madam . . .'

'I'm sorry,' Josh said grudgingly. 'But I'd still like to know what a shark like that has to do with you.' He nodded in the general direction of Diabolo.

'Well, I won't deny the ol' Moon Devil is a bit of a cold fish – ' Isis smiled faintly, 'but I wouldn't go so far as to say he's a shark.'

'Moon Devil?'

'It's just a nickname Tricksie and I came up with.' Isis nodded then to the woman in question; who, having obviously caught her own name, was smiling across at Isis. 'The devil bit from "Diabolo": a corruption of the Spanish and Italian words for devil. And the "moon" – well, Tricksie's noticed that whenever there's a full moon Diabolo always wants to fuck her.'

'Oh.' Josh was puzzled. 'I always thought it was strictly business between whores and pimps.'

'Not this whore and pimp,' Isis said breezily, 'Tricksie adores him. She's besotted. And as for Diabolo . . . God knows. I don't know if he feels anything for anybody. He's pure ice. But he's got a prodigious, if somewhat spasmodic sexual appetite, which Tricksie is more than happy to feed . . . when the moon's full, of course.'

'There's a full moon tonight,' observed Josh, glancing over his shoulder at the big picture window – and a full and strangely oversized moon hanging high in the City of Night sky. 'Looks like Tricksie might be getting an unpaid fuck.'

'Or something,' Isis commented quietly.

The other couple were barely speaking, yet seemed completely absorbed in each other; and this gave Josh the chance for some discreet observation.

Diabolo's facial features, skintone and hair all betrayed his Latin heritage. His hair was blue-black, longish and straight, framing an olive-complected face that was all fine, handsome angles and knifelike Hispanic cheekbones. It was the hardest, coldest face Josh had ever seen, yet the man had a potent sexual menace that seemed to hiss around him like a living flame.

Diabolo was also obviously quite phenomenally hung and obviously didn't give a damn who knew it. As if on cue, the man shoved one hand in his pocket and tightened his thin white trousers across his groin, emphasising his half-risen prick.

No wonder Tricksie's mad for him, thought Josh ruefully as his own prick throbbed. A tool like that could split a woman in two – even one who'd seen as much action as Tricksie.

Don't think about it, he admonished himself, but was helpless to stop his souped-up mind presenting him the naked Diabolo. The man would be thinnish, yet strong, his skin dark and gleaming, his body hair soot-black, his prick long, purple, meaty and substantial. Appalled, Josh found himself imagining what it'd be like to suck. How it would feel to take that huge rod inside him. In his –

Oh God, please! What's happening to me? he begged

silently. Moving uneasily on his stool, he imagined the transceiver probe in his backside, then sobbed inaudibly as his precocious imagination turned it into Diabolo's gigantic, throbbing cock.

'Are you all right?' enquired Isis at his side.

Josh snapped gratefully back to reality. 'Yeah, I'm fine,' he lied.

'You made a sort of moaning noise. It's not your time of the month too, is it?'

'What?'

'You moaned and wriggled about. You looked how I feel, as if you'd got the red rag blues.'

Josh took a pull of his drink and thought about Isis's words and a lot of other things – in particular a certain man in white. 'I almost wish I had,' he said quietly, giving in to the relief of confiding in her. 'It'd make some of the feelings I'm having more acceptable . . .'

'Don't worry, Josh,' she said softly, pressing her black-clad fingers over his. 'There's nothing to be ashamed of. There's nothing wrong . . .' She paused, seemed to consider, then went on. 'I often have sexual feelings about Tricksie.'

'You do?'

'Yeah. So I've done the logical thing. I've had sex with her to see what it was all about.'

Josh's mind boggled and his crotch pulsated. What a fabulous, fabulous concept. The most intriguing woman he'd ever met, making it with the one who was probably the second most intriguing – even though he'd never actually met her!

'And – and how is it?' he stuttered.

'Beautiful,' Isis replied simply. 'She's an accomplished lover, with either sex.'

'That I can well believe,' replied Josh in a low, awestruck tone, his attention on the crimson-haired whore now, rather than her erotically dangerous pimp. His imagination put up a panoply of steamy images: Tricksie and Isis entwined and loving in every imaginable way, kissing, sucking, fingering and stroking; using mouths, hands, dildoes;

119

giving pleasure and receiving it; blowing each other's minds. He set them top to tail, and the vision was as harmonious as it was sexy. Dainty red mouths nibbled at dainty red cunts. Both were pale women, yet together they were piquant: Isis's multicoloured hair shimmered like watered silk on Tricksie's white belly, while the whore's scarlet curls were a fire-cascade between her lover's long, graceful thighs . . .

'And do you . . . er . . . often? Josh offered tentatively, his eyes struggling to focus on reality.

'From time to time,' Isis answered matter-of-factly. 'Usually when Diabolo's giving her a hard time, which is what appears to be happening right now.'

'How do you mean, "hard time"? Does he beat her up or something?' Josh followed her look, aghast at the thought, yet unable to ignore his stereotypical ideas about the sex industry.

'He doesn't "beat up" as such.' Isis's voice sounded tightly controlled, under stress, and Josh wondered just how deep her relationship was with *both* the parties involved. 'But he does "hit" now and again.'

'Has he ever hit you?' Josh demanded in a sudden flash of insight. Maybe this Moon Devil was more than just Isis's colleague?

'No. But then again, the relationship between us isn't quite that deep.'

How deep was deep?

'Have you ever fucked him?' asked Josh as acute jealousy added itself to the stew of emotions churning his guts. The feeling was fiery and for a moment quite all-consuming, although he was at a loss to know exactly whom he was jealous of. And which of the three – at this precise instant – he wanted most, the whore, the pimp or the mad doctor?

'Yes,' she replied evenly, stunning Josh to the core yet again. Because she'd resisted him, his ego had slyly been telling him she didn't screw at all; and now in the space of a minute, she'd calmly revealed not only an ongoing lesbian relationship, but the fact that she'd had sex with a man she herself admitted was a stone-hearted sadist!

120

'Why?' he asked numbly.

'Because he's got a great big prick and he's a fabulous lay,' she answered with an edge of cruelty, 'and – because he's a misfit himself and he knows it. It never feels like a pity fuck.' On the word 'pity' she turned to face Josh square-on, as if to remind him graphically of what made *her* a misfit.

He imagined them then, two outcasts fucking like stoats. Elegant, intellectual Isis with her tragically flawed face, and lean, volatile Diabolo with his criminally flawed personality. It'd be like a clash of two ice gods: two characters who were so cool and detached writhing in a white-hot physical mesh. Two bodies, one pale and one olive . . . Cunt and prick. Sloshing and stabbing. Coming . . .

'And is it "beautiful" with him too?' he demanded savagely.

'That's not exactly the word I'd use to describe it,' she answered neutrally. 'And you know precisely why I can't fuck you, don't you, Josh?'

The bitch had read his mind again. Or at least some of it.

'Okay, already!' he snapped. 'But is it good with him then?'

'Yes it is,' she said at length. 'In a purely technical sense. He's been a male whore himself in his time – for both sexes – so he knows everything there is to know about fucking.' She paused again, then held Josh's eyes with her own good one, 'But there's no emotional involvement, if that's what's bugging you. It's just physical satisfaction on both sides. Sweat and orgasms. Feeding an appetite. Scratching an itch. Bodies – and minds for the stage direction – but no real soul involved. I doubt if Diabolo even has one.'

'Oh,' was all Josh could manage. His mind was a maelstrom of emotions and erotic images. He *did* have a soul! And that soul, along with his hard-driving physical need, was just one huge knot right now, an impossible ravelling of himself and three other, quite singular, human beings. He wanted sex and he wanted it soon and he wanted it with some, if not all, of this remarkable triumvirate. Isis was

121

adamantly locked out, of course, but tonight's adventure *must* contain the whore and the pimp, although in what combination, Josh still had no real notion.

'About tonight,' he began. 'The adventure. I . . .'

Isis glanced across the room as he spoke, and as Josh followed her eyes, he saw Tricksie gazing longingly at her white-clad companion. Diabolo was staring moodily into a glass full of something clear and decidedly sinister-looking, unaware, it seemed, of his companion's presence. When he did look up however, she tossed her head and assumed a mask of haughty indifference.

'Power games,' observed Isis, then turned back to face Josh. 'Do you want some of that?'

'I dunno.'

'You could find out something tonight, Josh, if you've got the bottle.'

'What do you mean?'

'I can run you a gay scene with Diabolo. And then you'd know how you really felt about it.'

Josh felt his erection throb at the idea, but his atavistic dread was stronger than the bizarre twistings of lust. 'I don't think so, Isis,' he said, biting his lip and not knowing if he was doing the right thing. 'I'm not ready for that. I don't think I ever will be. I can't explain . . .'

'You don't have to, Josh,' she said, suddenly gentler. 'Pleasurezone is about doing what you want. I can't force you into things you *don't* want. I was just suggesting an option.'

'But I'd still like . . . Oh God.' He pushed his hair back from his face in utter perplexity. 'It's the same old story, Isis. I really don't know what I want.'

'Don't worry, Josh,' she replied confidently. 'I've got a good idea of what to give you tonight. An "F & F". Trust me. I'll set some parameters to suit and give you free choice within them. You'll be all right. You'll see.'

Josh looked into those eyes then, those strange odd eyes, and knew he would be all right. And he knew he did trust her. 'Okay then,' he said, his heart lighter than it'd been all night, and his rod harder. 'I'm ready now. Can we get on with my adventure?'

'You bet.' Isis grinned and rose gracefully from her stool, her pain apparently gone. She led him towards the back of the room and the red-baize-covered door.

'What did you mean when you said Diabolo was your colleague?' asked Josh as he lay strapped to the treatment table, his arse impaled on the transceiver probe.

During most of his preparation it'd been difficult to think of anything or anybody but Isis. Her gentle hands had readied his body, and stroked his prick to renewed stiffness. Her soft husky voice had calmed his still-recurring colly-wobbles over restraints and drugs. Her slender, white-clad body had strengthened his erection just by being close to it.

But as the fat bung had slid deep inside his shuddering bottom, Josh's psyche had dragged him kicking and screaming back to thoughts of the nattily suited pimp and to what the invasive probe was so horridly reminiscent of. He felt himself hovering on the brink of an orgasm, helpless in the grip of an exotic full-sense vision of Diabolo bugger-ing him. His own prick shuddered as he seemed to feel Diabolo's penis remorselessly reaming his hole, its rigid length and width stretching him to a delicious but eye-watering openness . . .

'Oh God, Isis. Help me! I'm going to come,' he pleaded. 'Talk to me, tell me what you meant . . . '

'It doesn't matter if you do come, Josh,' she murmured soothingly as he stroked back a few stray locks of hair, clearing his brow for the mask, 'but all the same, I'll answer your question . . .'

Folding back his soft yellow shirt, she began placing the less intimate of the sensors, the one in his rectum and the one at his cock-tip being already unequivocally in place.

'I refer to Diabolo as a colleague because he is one. Who do you think looks after Pleasurezone's female clients?'

'Are you nuts?' Josh cried, struggling to sit up, realising he couldn't, then gasping for air as he sank back even

123

deeper onto the probe. When he could speak again, and Isis had wiped away the pre-come drooling from the end of his prick, he went on. 'The man's a psycho, a sadist. You don't mean to tell me you let him loose with naked women trussed up like this?' He nodded downwards to his obscenely spreadeagled body all festooned with its straps and wires and sensors.

'They're perfectly safe,' Isis said calmly as she primed a hypo and then injected the hallucinogen so skilfully that Josh barely felt it. 'I'll admit that Diabolo isn't perhaps completely "normal", but where Pleasurezone's concerned he's the best man for the job. It's hard to explain. He's a chameleon, a transformer. The Diabolo the lady clients all fall in love with isn't the same man who slaps Tricksie around. This is business to him; it's a separate compartment. And he's a superb therapist, a natural. I should know. Somebody has to prepare *me* when I try out the set pieces . . .'

Not for the first time, Josh imagined Isis secured to this very same couch, her beautiful naked body all aroused and plugged and wired . . . Then, due to the drug he supposed dreamily, the picture wavered and Isis's svelte shape became Tricksie's more sumptuous one; the soft tabby hair at Isis's groin became Tricksie's almost fluorescent scarlet bush . . . and over it, attaching sensors with an artistic delicacy, leaned the whip-slim form of the mysterious Diabolo. Jacketless this time and sans his stylish fedora, he'd rolled up the sleeves of his blue silk shirt and loosened the knot of the white tie he wore with it. His stark, Latin-black hair gleamed cobalt in the diffuse lighting.

'She loves him, doesn't she?' Josh mumbled, already drifting. 'He's a raving loony but she loves him. Tricksie loves him . . .' He could hardly see anything real now; the dreamscape was forming beneath the mask . . .

'Yes, she loves him . . .' a satin voice murmured nearby. '*You* love him, sweetheart. You love him like crazy and there's nothing you can do. You're his, Tricksie, all his . . . You love him, Tricksie, my sweet. You love the devil moon . . .'

7 Devil Moon

. . . the moon. The moon was so bright and hypnotising tonight that Tricksie Turing blinked and wondered if she'd fallen asleep while watching it rise.

'It's that ol' devil moon,' she sang softly to herself, shivering and burning in the same confusing moment. 'That old devil moon in my cunt.'

Wishful thinking, Trix old love, she told herself. But she still couldn't help hoping he was on his way now. The Moon Devil. Diabolo . . . God how she hoped he was coming.

He was like a narcotic to her, a drug her body screamed for. For Diabolo she'd do anything, or have anything done to her. Anything – by, with or to anybody. No outrageous or disgusting act was beyond her, just so long as it led, ultimately, to him.

Whether she took a punter inside her, in her mouth, her cunt or her arse, the man always thought he was the one she screamed for, or groaned for, or came for. Oh God, the poor deluded soul would think, a whore with orgasms. She's fabulous. She's gorgeous. She's the best lay I've ever had.

And back they came – the tricks that Tricksie tricked – again and again and again. And pay they did, in ever-increasing amounts, little realising that to Tricksie they were completely transparent. She never saw them. It was Diabolo's face she saw, his body she stroked or licked, his prick she took into her mouth or her snug, drooling vagina . . .

It was cold tonight and, feeling chilly, she cinched her silk kimono more tightly around her. The luxurious robe felt cool and sleek against her skin, and reminded her potently of its giver. Diabolo was strangely generous given the sterile nature of their relationship, and the brightly patterned kimono was just one of many gifts. The fabric was fine as cobwebs, and the design legendary: unicorns, dragons and triple-headed tigers pranced, slithered and stalked across her body, and Tricksie wondered, for the umpteenth time, why her pimp gave back so much of what he took, and how long this game of give-and-take had been going on.

Tricksie had no recollection whatsoever of ever actually meeting Diabolo. It was as if he'd always been there, and that he'd tampered with her memory to make the impression fit. Like a thief in the night he'd stolen her life and made it fiction. It was an effort to remember her real name.

Plagued by restlessness, Tricksie stared up at the full moon, watching it ride serenely through a troubled sky. It seemed bigger and brighter than usual. A sign, maybe? Had she been right to hope he'd visit tonight? That he'd decided to use her freely offered body, to slide between her ever-open legs?

Maybe, maybe not. She leaned towards optimism, though, because this pimp of hers had a peculiar affinity with the moon. Both were unfathomable and silvery, and both had control over women's lives. Especially this one's . . .

But therein lay a snag. As if to emphasise her lunar regularity, the muscles of her womb yanked her with an agonising spasm and Tricksie knew she'd started bleeding.

He'll come now just to spite me, the pig, she thought resignedly, reviewing her preparations for a full-moon fuck. She'd cancelled a late client, bathed at great length, spent hours taming her thick red hair. Perfumed and preened, she'd sat down to wait for his lordship – and now this!

Diabolo, bugger him, was almost unbelievably pernickety, which was peculiar, given the seamy world they both lived in. The man was fastidious to the point of being phobic, and Tricksie was astounded he'd even consort with one such as her, a vessel who'd held so many . . .

But consort he did, and fuck. He'd screw her with a blinding and beautiful ferocity, and after each coupling he'd leave her a small, white satin pouch full of fragrant dried herbs. These she'd infuse into a cleansing wash to use after her clients' attentions, and before those of Diabolo himself. She could feel its tingly freshness even now, being slowly eroded by the inexorable slither of her blood.

Oddly enough, Diabolo had never said a thing about the mysterious pot-pourri; it was as if he was allowing Tricksie just this one curious thing to work out for herself. She kept the mixture in a black lacquered box on her dressing table. This pretty *objet* – with a silver inlay in the shape of a peacock – was also something he'd given her one night when she'd given him a particularly special item from her repertoire.

She smiled ruefully. He'd hurt her. Holy Christ, he'd half-killed her! But afterwards he'd been heavenly. He'd returned for four nights in succession, fucked her to oblivion and back in a hitherto unknown phenomenon – and Tricksie had worked far, far harder for *his* pleasure than she did for even the best of her payers!

She ran her hand across the box, touching, remembering. By night, Diabolo and his mouth, his prick, his hands; by day, her own voluptuous devices. Lolling around the flat, waiting, wanting and touching herself; fingering the cunt that Diabolo had stroked and kissed and screwed; masturbating like a mad thing, then coming and coming and coming as imagination made her fingers into his.

But it couldn't last, of course.

After the fourth perfect night he'd said 'OK, back to work,' then disappeared for several long agonising weeks.

Right now, it was four days since Tricksie had last seen him. Or was it five? Her need for him could expand to fit any given length of time. Kicking off her pom-pommed slippers, she lay back on the bed and groaned. Sleep was impossible, yet she couldn't *do* anything. She could barely think. She'd got books, discs and holovid to amuse her, but with only a fraction of her attention available, they were useless. She lay still, inanimate, wanting Diabolo yet too numbed by her craving even to attend to her own seeping body . . .

Suddenly and shockingly, gooseflesh rose across the whole surface of her skin. Her heart went be-bump be-bump be-bump in her chest; then an invisible fist gripped it, squeezed it and held it tight. Across the room she heard the clicks of her digital lock.

Only one other person knew the combination. The door opened and a figure moved into the shadows, turned back noiselessly, and dropped the latch. The moon's light defined a male silhouette, a slim form which spun to face the room, then paused as if probing the darkness. Two steps forward – into the shaft of radiance – and there he stood . . .

In the stark blue-toned glow his face seemed carved from alabaster, and to Tricksie's besotted eyes he was everything godlike. An icon of Latin hauteur, this enigma could break her heart and churn her cunt with a single sharp glance. And she wasn't the only one he dazzled. When they were out together at La Selene, planning strategy, she'd seen both the sexes gaping at him, ogling him shamelessly, lusting for his pretty face and his lithe, sensual body.

And Diabolo, fully aware of his devastating looks, knew precisely how to dress them up. A street dandy of spectacular flamboyance, he had a penchant for sharp suits, and a cool, impressive way with hats. He carried himself like a marquis and looked out upon his world and its denizens as if they'd been created purely for his convenience.

But for all his style and sang-froid, Diabolo couldn't resist going over the top – and flaunting himself to breath-taking excess. He wore trousers cut from the finest cloth available, with nothing whatsoever underneath. The poor bewitched fools who perved at him didn't know where to look first: his soul-catching face or the clear, insolent outline of his rampant prick!

You're a slut, Moon Devil, she told him silently. A shameless, flashing slut! In that suit you might just as well be stark naked!

It was Diabolo's favourite ensemble: a pimp's cliché of languid, lightweight linen that he wore with a snow-white fedora hat. In the moon's light, his pale clothes made him a phantasm, but Tricksie knew nothing could be further from the truth. He was solid, real and deadly; far more dangerous than any apparition, and a pure erotic temptation she'd not a shred of strength to resist.

'What've you got for me, Tricksie?' he said softly, gliding forward.

At the centre of the room, he halted. He wouldn't come any further, because making Tricksie come to him was one of his strategies. Twitching with excitement, she almost wished he'd ordered her to crawl. The drug was at its purest when she had to grovel. Rising to her feet, she took her cache from the bedside drawer and said a silent prayer that it'd be enough, and then another that she'd get her reward. Oh God, please, yes!

Fighting her usual inner battle between pride and delicious subservience, she curbed an urge to run and fling her arms around him. This silent sexual war between them turned her whole body into a huge naked nerve-end. His cool look was like a caress flowing directly over her cunt. Should she beg? Whimper for his touch? Abase herself for his fingers, his lips, his prick? But instead, perverse as the man himself, she walked slowly forward, then stood in front of him. Waiting.

Tricksie and her pimp were nearly the same height; and with her in her high-heeled slippers, they now stood eye to eye. Stubbornly, she decided to resist him this time, defy him by holding his gaze and not looking down. His brown eyes narrowed minutely.

Oh God, I've done it again, thought Tricksie, recognising a perennial dichotomy. His bearing, his body language, his whole living aura implied that she should react as the classic sexual slave, but she hadn't. Intimately conversant with that scene, Tricksie could quite easily have assumed the appropriate role.

But then she'd have tricked herself.

Because it would've made Diabolo despise her. It was

only *real* defiance he liked. One thing she'd learned over the years was that he genuinely relished her pride, and because of it, got greater pleasure out of its eventual subjugation. His idea of a good time was seeing Tricksie – the empress of lust, who struck awe and trembling into her customers – fall to the floor and keen like a hound for the taste of his cock.

Tricksie had been so lost in her power calculations that the first strike caught her unawares. Diabolo grabbed roughly at the back of her neck, gripping it with one big hand and immobilising her. A moment ago she'd challenged him, but now her boldness was all gone. Something feral glared out of those huge almond-shaped eyes and she tried desperately to evade it.

But he wasn't having any. His fingers dug in, forcing and pulling, and he made her mouth come to his. He was slow and implacable, and when his lips took hers, her whole body became loose and bendy, and her dribbling cunt turned to pure liquid fire . . .

The kiss was his *tour de force*; he crushed her mouth, chewed on it, bruised it. His free hand slid into her robe and his fingers closed tightly on her nipple: pinching and twisting, his lacquered nails cold and deadly. It hurt, it really hurt, but hot need pooled like molten lead in her belly: thick, low and voluptuously sinking. She felt fluid stream freely between her thighs, and had no idea whether it was blood or the cunt-juice this man caused so easily to flow.

His nasty little cruelty took the last of her will, and her struggles suddenly became stylised, just part of *his* choreography. She tried to cry out but the sound tangled around their tongues. He deepened the kiss, made it harder, then harder still, heedless that he hurt his own mouth as much as hers.

Tricksie fought to smile, liking the idea of his pain, and knowing that in her own way, she was as twisted as he was. And even though her mashed mouth couldn't form a grin, she felt Diabolo react to the intent. He tightened his pressure on her teat, dragging delicately and pulling the whole breast into a tortured cone. Tricksie groaned and slavered under his lips, wanting to open herself, rub her running cunt against him, grind her stained flesh against that smooth white cloth.

When he let her go she nearly fell. Smirking unpleasantly at her weakness, he stood over her, waggling his long fingers in a 'gimme-the-money' gesture.

Bastard, thought Tricksie, gathering her wits and holding out the cash. He took it slowly, courteously; then his free hand whipped out, grabbed her shoulder and pushed downwards.

A grip like death put her on her knees. She daren't look up, but it was no great hardship. Diabolo's white-clad crotch was almost touching her nose, the immaculate cut of his trousers enormously disturbed.

Her tormentor released her shoulder but only so he could count the roll of money. She could hear the notes flicking above her head. He loved the feel of real currency and insisted she accept only cash.

Would he be pleased? Would it be enough? Could she resist the urge to press her lips against that straining bulge and mouth his prick through the milk-white fabric? Diabolo's voice, quiet and menacing, halted her silent ramblings.

'Get it out.'

Obedient, she unzipped his trousers and eased out his tool.

He was hard as life, his member rising from his crisp white flies like a great red prong. The tip looked so hot, and so velvet-slick, that Tricksie had to swallow a rush of saliva. Gulping a second time, and a third, she felt her cunt undulate in concert, anticipating the nether-taste of him as much as her tongue did his flavour.

'Suck it.'

His voice was curt, businesslike, but the quaver in it betrayed him. Tricksie smiled, and did as she was told.

Gotcha, mister. She couldn't see that glorious face but she could imagine it. He adored this. He was a vicious hard-nosed brute but he still fell down before her superb expertise.

She pictured him now, sweetness and ecstasy floating across his fairytale countenance, his face a poem of pacific tenderness so completely at odds with his harsh, insensitive words. Then, for one instant, she imagined something she couldn't name for fear it would evaporate.

His searching fingers confirmed her mindview: a feather-soft touch on her cheek, a slow, slow tracing of her jaw. His thumb outlined her lower lip and brushed against his own embedded flesh . . . Tricksie relaxed, let her mouth be pliant and encouraging. His other hand cradled her head and she felt the banknotes crinkling against her tangled curls. It was Diabolo's instruction – take me deeper . . .

And she did. Her lips and throat opened in a welcome of heat and moisture. She drew him in, worked on him with her dainty, darting tongue, and wrenched a long, low howl from the very heart of him.

Triumph! The money, so efficiently counted, went fluttering to the floor. Diabolo stood in the centre of his whore's boudoir with his cock in her mouth and his multi-credit bills scattered all around her. And Tricksie – queen, whore and slave – had conquered her sleek, felonious lover, as she always did.

Her tongue flickered and he gasped. She hollowed her cheeks, sucking and slurping without qualm or mercy, and his magical, musical voice soared moonwards in a litany of startled yelps and moans: chuntering broken-up phrases of pleasure, excitement, abandon.

'Yes yes yes, baby, that's it. Go on go on go on . . .' He was balanced on the pinnacle of his own orgasm. Inches from Tricksie's face, his thighs were twitching and trembling, and beneath her clutching fingers the muscles of his perfect arse bunched and spasmed . . .

'Ayeeeeeee!'

He clawed at her, his fingers digging mindlessly into her scalp. Tricksie embraced his slender body, exulting in the force and savagery of his thrusts, praying to love that she could take their depth and power.

'Mama, Mama, Mama,' he shouted, his hips jerking, his body jumping like a demented puppet. Tricksie felt semen

132

in her throat: first spurting, then slipping, trickling, flowing . . . Diabolo's semen. Tricksie swallowed it convulsively, absorbing his essence into her, drinking down his very soul.

For an aeon, they were motionless . . .

Diabolo was soft now, sated, and Tricksie let his prick slide from between her lips. Her lover was a statue before her, a scorched but frozen mannequin: his head tipped forward, his eyes obscured by the deep brim of his hat, his hands hanging nerveless at his sides. He made no attempt to cover himself, and Tricksie took a tissue from her pocket and gently cleansed the stickiness from his wilted flesh. Indulging herself, she dropped a tiny kiss on the silky tip, then returned the source of her pleasure to its white enclosure. Neatness and order restored, she rubbed the tissue across her lips, crumpled it and flung it across the room towards the wastebin. The missile hit its metal target with a muffled 'patt' and the minute, barely audible sound seemed to wake Diabolo from his coma.

'Tricksie, Tricksie, Tricksie. You're somethin' else,' he whispered, stroking her head as if she were a well-trained pet. With a fluid shimmying movement, he squared his shoulders then plucked off his hat and studied it thoughtfully for a moment. He nodded slightly, then, flicking his lean wrist, sent the hat spinning through the air towards Tricksie's old armchair.

'Gonna take a shower, babe,' he said as it landed. He sauntered across the room, discarding his clothes as he went and leaving a trail of designer tailoring on the floor behind him.

Tricksie sank back on her heels and stared at the after image of his already naked body. Uh huh, what am I going to do now? He's staying – and I've got a quimful of blood.

And as if her body had heard her silent question, it reminded her tangibly of its condition. Tricksie felt a hot, slithery sensation in her vagina and in a panic she clenched the muscles of her cunt and arse. If his lordship found her in a bloody kimono it'd gross him out for sure. He might hit her – which she didn't really mind – or perhaps freeze her with the cold acid edge of the voice he used so sparingly.

Physical pain would be preferable, infinitely so. At least when he slapped her it usually ended up in some kind of sex. And even though she was bleeding, she of all people knew ways to amuse without penetration or even without touch. One of Diabolo's favourite tricks was to make her lie on the floor while he stood over her, fully clothed, and ejaculated on to her upturned face. He'd aim for her mouth, then laugh softly when he missed. After that, he'd usually zip up without a word and leave. Tricksie would remain where she lay, licking her semen-coated lips and rubbing herself to a furious, gut-wrenching orgasm.

But still, as she glanced idly through the window at the high coasting moon, Tricksie realised that by some freak chance this was the very first time he'd turned up while she had her period. Tonight was an unknown ball game, an undiscovered country. Would he still stay when he found out she was bleeding?

The slipping sensation came again between Tricksie's legs and suddenly things were crucial. Moving across the room, her body crouched and her gait ugly and crablike, she opened her dressing table drawer and pulled out a large white linen handkerchief. Flipping open her robe, she jammed the snowy cloth between her thighs and held it wedged against her cunt while she wondered what on earth to do next.

She was stuck in a classic Catch–22 situation. The smell and sight of blood might well send Diabolo running, both for cover and the cunt of a non-menstruating woman. Yet the very same female function that effectively put Tricksie out of action also made her unbearably and agonisingly randy. The yearning, the physical need for sex, was acute. Her surging hormones made her so sexy she could cry with frustration; her clitoris seemed to scream for pressure, the rougher the better. It was twitching furiously right now, and she could remember many a time past when she'd spent whole days with her hands plastered in blood as she worked unceasingly between her own legs.

Surreptitiously, fearing that any second now the bathroom door might fly open, she began to rock the wedged handkerchief against her sensitive membranes. Sinking to the carpet, she braced her back against the sturdy dressing table, and tucking one end of the makeshift pad under her bottom, started scrubbing her clit in earnest with the other. Through half-closed eyes she peered at the trail of expensive clothing that straggled towards the door, and as the pleasure massed in her crotch she imagined the strange, coldly beautiful creature who had so recently been inside them.

Try as she might, she couldn't remember a time when she hadn't hungered for Diabolo; and as she glanced down at her cunt, and the impromptu sex-aid moving rhythmically over it, she thought of all the ways he'd used and demeaned that cunt in the course of their long and peculiar relationship.

For instance, a client had expressed a wish for a particularly 'juicy' woman, and so, prior to the appointment, Diabolo had simply pulled Tricksie into a barely private alcove in the Mall outside La Selene, thrust his hand unceremoniously into her panties and quickly frigged her to the required state of wetness.

It hadn't taken long – just the sight of him made her slippery, never mind his touch – but people were passing by them all the time, and one tiny sound would've advertised the fact that a young woman was being brutally masturbated in a completely public place. Tricksie had had to bite her lip to keep in her groans while Diabolo had expertly pinched her clitoris and worked it up and down between his finger and thumb, digging delicately into it with his nails so the knifelike pain just prevented her from coming. Juice had been dribbling down her legs as far as her knees by the time she was eventually 'presented': a fact that filthy beast had acquainted the punter with in crudely graphic detail. Not only had he described exactly how it'd been achieved, he'd also invited the delighted client to insert his hand into the liquid evidence right then and there in the bar!

On the same juice-loving client's next visit to the City,

Diabolo had used a different ploy; although this time, thankfully, the moistening had taken place in the privacy of Tricksie's flat. Lying on her back she'd been forced to remove her knickers, pull her knees up tight against her chest, and ensure that the whole of her slit was completely exposed. Then, not deigning to stimulate her in any way whatsoever, Diabolo had simply pulled out his dick, wanked himself vigorously, and had spunked copiously and with deadly accuracy straight on to her naked pink vulva. Once again she'd been dripping all down her thighs for the paying customer.

Yes, the Moon Devil had a thousand different ways to bring his charge to heel; whether it be for her clients' benefit or purely for his own warped entertainment. Shockingly, thoughts of his various methods of subjugation were intensifying the sensations between her legs. She moaned, in the grip of a slight precursing spasm, and let her mind flow back over some of his more recent outrages.

Always one to inflict casual pain, Diabolo had decided one night that it'd amuse him to spank her. At his instructions, she'd dressed in one of her most chic outfits: a tailored suit, a hat with veil, and close-fitting gloves. But no sooner was she clothed than he'd issued a curt order that she strip off every stitch from the waist down.

'How elegant you look,' he'd drawled, forcing Tricksie to look at herself in the mirror.

Standing behind her, regarding their images balefully in the glass, he slid his hands around and took hold of her high, round, linen-clad breasts.

Tricksie didn't think she looked elegant at all. She looked indescribably lewd, her primly covered top half accentuating the obscenity of her naked loins and thighs. Reluctant to see the even grosser sight of juices beginning to dribble from her lush vermilion bush, she'd looked away, only to feel her breasts excruciatingly crushed and a bulging erection being jammed against her bare bottom.

'Look at yourself,' he snarled, shoving her knees apart with his own to exhibit her more shamefully.

They stood like that for five long minutes. Tricksie stared

transfixedly at their reflection while Diabolo continued his cruel gouging of her breasts – at the same time delicately licking the soft skin of her neck and humming a familiar little tune to himself. Her cunt was drooling by now, love-juice hanging in heavy silvery strings, her flesh almost burstingly aroused; but she daren't touch herself for fear of incurring his wrath.

At long last he pushed her away, strolled over to a straightbacked chair and sat down. An imperious gesture brought her to him, and as she stood waiting and trembling, he'd stripped the glove off her right hand, then arranged that hand meticulously over her own slimy crotch – very carefully positioning her middle finger directly on her clitoris. Thus readied, he'd ordered her to lie across his lap, with her hand still between their two bodies. His last instruction was that she rub herself continuously, without a single second of let-up, while he administered a prolonged smacking to her pale, shivering rump. Within moments she was coming – violently and repeatedly – as Diabolo turned the whole of her exposed backside into a mass of flaming agony . . .

One consolation, however, over the long, painful hours that'd followed, was that the punishment had made Diabolo's right hand sore too – and Tricksie had had to take his penis in her own hand to wank him to his climax.

Reliving that memory, and almost feeling that stiff, yet velvet-skinned rod beneath her fingers now, Tricksie was suddenly whirled into orgasm. The delicate pulsing contractions tore furiously through her cunt, and a vivid down-pushing squelch sent blood and sexual juices streaming out into the handkerchief. She moaned as her clitoris fluttered, then eased the cloth away to watch the wild beating of her own glistening bud. The blood was red on red, scarlet on scarlet as the tiny organ jumped in time to the steady pounding of her heart . . . Pressing the cloth against herself once more, Tricksie rolled silently on to her side and lay, breathing slowly and returning to earth, as her spasming body grew still and her menstrual flow oozed out on to the fine white handkerchief. Diabolo's handkerchief . . .

The spanking had been just one occasion amongst many. Almost sleepily, she recalled an instance three weeks ago, when Diabolo had decreed she take a night off to spend watching holovid with him.

A cosy evening in front of the box?

Sort of. Diabolo had watched a pornographic film, a boxing match and an episode of a popular soap, while Tricksie spent the whole evening on her knees, with Diabolo's prick in her mouth and her finger lodged up his anus. He ejaculated seven times in the course of his viewing – although the last few comes were virtually dry – and Tricksie ended up with cramp in her finger and tongue, and such an appalling ache of sexual frustration that she finally broke down and wept. Only then, and with no discernible acknowledgement of her tears, did Diabolo quickly and roughly frig her to orgasm.

Tricksie knew she ought to get up, and do something about herself. But the recollection machine was running now, and she was helpless in the grip of her beloved's past cruelties, the cruellest of which occurred when they weren't even together. When Diabolo plunged his cock into another woman's cunt, he first made sure that Tricksie knew full well it was going to happen. And knew to the precise instant *when* it was going to happen, so she could eat her heart out as she imagined the scene.

Yes, Tricksie was so familiar with his demonic perversity that she knew beyond doubt that if Diabolo said he would be penetrating a woman at a certain moment, he would be. She could look at her chrono and know that at that very instant he would be pushing his tool between some lucky woman's sleek, glossy labia.

His most notable atrocity of recent months was to screw the only woman Tricksie could possibly count as a friend. She'd rationalised the event since, but at the time it'd seemed a double-handed blow. Not only was Tricksie jealous of Isis being fucked by Diabolo, she was also jealous of Diabolo for screwing a woman she herself had had sex with.

Yes, it'd been a dark green hour when he'd left Tricksie

alone in La Selene with the knowledge of where he was going. Yet she couldn't blame her friend Isis, because when he'd made his mind up, Diabolo was completely irresistible: to women, to men, and even to those who weren't quite sure!

It'd also helped to kid herself that Diabolo was merely bonking Isis as a favour, because, being badly scarred in an accident, she couldn't pull a sex partner in the normal way.

Which, Tricksie had to admit, swigging down Campari after Campari, was a complete bunch of crap. Because scar or no scar, Isis was gorgeous. Not only was she slender, elegant and charismatic, she was also deeply mysterious, dazzlingly intelligent and involved with Diabolo in some kind of exotic business enterprise to which Tricksie had not been made privy.

And on top of that, the generally all-round amazing Isis was also sensational in bed. Inventive and graceful, the scarred woman had, perhaps, the prettiest cunt Tricksie had ever seen. Or tasted . . .

Yes, Isis was a delicious lady, and with her taste on his lips, Tricksie suspected Diabolo would be quite a different man. Because Isis was a lady, he'd most likely be tender and respectful, and make love to her with the sort of consideration and delicacy he didn't waste on his whore. Yes, that was it! He'd make love to Isis. Not shag, fuck, poke, or screw – the terms best employed to describe what he did to Tricksie.

Not that she'd even get those when he found out she was bleeding.

Dropping back into herself, Tricksie realised that the shower had stopped running, and with practised efficiency she brought herself to a quick but fairly automatic orgasm. The physical throb relieved some of her distension but it was a far from transcendental experience. With no stage of hazy repletion to go through, she made swift calculation and squinted across at the door . . .

All clear. Time to check out the state of her cunt . . .

Surprisingly the handkerchief was only slightly bloodied.

After a quick rummage in her knicker drawer, Tricksie pulled on a pair of red stretch-lace panties to keep it temporarily in place, and, safely padded, she set about retrieving and folding Diabolo's scattered clothing . . .

And now the water was no longer running, she could clearly hear that most curious and unlikely sound – the king of stone-faced cool singing his heart out as he towelled himself dry. When his ablutions were over, there wouldn't be another such sound out of him, so Tricksie made the most of his strangely harmonious voice while it was available; and wondered, as she often did, why Diabolo had never become a rock star. If he'd been a singer instead of a pimp, they might've had a more normal relationship . . .

When silence finally fell, she waited a couple of moments, then pushed open the door to the bedroom.

Diabolo was lying stretched out on her bed, stark naked and relaxed, his lean olive-skinned body an exotic graven image against the ivory satin quilt. As ever, he was bright-eyed and wide-awake, and his current occupation was the study of his long, slim hand and its slow, rhythmic movement between his legs . . . Tricksie's eyes widened. Wrapped around his thick dark prick was the pale pink raw silk camisole she'd shed earlier and left draped across the bed . . .

'I was tidying your clothes,' she murmured, anticipating a query over her tardiness. Smoothing her robe securely across her front, she walked towards the bed and met the neutral gaze in Diabolo's large brown eyes. He appeared to be listening to her, quite intently in fact, yet his smooth, deliberate masturbation remained uninterrupted. His prick was already almost fully erect, towering out of the crumpled silk, its chunky knob glistening with his carefully spread juices.

'Is that a fact?' he murmured absently, in a tone that could have implied anything but at least wasn't overtly angry. 'Care to join me, Trix?' With his unoccupied hand, he patted the space at his side . . .

For a moment, Tricksie found herself stunned to immobility, transfixed both by the physical beauty of the man before her and by the unexpected gentleness of his invitation. Diabolo was never this benign. Orders were what she usually got, and this languid, laid-back amenability was almost as scary as it was unexpected.

And the timing was lousy.

Tricksie felt like breaking something. For the first time in all the years she'd known him, Diabolo seemed dangerously close to being nice. And just when she should've capitalised on this, and been able at last to enjoy lovemaking instead of cold, contemptuous copulation, she was lumbered with her period. It was no bloody wonder they called it 'the curse'.

'I . . . I'll . . . I won't be a minute. I need to wash,' she stuttered, too stunned by malicious irony to make proper sense.

'I thought you'd be clean already, babe,' he said quietly, and Tricksie whirled around, anticipating his censure.

But Diabolo merely smiled a small, contemplative smile and continued to slide her delicate, lace-trimmed garment over his prick.

'I'll be as quick as I can,' she replied, trying to sound as unconcerned as he did.

'No problem,' he murmured, sinking back into the bed's softness as his hips began to lift in time to the regular stroking movements of his silk-covered fingers.

But I'm afraid there is a problem, thought Tricksie in the privacy of her bathroom as she tried to achieve the impossible – an immaculate, blood-free cunt to present to Diabolo. Her orgasms seemed to have stemmed the flow a little; but there was still a slight trace of red when she passed a cloth between her thighs. She was dainty, exquisite and perfumed in all other respects, but the scarlet stigma lingered depressingly on. There was nothing to do but go back in there, admit it was the 'wrong time of the month' and accept his lordship's decision. There was always a chance he'd deign to be sucked off, or wanked . . . or even that he'd simply ejaculate over her as he so often did.

Allowing herself one final sigh, Tricksie jammed a couple of tissues tight between her labia, slid the red pants snugly into place and put her robe back on. Then, with a deep breath, she drew herself to her full height and prepared to return to the bedroom. Okay, so tonight was probably a complete screw-up, but she was still Tricksie Turing, the queen of whores, and she had one hell of an image to maintain.

'What's up, babe?' Diabolo enquired, his fine eyes narrowing as she approached the bed. As usual nothing was escaping his seemingly omniscient notice.

In the split second of framing her reply, Tricksie observed that her lover – if she could ever call him that – was no longer erect.

Had he come? she wondered, then decided he most likely had. There was a lacquerlike sheen to the surface of his belly which suggested that the semen had skipped the now-discarded camisole and landed there on his smooth brown skin. He'd probably massaged it deep into his pores and threaded it through the glossy black hair of his pubis . . .

What do you want me for then? she felt like shouting, but knew she never would or could. He'd mark her if she sassed him, and he'd probably be ready for sex again in a few seconds anyway. He was capable of several orgasms in fairly quick succession, and it wasn't unusual for him to have at least half a dozen in a night. His powers of recuperation were about as inhuman as the rest of him.

'What's bugging you, Trix?' he persisted in the face of continued silence.

Tricksie made as if to turn away, but Diabolo like lightning, reached out and grabbed her robe. The slippery sash unwound itself and the silky garment fell open to reveal her lush breasts, her slim waist and thighs, and, where her usually naked cunt was, the flimsy crimson lace panties.

'What's with these?' he asked, his voice cool as he pulled her down on to the bed beside him and began to play – ominously – with the fine elastic that spanned her belly. 'I like to see your snatch, babe. I like you available.'

Tricksie tried to pull away and escape the long probing fingers, but Diabolo's arm was like an iron band around her waist.

'But I'm not available,' she said, turning in his hold. Scared, but still proud, she looked straight into those enormous, unfathomable brown eyes and said her piece. 'I don't think you'll want to fuck me tonight, Diabolo. I've got my period. My cunt's full of blood.'

It was almost impossible to quell her trembling, but she managed it, and waited, motionless, in his arms for what seemed like a lifetime.

His long black eyelashes flickered once or twice, but otherwise the perfect face betrayed no trace of emotion.

Finally, Tricksie lost her nerve.

'I'll do anything else you want, though,' she breathed, reaching out boldly to touch his cock.

Expecting rejection, and possibly a violent one, she was shocked to the core when his fingers closed gently around hers and encouraged a familiar motion. His flesh stiffened immediately.

'That's cool, baby,' he murmured blandly, sliding her slender fist smoothly over his still-moist tool. 'Let's just see what happens, shall we?'

A million questions rose to Tricksie's lips but she banished them all. Don't ask, she told herself silently. Just take what's on offer. You might never get a chance again . . .

Still slowly masturbating him, she pressed her mouth to Diabolo's lips and slid her tongue between them. He remained strangely quiescent under the kiss and the manipulation of his cock; falling back, he let his hand slip away from hers, and his mouth relaxed to allow a complete exploration of its soft, wet interior. For the first time ever, his tongue didn't fight her, but lay deliciously submissive and teasable . . .

Feeling a sudden, primal excitement, Tricksie gorged herself on him, tasting, plunging and ravaging as her fingers moved on his rigid, velvety cock. It was unbelievable that he was allowing this, but there was no time to wonder why . . .

After a few moments, Diabolo inevitably took control again, but in a new and oddly tender way. Gently disengaging her fingers from his erection, he slid off Tricksie's kimono and ran his hands quickly but lightly over her longing body. He hesitated at the panties, seeming to examine the fragile texture of the lace; then, muffling her protests with their still unbroken kiss, he eased the minimal garment down her thighs and completely off her body.

'No,' she protested into his mouth as she felt him pluck the tissue out of her cleft and fling it away.

'Yes,' he replied, then pushed his tongue deeper into her mouth, and his fingers into a well of blood and pungently scented juices.

This can't be happening, thought Tricksie wildly as her body told her in a thousand ways that it was. Her hips writhed of their own accord as he caught up the rich stickiness from her vagina and spread it carefully up onto her unsheathing clitoris. She moaned in her throat, blessing her tormentor's name as he slowly and delicately caressed the lubricated bud, circled it and rocked it in a motion Tricksie knew would soon bring her most sublimely off.

Thrashing her head like a madwoman, she shook away his kiss and screamed 'Diabolo!' at the top of her voice as the whole universe fell blazing though her loins and her pulsing womb sent blood pouring out onto his possessively enclosing hand . . .

It was several minutes before she was conscious enough to worry about the mess, although she was fully aware all the time of his warm fingers still pressed soothingly against her vulva.

Looking down at last over their entwined bodies, Tricksie shuddered at the gory state of them both: her pale thighs were slashed with bright bands of red, and Diabolo's right hand was just one shimmering mass of blood. Struggling to rise, she wondered frantically where to begin the immense task of cleaning up, aware, as the silk sheet clung to her thighs, that it too was daubed with her flow . . .

'Take it easy,' he said quietly, pinning her easily where she lay. 'Where's the fire?'

'We're all messed up,' she mumbled, hiding her face and clenching her thighs in a futile attempt to contain the bloodiness. 'I'd better get a towel or something.'

'There's no rush for that, Trix.' Pressing his smeared fingers to her face, he made her look at him.

'But – '

'But nothing.'

Slowly and deliberately, he brought his crimson-coated fingers to his lips and sucked each one with a bizarre show of relish.

Oh God, what kind of kinky game was he playing now? This was the hyper-fastidious Diabolo and he was lapping her menstrual blood as if it were the finest heather honey.

'My . . . my blood . . .' she stuttered, her mind boggling.

'Yeah,' he murmured, licking the tip of his little finger and regarding it thoughtfully. 'Okay babe, on your back. I'm gonna drink from the spring.'

Uncomprehending, Tricksie let him push her on to her back. It wasn't until he scooted his slim body down the bed and crouched between her red-streaked thighs, that she deciphered what he'd said.

'No! You can't!' she cried, attempting to close her legs.

'I can,' he observed as he held her open effortlessly. 'Believe me, Trix, I can.' He laid his hand fleetingly over her mouth. 'So let's keep this closed and these . . .' He trailed one finger between her blood-covered labia, 'and these wide open.'

Before she'd time to protest further, his unsullied face was pressed between her stained thighs, and his tongue was seeking her trembling clitoris. In an instant he was sucking furiously where before only his finger had pleasured . . . and Tricksie's disbelieving horror had turned to the most voluptuous of pleasures. Her sticky thighs and hips flaunted into the rhythm of his suckling mouth. Diabolo had never been a great one for cunnilingus at the best of times, but that he should do it now was almost as unthinkable as it was fabulous.

Within seconds she was beyond reason, beyond thought, and well beyond fathoming the enigma feasting on her bloody crotch. In raptures, she wrapped her legs around his head and dragged her heels convulsively over his strong brown back – as for the second time in half an hour, he brought her to a long, massive, flaming-scarlet orgasm.

Coming and coming and coming, she was a rag-doll who existed only to do his bidding; her cunt was still palpitating, and her mind unfocused, when she felt him slide himself up her, hooking her long legs as he went, and almost double her supple body under his. Caught in this vulnerable flexion, with her vagina offered to his demanding tool, Tricksie opened her eyes and saw a blood-smeared face hovering over hers, smiling slightly.

'Relax, baby,' he murmured absently as his prick went slip-sliding deep into her trembling hole. 'Relax for Papa. This is what you want. This is what you've been waiting for.'

Pleasure piled on pleasure as her oozing flesh fluttered around his sure, stiff rod. It *was* what she wanted, what she'd always wanted! Hurling her bleeding body into his thrusts, she exalted in the audible squelch of cock and cunt, the ancient liquid joining of man and mate. In this at least he was hers, and weeping with joy, she drank her own blood from his kissing lips and surrendered all her senses to a pure uncomplicated ecstasy. Through its mind-numbing haze, she felt Diabolo's sudden violent plunge, and her vagina, already awash, received the heavy pulse of his semen. The whole universe echoed with his high inarticulate cry, and with it they were lost, together and one in a magic blood-stained maelstrom . . .

When next Tricksie opened her eyes, she stared downwards over the bodies of two painted savages. Long crimson daubs adorned both Diabolo's lean frame and her more sumptuous one. She hardly dare look him in the eye, this man who shared her ruined sheets.

Yet when she did, he returned her gaze steadily, and then reached out to rub gently at her lower lip. Removing her own stain, no doubt, absorbed through that long orgasmic kiss.

'We need a shower,' he said, 'but I'm too bushed to get one just yet . . .'

Tricksie had all she needed, in spite of her messy state.

Being held so comfortingly was completely unprecedented; Diabolo usually rolled away immediately after pulling out, and yet now he was actually cradling her in his arms . . . as if he really cared for her.

'So am I,' she whispered, cautiously edging closer. Her heart thumped happily when he didn't push her away.

Why? she thought blissfully. Why? She allowed her mind to ask the question but wouldn't let it spoil the moment.

'I saw a man die today,' Diabolo said suddenly, as if he'd heard her silent query. 'Killed by an old-style projectile weapon. The bullet missed *me* by inches. I could've been the one who bought it.' His voice quavered, and Tricksie realised that this too was unprecedented. Ice-cool emotionless Diabolo had been and still was scared. He went on almost absently, as if working out his own feelings rather than simply recounting a happening. 'There was blood everywhere. Blood . . . and he died . . . It could've been me.'

He said no more for the moment, but Tricksie felt his hand move lightly on her hair . . . and heard the words he hadn't spoken.

That was what all this was about. The silence was more eloquent in its way than any of the few sparse utterances this man had ever made. He'd nearly died . . . and he'd come to her, Tricksie, for the ultimate affirmation of his continued existence. He'd seen the blood of death today . . . but with her he'd found the blood of life.

'Kinda makes you think about what's important,' he began again cryptically; yet to Tricksie the message was loud and clear.

She was important to him. He'd turned to her rather than any of the other women he must surely have . . .

'Some shuteye now, babe,' he muttered, touching her hair again as she felt his body relax against her. 'Then we'll have that shower . . .' Was this another first? Was he actually going to *sleep* with her?

Glory halleluiah, it's true, she exulted behind sealed lips as within seconds Diabolo began to breathe steadily and, miraculously, was fast asleep.

147

So you're human after all, Diabolo, Tricksie mused drowsily as she followed him down into slumber. Not a demon, not a spook or a zombie . . .

You're a man, my love. Not a Moon Devil at all. Just a lovely man . . .

8 *Intermezzo III*

. . . a man . . . Just a man . . . a lovely lovely man . . .

'Of course you are, Josh. Of course you are,' said a voice that didn't sound a bit like Diabolo. It didn't sound much like Tricksie either . . .

So who . . . What?

'Take it easy, Josh,' Isis said kindly, and in an instant Josh knew who, what, where and how.

'Sheesh! That was an incredible trip,' he mumbled, sitting up and rubbing his eyes to get rid of some bizarre after-images. Red splodges hung in his vision, and made him feel quite peculiar. Looking down, he sighed with relief. He was half-naked still, but at least there was no blood on him.

'Look at me, Josh. Look into my eyes. Let's make sure you're back in the real world,' Isis ordered crisply. Still not quite with it, Josh meekly obeyed.

Her scar made him panic for a second – its red-purple whorls looked far too gory for comfort – but then he remembered that was a mark that could never be showered away.

This is wild, thought Josh as Isis handed him a blanket and he wrapped it around his exposed hips and thighs. He'd woken in the lounge again, so she must already have cleaned him up – but obviously he'd come to before she'd had a chance to settle him on the settee.

I wonder if they're in the shower yet? he mused, then shook his head again.

This is driving me nuts, he thought, grinning at the wacky internal paradoxes of 'adventuring'. 'They' existed, but the just-finished episode had never happened to either of them.

'Your boyfriend is one helluva guy,' he observed to Isis as she put a glass full of a familiar amber fluid into his hand.

'So is my girlfriend.' She winked impishly, an action that looked positively weird with her odd eyes. The weirdness made Josh shudder and feel good – both at the same time. 'As you're probably well aware . . .'

'God, yes,' he said with feeling, and took a long pull at his drink.

The transition from woman to man had been cleaner this time, had taken mere seconds, but it was still dangerously easy to 'feel' as if he was Tricksie. Her larger-than-life persona, and her mature, animalistic sexiness were far more vivid in his mind than memories of young, virgin Layla.

It's probably because she's real and I've seen her in the flesh. He sipped appreciatively at his whisky, considering the difference between seeing and being.

'Isis?' he began tentatively.

'Yes?'

'Is what just, er, happened a true picture? Are Tricksie and Diabolo really like that?'

'It's possible. Diabolo helped compile the database, so his personality will have been pretty accurately incorporated. And,' she paused thoughtfully, smoothing her finger along a crease in her crisp white smock, 'and I should think the "Tricksie" I gave you was pretty close too. She doesn't really know much about Pleasurezone, but there's been plenty of input on her from both me and Diabolo.'

Between them, they probably know everything about her, Josh thought ruefully after Isis had left him to relax. In a flash of *déjà vu* he didn't really know who to be most jealous of: Tricksie for having had Isis, Isis for having had Tricksie, or that moody bastard Diabolo for having had the pair of them.

There was no getting away from it; Pleasurezone was incredible, but it was gradually shaking up his mind. One minute he was a man, the next a woman; one minute he'd the hots for a cool mean pimp with an outsize tool, the next he was going crazy over a mad but unfuckable doctor.

She'll be as randy as hell tonight, thought Josh, exploring his new enlightenment. Menstrual hormones were known to soup up the female libido; he'd read it in books. And now he'd felt their effects for himself. Isis was ripe for fucking, blood or no blood, and that same flow would make her hot, wild, and easy to slip into. Just the way Diabolo had slid into h–

'Get your head straight, Mortimer,' he snarled aloud, snatching up his clothes and stalking into the bathroom.

But how would Isis deal with her enlarged sex drive? he pondered, unable to stop taunting himself. Was it worth another crack at her?

No, he decided regretfully. Her willpower was probably as steely as her body was sexy.

Maybe she'll fix herself up with Mister Iceman, thought Josh sourly. The all-fucking, all-slapping, all-belittling Diabolo. At least that way she's sure of a great lay. Trying out the idea of Isis with Diabolo tonight, Josh cursed himself for being a jealous idiot and great big sentimental old softie. If the truth be told, he rather hoped the pimp would be servicing his whore tonight . . .

Back in La Selene, it occurred to Josh that Isis too might have a boyfriend waiting somewhere; some guy she was free to fuck because he'd got nothing whatsoever to do with Pleasurezone. There were several men drinking alone, and Josh eyed them all suspiciously. Any one of them could soon be enjoying the one thing he couldn't get from his orgasmic 'adventures' . . . the privilege of sliding between Isis's long, slim and utterly glorious thighs.

And as he sipped moodily at his drink, his sixth sense suddenly told him those thighs were approaching, even as he lusted for them.

Sure enough, when he turned from the bar, she was making her way towards him, weaving elegantly through the tables and drawing admiring glances from each male she passed, in spite of the purple stain on her face that she was so convinced was hideous . . .

'Hi again,' she murmured, slipping on to the stool beside him and settling herself comfortably. He made to order her a drink, but she was already reaching out to catch Guido's attention. Josh felt a fresh jolt of arousal as her silk blouse tightened across her slightly swollen breasts. The thin blue cloth formed to the stiff outline of her nipples, and Josh could almost taste their budding heat. Oh God, she was in fabulous shape. Her body was just bursting with sex.

Looking around, Josh wondered where her more regular bedmates were.

But . . . no Tricksie. No Diabolo. Were they together after all? Making love instead of poking, fucking and screwing? For the red whore's sake he hoped so.

'How are you feeling now?' he asked Isis, suddenly realising she seemed a thousand per cent more relaxed.

'Shouldn't that be my question?' She smiled over the rim of her wineglass, and Josh realised something else too. It *was* wine she was drinking . . . so obviously she wasn't planning on taking any more of her heavy-duty painkillers.

'Oh, I feel great,' he murmured, half lying and half telling the truth. 'I was just wondering about – ' he flicked a glance at her belly. And the soft vee where her black velvet trousers encased her groin, 'Well, I was just wondering if your painkillers had worked. You don't seem quite so uptight.'

'I'm fine now, thank you, Josh,' she replied with a slow, rather smug little smile. 'The painkillers help, but . . . Well, I've taken a more effective remedy.' Her voice tailed off mysteriously and Josh's prick tingled as his suspicions ran riot.

'And what would that be?' he enquired, wondering whether he'd get an answer.

'Having an orgasm.'

He watched the smooth undulation of her throat as she swallowed her wine. And imagined her arching, groaning . . .

'But when – how?' he stuttered, knocked sideways by a tidal wave of lust. He felt faint with a need to see her, to

152

see this luscious woman climaxing, by his efforts, or her own.

'For a sophisticated man, Josh, you're very naive,' she drawled, placing her glass neatly on the coaster in front of her. From beneath her long black lashes, her good eye twinkled mischievously. 'I diddled myself, didn't I?'

'But when?' Josh took a healthy swig of the fine single malt he'd indulged himself with – and hardly tasted a thing. 'Just now?'

'Not exactly.'

'When?' His voice went hoarse as a delicious churning in his balls told him he already knew the answer.

'While you were dreaming.' Isis's voice was faint too, barely more than a whisper. And beneath the livid scar she was actually blushing.

Josh's spine went to syrup and suddenly he'd an iron bar in his pants. He wanted to know how and where. He wanted the details.

'Were you near me?' he asked, his voice controlled as he reached out and grabbed her hand, hurting her with his nails yet barely aware of it.

'Quite near.'

'How near?' he demanded roughly, resisting her attempts to shake herself free. 'Tell me!'

For a moment they locked eyes, glaring at each other like boxers in a clinch. But Josh felt full of power, and for once, in ascendance over her. And Isis, ever the tactician, succumbed.

'On the stool in the treatment room,' she replied, her voice absolutely level and quite clinical in its lack of expression. 'Almost a metre from your erection, I'd say.'

'Go on.' Josh's tone matched hers even though jungle drums were pounding in his crotch. It was an effort to sit up, to hold Isis's hand and his own glass. The riot in his penis was at that second the single greatest sensation in his life. His flesh need handling, touching, caressing, just as Isis's body had needed the healing stroke of her own fingers. How excellent it'd be to unzip and ease out his aching tool, to expose that stiff veiny rod and then draw her slim leather-covered fingers to his body and make them minister to his need – at first delicately, then, as the fever rose, with a furious jerking brutality.

Isis stared at him, her eyes as round as a scared fawn's, her breasts heaving with the effort of confrontation. Josh marvelled at the peerlessness of her shape, the perfect, gravity-defying curves that scorned the support of any bra. Her nipples were so clear to his eyes and so hugely distended that even the thin silk of her shirt was probably acting as a discreet stimulation. They'd be so sensitive right now, so vulnerable to pleasure. He wondered urgently if she could make herself come just by touching them?

'Go on,' he repeated.

Her rosy mouth opened as if to protest, but Josh silenced her with a look.

'You won't fuck me. At least give me this!'

For a moment she was utterly silent, her tongue peeking out, touching her full lower lip . . .

'Isis, please!' Domination turned to desperation and the transformation worked.

'Okay. Where do you want me to start?'

'Wherever. Just start.'

'Well . . . I always feel horny at this time. Which I guess you'd know all about after tonight.' She shot him a sideways glance. 'And it's not easy to be ethical when you feel hot for a guy . . .' She paused on Josh's indrawn breath of protest. 'Okay, I know you think I resist you just out of cussedness, but I do believe I'm right to. Anyway, I was feeling randy as hell to start with and then seeing you strapped to the couch, with that great body of yours half-naked and your cock reaching for the ceiling . . . Godammit, Josh, you're one helluva sexy sight when you're wired . . .'

'But if you want me so much, why – '

'No, Josh, and you know why.'

'Okay. I'm sorry. Please, go on.'

'It just got too much, unbearable . . . I had to touch myself. Then. There. I had a little plug in of course, but I could feel the juices oozing, the glands working overtime, the tiny ones just on the outside . . . My clit was so hard and high it was killing me. I tried a sneaky rub through my clothes, my smock and my panties, but it was no good. I need lots of direct contact, hard action right on the tip of my clitoris . . .'

Oh God in Heaven, Isis, I could give it you, Josh howled silently, gnawing on his lip to keep lustful protests to himself. If he interrupted her at a crucial moment, his chance might never come again . . .

Isis stared at her gloved hands for a moment while Guido answered Josh's summons for fresh drinks; but when the barman had served them and was safely out of earshot, she shook herself free of Josh, took her second glass of wine in both hands, sipped deeply and went on.

'I could see you were settled and stable and that everything was going smoothly. You were muttering things too and that made me feel even sexier. So I decided I'd do it properly, frig myself to orgasm while you were safely out of the world.

'I got off the stool for a moment and took down my panties. I knew there'd be lots of time to put them on again before you came round. I climbed back on to the stool with my skirt rucked up. The leather felt nice against my bottom. Just the way the couch does, Josh.' For the first time she looked him in the eye, and he felt an even greater pang of lust. There was so much fire in that lop-sided face . . . so much sex. 'I could feel my juices trickling on to the seat, so I eased myself to the edge, spread my legs more. That way I could get my fingers right into my fanny.'

The picture formed in Josh's mind and his cock twitched wildly, his own juices oozing just as hers must've done . . . That white smock, Isis's long sleek thighs, the furry patch between, her clever fingers seeking . . . entering . . . rubbing in a sweet, fast rhythm.

'And then?' he demanded impatiently. His excitement was on a knife-edge. She couldn't stop now!

'Josh, I – '

'Go on,' he pleaded.

'Then I touched myself.'

155

'How?' he persisted, even though his imagination was already directing the action. He saw the glossy mat of reddish-brown curls, her labia quite clear through the hairs, plump and swollen as her long fingers dove between. Even her hands were sexy to him now; in spite of her scars, she kept them beautifully, with nails painted and the flawed skin exquisitely soft as if she creamed it several times a day.

'I . . . I rubbed my clit,' she stammered, her whole face pinkening. Josh wriggled in ecstasy on his stool, her embarrassment like a caressing hand on his aching rod.

'Fast or slow? Hard rubs or just teasing?' Detail! He had to have detail! And he'd drag it out of her even if it meant the pair of them coming right here in La Selene.

'All right,' she hissed at him, her eyes going narrow and hard. Josh shuddered under her fury, biting hard on his abused lip to stop himself climaxing there and then. The danger spiralled higher when she clomped her glass back on the bar and twirled her fingers with the obvious intention of illustrating her account with gestures . . .

'You asked for this, you bastard, so here it is. First I slip this hand between my thighs.' Lifting her right hand, she set her thumb at a wide angle, 'I'm a left-handed wanker, by the way, Josh, so I use my right hand to spread myself open, to part my pussy-hair and hold the lips apart. It's pretty slippery down there, but I manage . . .'

Josh was acutely and intimately aware of her sudden use of the present tense. He'd no idea if this was a true account of what'd happened while he was under, but as she continued in a low, red-hot voice, he no longer cared.

'I hold my labia as wide open as I can, Josh. I like to be able to look down and actually see my clitty. See it there, all red and wet, like a juicy little berry ready to be sucked. I wish sometimes that I was a contortionist, a gymnast who could bend double and eat my own twat. I'd like to lick my own clitoris, Josh, especially when there's a hunky big-pricked man strapped to a table next to me. But he's asleep. He can't see what I'm doing to myself. What a shame. He can't see me looking down at my own snatch, watching as this finger,' she raised her left hand directly in front of Josh's almost-crossed eyes and waggled her middle finger lewdly, 'as this finger dips into the gel-pot, takes up a nice gluey load and then slips neatly between my cunt lips and straight on to my clit.'

Between Josh's thighs, the situation was critical. His balls were tight up against his body and he could feel his orgasm speeding towards him in a shimmering cometary mass. His penis was a pole of fire compressed agonisingly into his tight pants . . . It felt absolutely fabulous.

He daren't move. He hardly dared breathe. The slightest agitation and his tortured rod would yield itself up inside his stretch-silk underpants. He suppressed a sigh, imagining the sticky and mortifying state he'd soon be in, sitting in a pool of his own spontaneously ejaculated semen . . .

'I like the first touch to be hard, a long hard press . . . no motion, just pressure. Testing the limits. Assessing.'

Josh's knuckles were white now, his nails digging painfully into the edge of the bar. It was either that or hold his crotch, with the instant and inevitable consequence . . .

'And when I know what I need, that's when the action really starts. The gel feels nice. Cold and slippery and kind of soothing. But I like to use my own juices too. It feels less mechanical that way, more like an art. Makes it lovemaking, not just a reflex . . . Do you understand that, Josh?' Her eyes, both sound and spoiled, blazed into his, and Josh nodded with extreme care.

'So I slide my finger down to my hole and scoop up some more liquid . . . Of course when I've got my period I just flick around the edges, take it off the little lips . . . but when I haven't I stick my finger right inside myself, right into my vagina to get the thickest hottest juices. By then, my clit's all swollen, really big, out of its hood. So I bring up that load of lovejuice and massage it in. Rub it in and in and in until my hips start pumping and I – '

'Oh God! Oh God!' Josh doubled over his tormented body as his own hips tried to mimic her words – and his penis pulsed helplessly inside its prison. Tears squeezed out from his closed eyes as his loins erupted in an exquisite volcanic rush and the crotch of his silk briefs was filled with a warm slippery wetness. For the first time since adolescence, he'd come in his pants . . .

Dazed, Josh bowed his head almost to the bar counter, and just sat there, hunched and gulping in air, for several long moments. Isis had blown him away, all over again, and he sighed as she laid a gentle stroking hand on his shaking back.

'Are you okay, Mr Mortimer?' enquired a male voice and Josh looked up into Guido's concerned face.

'I . . .' Josh began, with not the remotest idea how to continue.

'Is it that headache again, Josh?' Isis intercepted smoothly. Josh could only nod, then cover his eyes once more; he wanted to kiss her and strangle her at the same time.

'Could we sub a couple more of those painkillers of yours, please, Guido?' she went on, then touched Josh's back again as the barman retired in search of more pills.

'You just climaxed, didn't you?' she said softly, her fingers moving lightly on his shoulders, soothing and massaging.

'I sure did!' he snapped, whirling and straightening up in one jerky movement. 'Why did you do that? You won't go to bed with me but you're quite happy to make a damn fool out of me in public, talk dirty to me until I spunk in my pants like a horny kid! What kind of pervert are you, Isis? Do you get off on tormenting men like this, working them into such a state that they can't control their own pricks?'

Isis held her ground, uncowed by the fury that shocked even Josh himself.

'I said what I said because you asked me to,' she replied calmly, meeting his glare, her scarred face impassive.

'I'm sorry,' Josh said softly as his anger dissolved into awe. Again. What was it about her? She had him around her little finger . . . Or was it the middle one, he thought, eyeing her gloved left hand as his reviving prick gave a

158

tiny spasmodic lurch. 'Was it true? What you, what you said . . .'

'Yes,' she replied evenly, as she too studied her hands. 'It's what I did while you were under. Exactly what I did.'

Josh believed her, and went on dwelling on the revelation for the rest of the fairly subdued evening. Nothing more was said – on either side – about Isis's masturbation or the need that had initiated it. Very little was said on any topic aside from the time of Josh's next appointment. They both spent much time in silent contemplation of their respective drinks.

Their parting was sparsely worded, but when he reached the door, Josh paused, suddenly deciding he did have more to say – even if he didn't know precisely what it was.

But when he turned and looked towards the bar both the stools they'd occupied were empty. Like the mystery she was, Isis had already disappeared.

From the bar maybe, but not from Josh's mind. And as the hours passed, he realised, more and more, that the good doctor Isis was now a permanent resident in this upgraded imagination of his. Both Isis and the crazy dreams she took him through, were his constant mental companions during the fast elapsing days of his furlough. Not that he objected to having Isis in his mind, but the resulting and almost continuous state of erection sometimes made him long for the damped-down torpor of Libidox. It was hard work being rampant all the time, wanting a body he couldn't have . . .

There was no let-up. If he saw a veiled woman across the Mall, he felt like charging across to her, ripping open his pants and screwing her then and there. If he heard a voice in a crowd that sounded even remotely similar to Isis's husky provocative drawl, he felt like racing to the nearest men's room and wanking himself off to a solitary, sobbing climax.

Jumbled into this obsession were fragmentary visions of his 'adventures': pictures of Suleiman and Layla, Kenny and Rio, vague yearnings for the voluptuous Tricksie, and finally and most disorientating of all, a real desire to relive the encounter with Diabolo. The dodgiest thing about this being that he wasn't quite sure if he wanted to *be* Tricksie . . .

He could answer all this via Pleasurezone. In the crypto-reality of 'adventuring', he could finally – once and for all – settle the suspicions that'd niggled him since his one teenage encounter with homosexuality.

A gay trip would be the answer, but it all seemed distinctly unappealing beside his red-blooded craving for Isis. In spite of his submission and her ordering him about, his prick seemed to shout every time he thought about her . . .

It was yowling now as he walked into La Selene at the appointed time. Cock, heart and spirits lifted as he saw her familiar face and body, and then drooped, all three, when he saw she wasn't alone.

What are you up to, he thought furiously. She was completely oblivious of his arrival and deep in conversation with a – well, with perhaps the most sexually undefinable creature Josh had ever set eyes on. With a conscious effort he shortened his usually long stride and almost crept across the softly carpeted bar. Anything to give him time to take in the strangeness of Isis's new companion . . .

As he drew closer, the strangest thing of all was that Isis and the unknown 'person' seemed, in a rather subtle way, to resemble each other. In the best split-second reconstruction job he could do, Josh subtracted the scar from Isis's fundamentally exquisite face, and found that her underlying features and those of the peculiar newcomer were indeed incredibly similar.

To confuse him even more, they were even wearing the same sort of clothes, although Isis's trousers, shirt and waistcoat looked – as ever – almost sinfully feminine, and her companion's immaculate pin-stripe suit was sharp-tailored to the point of severity.

The closer Josh got to the pair, the more his reaction-shock-fascination grew. He was seeing Isis and yet not-Isis, and consequently he experienced the coiling attraction he already felt for *her*, combined with an atavistic revulsion for the complete 'otherness' of her companion. He was just about to turn and make an unnoticed getaway when Isis called out.

'Hi, Josh! Over here. There's someone I want you to meet.'

With a thrill of dread Josh closed the distance between them, becoming more and more aware, as he approached, of being intensely scrutinised by the weirdo at Isis's side.

And when he at last stood between the unlikely duo he almost lost his nerve altogether. Isis's 'someone' was smiling at him with a blatant and thoroughly undisguised sexual interest. Large hazel-gold eyes, so similar to Isis's one good eye, checked out Josh's jeans and leather-clad person; then, with a unmistakably lascivious glitter, locked on his already-swollen crotch.

'Josh,' said Isis, breaking what seemed far too much like a spell, 'I'd like you to meet my cousin, St Etienne.' She gestured at her ambiguous relative with a purple suede-covered hand.

More snazzy gloves, thought Josh inconsequentially as he held out his own naked fingers for a handshake he really didn't want. 'Ett, this is Joshua Jordan Mortimer. You might say he's an associate of mine.'

'Pleased to meet you,' Josh muttered grudgingly, then was surprised to find his hand gripped in a firm, brief and unexpectedly pleasant-feeling hold.

'Charmed,' replied St Etienne in a light, yet melodiously husky drawl that had much in common with 'his' cousin's alluring voice, and seemed at odds with such a strong, assertive handshake.

'Ett's my only living relative, Josh,' said Isis chattily. 'We often meet here for a bevvy . . .'

'Ah yes, Ice my dear, we *"outlandos d'amour"* really must stick together. Don't you think so, Mr Mortimer? I'm deeply concerned, sometimes, to think of my cousin living alone in the City . . .'

Josh nodded a vague assent, not quite sure what Isis's painted cousin was on about, but fascinated all the same. Close up the family likeness was striking, and although St

161

Etienne had straight hair, styled in a heavy blocky fringe that skimmed the eyebrows with the rest gelled back austerely and caught in a tail at the nape of the neck, it appeared to be more or less the same unusual multicolour of Isis's luxuriant waves. They certainly both had the same clever hand with cosmetics even though St Etienne of course had no awesome scar to deal with.

'May I get you a drink, Josh?' asked the sartorial one, entirely unabashed by Josh's just-short-of-horrified stare. 'Hmm. Josh. That is what Ice called you, isn't it? Personally, I think "Jordan" sounds far more distinguished, but of course it's not up to me is it?' Josh's mouth dropped open in amazement as the other one placed a long lacquer-tipped hand on his arm, and accompanied the gesture with a brazen fluttering of long black mascara-ed lashes.

Josh's heart did a somersault, and then seemed to drop through the pit of his belly, as, to his appalled astonishment he felt his prick reply with a loathsome throb.

It's because he looks like Isis, godammit, he shouted inside. It's got to be! He could almost accept fancying a brutally masculine type like Diabolo, but to get the hots for this nancified oddball? Oh no. Oh no no no . . .

'Behave yourself, Ett,' Isis admonished lightly, smiling at both of them. 'Didn't you say you were waiting for Bobbie?'

'Yes, and she's late again, the little bitch. If she doesn't get here in the next five minutes, I'm going to ask Guido out instead,' St Etienne said in mock petulance, smiling coyly at the barman who'd just come up to take orders. For Josh, shock piled on shock as, instead of the expected disgust, he saw a flare of positive response in the young blond's eyes.

My God, he's one too, thought Josh as he slid further and further out of his sexual depth.

'What will you have, Josh?' asked St Etienne again in the face of Josh's continuing and flabbergasted silence.

'Josh?' prompted Isis, grinning at him, with what seemed like unwarranted mirth.

'Yes. Er . . . thanks, I'll have a white wine, please.'

'Guido, sweetheart, a bottle of your finest, if you will?' St Etienne reached out to stroke the barman's cheek affectionately, then hopped off his stool and pulled up the one beyond. 'Here, Joshua, sit between Cousin Ice and I.' And when Josh was established on the plush-covered and faintly warm seat, he continued rapturously, 'What a glorious profile you've got, Josh. I could just die for a nose as straight as yours.'

'Don't be so silly, Ett,' Isis chastised as the wine arrived and was poured. 'You've had yours fixed twice already, you surely don't want to change it again.'

The banter continued in this teasing vein for some time, but Josh contributed next to nothing. He was acutely aware of sitting in the heat so recently emanated by St Etienne's trim backside, and the sensation was uncomfortably delicious.

Yet confusing as at first the whole scenario seemed, while Josh sipped his wine and observed the two cousins' interplay, he recorded several at first comforting, and then downright arousing facts . . .

St Etienne and Isis had even more in common than was initially apparent: the same slender elegant neck and throat . . . the same narrow delicate wrists . . . And when St Etienne gracefully half turned and reached across the bar for a cocktail titbit, the fine cloth of a close-tailored waistcoat stretched across the same lusciously rounded curves!

Isis's flamboyant cousin wasn't an effeminate homosexual at all . . . She was a woman! And a thoroughly desirable one, in spite of her cross-dressing and her outrageous mannerisms. More than that, she seemed a genuinely likeable soul too: with a wicked, yet utterly contagious sense of humour and a concern and affection for her scarred cousin that was writ in letters too large to ignore.

Within minutes, Josh found himself positively fancying St Etienne, despite Isis's potent presence at his other side. The two cousins shared the same brand of sexual charisma: in St Etienne it was atrociously blatant, and in Isis more subtle and mysterious. In Isis their charm gleamed softly and tantalisingly, while St Etienne blasted it out like a multicoloured searchlight that rather nonplussed those it fell upon . . .

'Oh, I'm so sorry, my dears, I'll have to leave you,' the bright one said at length. 'There's Bobbie over there . . .' She gestured grandly in the direction of a rather odd-looking young woman who'd just entered: a pallid punkette with a black bird's nest of hair and even more elaborate make-up than St Etienne's. 'And she's pouting. I'd better go and pacify her. Cheerio, Joshua, divine to meet you. We must get together some time . . .'

Intrigued, Josh watched St Etienne make her way across the crowded room towards what was presumably her girlfriend. Many sets of eyes followed her, and it was clear that some of them were as puzzled as Josh had been. Isis's cousin had a fine, bold walk that could easily have been assigned to either gender, and the clean pure lines of her face made her an attractive member of either sex. The whole signal was even further scrambled by the kiss she gave the very obviously female Bobbie.

The unknown girl appeared from a distance to be rather worked up about something and on the verge of tears; and as St Etienne began to comfort her, Josh turned back towards Isis and caught the tail end of an arch little grin.

'Okay, I admit it.' He reached for his drink, 'She had me foxed there for a minute. I really thought she was a man, and that you were setting me up for a gay trip.'

'Would I do that?' Isis's voice was pert and her good eye twinkled roguishly.

'Probably.'

'Yes. You're right. It'd crossed my mind to see if I could trigger you into a homosexual "adventure" for your own good. But believe me, Ett isn't part of the plan. She just happened to be here.' She raised her glass to her already moist lips and Josh's lurching prick suddenly reminded him which cousin it was he really wanted to screw. He watched the undulation of Isis's pale throat as the wine went down, and imagined her swallowing his come . . .

'Josh! Are you listening?'

'Sure,' he said honestly. He was actually listening to her; it wasn't his fault that his mind was showing him so graphically what could've happened if things were different. Shifting slightly on his stool, he tried to manoeuvre his engorged cock into a more comfortable position. 'Tell me about your cousin. Does she always dress like that? What's she – well, what's she into? Is she a lesbian or what?'

'All right, here goes. Ett started cross-dressing in her teens, about the time she abandoned her Christian name. She's Mary-Rose St Etienne, by the way, but she absolutely hates it. And as far as I know, she's omnisexual. She's had boyfriends, girlfriends, and various other "friends" who were hard to put labels on. I don't know precisely what she does with all these people, but I suspect everything would be a fair bet. She's very arty; she writes novels, and her imagination is unlimited, both in bed and out. Oh, and in case you hadn't guessed, she's got a scene going with Guido . . .'

'What? When she's not seeing Bobbie?'

'Oh, no. At the same time, I gather.'

'What kind of a ménage is that?' Josh's imagination instantly supplied several lurid images; and most of them sped directly to his already-trembling tool.

'Who knows? Sex isn't algebra, Josh,' said Isis blandly. 'The equations don't always have to balance. Ett's never described the actual plumbing of her sex-binges, but, believe me, knowing her, the possibilities are limitless.'

'Yeah,' breathed Josh, his mind's-eye seething with gymnastically entangled bodies, contorted limbs, sweaty arrangements of mouths and genitals . . . He jumped and almost spilled his drink when Isis gently touched his hand.

'Pleasurezone could make you a part of it, Josh,' she said softly. 'If that's what you want?'

'You mean *they*,' he nodded to the still-talking St Etienne and Bobbie, 'they could be my adventure?' He looked down at the suede-clad hand on his arm, centred his spirit on the slight contact and wished. Hard.

But when he looked up again, Isis was shaking her head,

despite what he took to be a tinge of regret in her mismatching eyes.

'With my cousin, Josh. And her friends. That's all I can offer.'

'Okay, then, Boss Lady,' Josh answered decisively, draining the last of his wine. 'I'll take the deal. Give me an adventure with St Etienne and Co. One of your famous F & Fs. If I can't have you, I'll have your kinky cousin.'

'Have St Etienne?' she enquired with a smirk. 'You fuck St Etienne? Haven't you been listening to me at all, Josh?'

'How do you mean?' Josh demanded. 'No offence, but I was assuming we'd be following the usual modus operandi. A sort of "you let me see her, then I dream about sticking it up her" scenario?'

Isis chuckled behind her suede-covered fingers and studied him impishly over them, her good eye sparkling with mirth.

'Joshua Mortimer, you don't seriously believe that after all I've told you about her, my cousin is into boring old, two-dimensional bog-standard intercourse, do you?' She nodded in the direction of her be-suited relative and the now starry-eyed Bobbie, who were just leaving the bar with their arms around each other's waists. 'This isn't a spread-your-legs submissive female you're dealing with here. Get in the sack with Ett, Josh, and *she's* the one who'll be doing the screwing.'

'Doing the screwing . . . Doing the screwing . . .' burbled Josh, feeling exquisitely out of it as the hallucinogen made its presence felt.

'You okay?' Isis enquired over her shoulder as she prepared the final calibrations.

'Absolutely divine, ducky,' Josh giggled, quite giddy now that the various inhibition-busting drugs had loosened him up.

In more ways than one.

He wriggled down on to the probe, opening both his mind and his fluttering anus to its possession. He did get off on it, he did! He loved being filled, and stuffed, and stretched . . . and that mad woman, St Etienne, could probably do things that felt even better. She could use . . . Oh God, oh God! Yes, that *would* be even better . . .

'Even better,' he moaned, smiling like a ninny and watching his tool bob in its restraining transceiver cuff.

'Pardon? What's that? Are you sure you're all right, Josh?' Isis was bending over him now, checking his pulse, pupil dilation, temperature. In her white smock, Josh thought she looked a streetwise tattooed angel, a piece of heaven on two legs and – as his vision wavered – extraordinarily like her bizarre cousin.

'Will cousin Ett do stuff that's better than this?' he burbled, bouncing on the probe, then squealing as the sweet sensations churned in his arse.

'Look, Josh, are you sure about this? I've another program all backed up and ready to run. I think you'll like it. It's one of my own but it's a bit special.'

'Nope, I've made my mind up,' whispered Josh dreamily, nodding to the mask that Isis was clutching with less than her usual decisiveness. 'I'm gonna boldly go where I've never been before.'

'All right, Josh, so be it,' she said, gently positioning the velvet-lined mask. Josh smiled, enjoying the soft purr of her voice. In the utter blackness it seemed so rich and sensuous it was almost solid. 'This time you're still yourself. Just lie back, relax and let it all happen. This is you, Josh, and my cousin can be anything. Absolutely anything . . . and everything. Just remember that she likes to play. It's all a game to her, Josh, and you're going to play it with her . . .'

'Yeah . . . Play . . . That's it . . . I like it . . . It's funtime . . . Time to play . . . Playhour . . .'

9 *Playhour*

. . . Jordan shook his head. What? Oh God, had he blacked out for a moment?

Where on earth am I? his befuddled mind demanded, as his body started answering questions he hadn't yet asked. He felt hot, sexy and hungry, yet he didn't know why and he didn't know who for. All he did know was that he wanted action. Lots of it.

I want some fun, he told himself indulgently. I want something different and I want it now. He started to get a grip on his memory.

Well, a partial grip . . .

He didn't just *want* something different, he *felt* different. Maybe that was why he'd said 'Jordan' when the stranger had asked his name? It wasn't the one he usually used.

'New scene, new name,' he said quietly, trying to work out if he'd had too much to drink. Or not enough. Yeah, he was Jordan tonight all right, but how the hell had he arrived at this place?

Looking around the subtly elegant room, though, the blanks started filling in. The soft lighting reminded him of the bright lights of a club . . . flamboyance all around him, outrageous sights and colours wherever he looked. The discipline of classical music, lilting quietly in the background, took him back to a pounding overload of sound. Hi-energy retro sounds from the 20th century, classics from Bronski Beat, Erasure and the Pet Shop Boys, combined with hot new fuck-music like the Kenny Jayston Krew and Red Cat and the Slaves; all of it loud, sexy and heavy with bass . . . He was alone, now, but he remembered being crushed in the centre of a crowded dancefloor, a vibrating handkerchief of sprung wooden boarding that contained the weirdest bunch of people Jordan had ever set eyes on . . . Men dancing with men. Women dancing with women. Straight couples in the bentest of clothes. Leather. Vinyl. Rubber. Moulded metal. Lace and chains. Males in frocks. Curvy girls in crucial suits . . .

Oh, God yes! Women in pinstripes, severe tailoring, waistcoats . . .

Now that is a turn-on, old son, isn't it? he thought with feeling. His prick went 'yow' as he remembered exactly whose flat he was in . . .

'Hey, Jordi, you haven't got a drink yet. What can I fix you?'

Jordan flinched, suddenly and fully back in reality. Lost in his musings he'd never noticed her soft-footed return, but his breath left his body as he looked up at the one he'd soon have sex with . . . 'Whisky, please,' he croaked, feeling a silky shiver in his gut.

She'd changed her clothes, got into something a little less comfortable.

'Great! I've got a Hebridean single malt that you'll just adore,' his new friend answered in an arch drawl, seeming to ignore his confusion.

Jordan had felt uncomfortable at first around the cool-eyed, be-suited woman who'd picked him up so confidently. But some time during the evening – he didn't know precisely when – there'd been a curious shift in his perception. He'd stopped being surprised by her husky, seductively domineering voice, her brisk expansive gestures, and her immediate and unthinkable intimacy. It seemed like blind fate that St Etienne should touch his body so freely. Touch parts of him other women would have touched only in the bedroom.

Yeah, it'd been shocking. Hackle-raising. Then, suddenly and crazily, it'd started being fabulous. Unbearably exciting. His groin had turned to throbbing agony, and he'd found himself playing up to her every outrageous utterance. Wanting those touches. Flirting and seducing . . .

'Thank you,' he said softly, 'But anything will do. Have you . . . have you phoned your friends?'

'Sure,' replied St Etienne with a smile that teased and promised, 'They'll be over in a few minutes. They don't live far. But in the meantime, why don't you and I have that drink and get more comfortable?'

Jordan wondered again just how comfortable it was possible to be in those clothes of hers. There was certainly no scrap of ease for him!

He studied her as she crossed to a small built-in bar and began to mix drinks with an almost scientific precision.

When he'd first seen her, earlier this evening, he'd stiffened immediately, intrigued by her immaculately tailored English wool man's suit. But now, his groin throbbed mercilessly, his prick goaded by her new and frankly erotic clothing . . .

Buttersoft leather. Everywhere. Fashioned into a cut-off vest and jeans-cut trousers, the living fabric was so tight it went beyond the usual cliché of 'sprayed on'. Far beyond!

St Etienne's leathers looked as if they were electrostatically bonded to her body; they were a sheer black animal film that floated obscenely on the surface of her skin. Her bare arms and midriff looked stark white in contrast, their smooth pallor thrown into high relief by the raw aggression of a heavy, studded silver-buckled belt and short, close-fitting fingerless leather gauntlets. Her boots were low, soft and slouch-style, their menacing workmanlike quality far more erotic, somehow, than the classic needle-heeled stilettos.

It was the first time Jordan had been this close to a 'leather goddess' . . . and he knew, all over again, that St Etienne was exactly what he'd been looking for . . .

He'd set out tonight determined to find sex in a kinky new package. That 'something different'. And Peacock City, the nightclub, had been the perfect place to find it. Heaving with party-people, the venue's name was particularly apt; it'd been stuffed to capacity with people dressed

170

to the nines, the tens and beyond, as well as those men, women and various indeterminates who, like Jordan himself, appeared fairly conventional, at least on the outside.

St Etienne wasn't anything remotely like conventional and had entranced him from the very first second. A one-off in both dress and manner, she was, to his newly opened eyes, far more beautiful than the usual type of woman he went out with.

Tallish, just a little short of Jordan's own height, she'd caught his eye as athletically built, but beneath her waistcoat, jacket and shirt, quite deliciously curvaceous. From a distance, and through the crowds, he'd thought her an effeminate man – and been shocked by his own genital response. But up close, he'd soon perceived the delicacy of her bones, the finesse of her wrists and throat, the luscious thrust of her breasts beneath fine grey suiting. And now, as she turned towards him, Jordan saw, once again, a face that was powerful, yet exquisitely sculpted, and a body that surpassed both its early promise and Jordan's wildest flights of masturbatory fantasy.

'Here. Try this,' St Etienne said, crossing the room, her stride purposeful and sensuous. Giving Jordan the drink, her hand lingered on his, half-caressing, wholly exciting, and as he took the glass to his lips, his prick trembled precariously. Jordan gulped the whisky far faster than the smooth brew deserved. Never, ever had a drink been so needed.

'I saw you eyeing the leather brigade in the City. I thought *this* —' She ran one finger slowly along the inside of her leather-coated thigh, and right up into the vee between her legs, 'might appeal to you.'

'I . . . I . . .' Jordan couldn't speak. St Etienne's lewd gesture had quite stunned him; she'd touched her own cunt through the wafer-thin hide, let her finger point to the hot place he wanted so much.

'Don't be scared, little Jordi,' she said suddenly, her voice strong yet kind. 'We'll look after you. It's the first time you've done this sort of thing, isn't it?'

What sort of thing? Jordan nodded, still struck mute.

'Don't worry. You'll be all right with us.'

St Etienne sank gracefully on to the settee beside her prey. 'We know what to do, Jordi. We'll make it good for you. Very good. Better than you could possibly imagine.' She took the empty glass from Jordan's frozen fingers, put it with her own on the coffee table, and leaned forward with unmistakeable intent.

Jordan just let it happen. Through the course of the evening he'd swung from an initial shock at St Etienne's casual unsolicited caresses – a touch of the cheek, a stroke along the back of the hand, a long, assessing glide along his thigh to his crotch – to actively desiring them, and manoeuvring his body so they were inevitable. But this was the first time she'd gone so far as to kiss him . . .

And once kissing, St Etienne assumed complete and utter control. Her lips were like the rest of her: a heady combination of softness and power. She opened Jordan's mouth with her tongue and pushed moistly inside. And as she first probed, then sucked, nibbled and grazed on his lips, face and throat, her hands began travelling over his hot, unresisting body . . .

Jordan had shed his jacket on arrival and his fine lawn shirt was little hindrance to her strong, assured fingers. The caresses were gentle and tantalisingly skilful, tracing the contours of Jordan's chest and back, pinching his nipples through the ultra-sheer fabric of a very costly shirt. He'd dressed so carefully for tonight . . .

Suddenly a hand closed over his sensitive groin and he was shaking again. The kissing stopped, but the hand stayed where it was, its hold as light as silk yet infinitely promising.

'Easy, baby,' murmured St Etienne against his ear. 'I know this isn't what you're used to, but just relax, sweetheart. Go with the flow . . . I only want it to be nice. For both of us.'

'I'm sorry,' muttered Jordan, unconsciously pressing his crotch into her fingers, 'I've never . . . I usually . . . I'm not sure.'

'Be sure,' St Etienne answered, her own sureness complete. 'You just did *this*!' Her hand rotated ever so slightly, answering Jordan's thrust, 'Trust your body, Jordi, it knows what it wants.'

'But the others, St Etienne. I've only ever made love one on one . . .' He stopped short, embarrassed by his own naivete. As if in answer she squeezed lightly, and as Jordan squirmed, the words came tumbling out: 'I've only ever had sex with one person at a time.'

'Don't worry, Jordi. Bobbie and Guido are like minds, sensitive. They understand. They know it's your first time in a group . . .'

Jordan didn't know whether to feel better or worse at this, but his fears seemed to melt as St Etienne's hand moved beguilingly. It was so sweet to give in, to relax . . . forget responsibility, let another make the decisions, give the pleasure . . .

All through his adult and sexual life, Jordan had felt the burden of having to make things work. The initiative had always been his and though power had sometimes been thrilling, he'd longed, oh, so often, just to lie back and let somebody else take control . . .

As St Etienne had taken it now.

Jordan moaned as gentle but determined fingers explored him through the denim of his jeans. He was examined – it was the only word to describe her methodical approach – along the whole length of his trapped, aching shaft; then a grip of quite piercing delicacy enclosed the head of his cock, more intense through the rough fabric, perhaps, than it would've been on his bare flesh.

'Oh God, Jordi, you're beautiful,' St Etienne whispered, her light voice more husky now, more male-sounding as she rose into the role Jordan had prayed she would.

'I've been dreaming of your prick since the first moment you walked into the club, Jordi. I've been going crazy for you. Wanting to touch you, bare you, lick you . . . I wanted to do nutty things to you, Jordi, real nutty things . . . I wanted to strip you naked right there on the dancefloor. Expose you and exhibit you to everybody. To all the cruising nymphos and cock-hungry queens and say "Hands off!

This is mine!" Then I'd show them just what I could do to you. I'd stroke your prick. Lick your beautiful balls. Bring you off and drink your luscious cream, then, while you were still sobbing, I'd slide my fingers deep inside your arse and fuck you with them right there and then in front of everybody.'

Fire lurched through Jordan's blood-gorged prick, and as it pulsed uncontrollably, spewing semen, his legs turned to water. Like a sex-hungry kid, he'd climaxed from the sheer power of St Etienne's dirty, evocative words. He whimpered, burying his face against the smooth leather of her vest and unconsciously pressing his blushing cheek against her nipple. 'I'm sorry.'

'Hush, baby, hush,' she soothed. 'There's nothing to be ashamed of. I wanted it to happen. You'll take longer to come later. We'll be able to do more. It'll be much, much better.'

Jordan felt a great tide break inside him, a deep singing joy at submitting, at last, to his fate, and to a power far greater than himself. He snuggled closer, feeling peace and a deep and novel eroticism at being held in St Etienne's strong, musk-scented embrace. Nimble fingers moved at the nape of his neck, and suddenly the tie that held his hair slid away and St Etienne's hand was running through his thick black curls.

'Such lovely hair,' she murmured, pressing her lips to Jordan's brow.

The moment was electrifying. The kiss, the nearness of their bodies, and the sticky heat inside his shorts were a combination so intoxicating that Jordan almost fainted. He wanted to fall to the ground and abase himself before St Etienne's magic. He wanted all the things she'd described so vividly . . . and more. He wanted to be a plaything; pure flesh to be served, used, entered. He wanted to be naked and feel her fingers and her flesh all over him. Her presence against his mouth, his loins, his arse.

'Please,' he whispered, gazing up into the fine painted face and the glowing gold-brown eyes, as his mind sought a new lexicon. 'Please . . . take me.'

'I shall, my sweet. Very soon.'

'Oh God, St Etienne! I want it . . . you . . . now.' New life flooded into his cock, and as it stiffened, he was sharply aware of his bottom too: a raw 'needing' sensation in the hole itself and an increased sensitivity throughout the whole surface of his backside. He imagined her gentle hands fondling him, cupping the cheeks, moulding, parting . . . He moaned, soft and low, almost torn apart by the urge to reach round and manipulate his own rear . . . then froze like a startled animal as the bell-like tones of the door alarm cut through his fever.

'They're here,' St Etienne said quietly; then, touching her finger to her rose-stained lips and transferring the imprinted kiss to Jordan's mouth, she gracefully disengaged their tangled limbs and went to answer the door.

Jordan slid back weakly, stunned into reality for a moment as he realised he'd been wound around St Etienne like a vine, clinging to her like a frantic love-lorn girl.

What's happened to me? It seemed so right, so true. And now, out of her immediate orbit, he felt lost, adrift and confused. Had he blown it? Lost his nerve . . . misjudged his own needs?

Soft voices refocused his attention, and he looked towards the door and the couple who'd entered. One dark, one fair, one female, one male, they both exchanged kisses with St Etienne, and the depth and blatant sensuality of those kisses made it obvious to Jordan that unlike himself, they were completely at home in this strange erotic milieu . . . Group sex and gender confusion weren't different or strange to them – they were the accepted norm. And as the newcomers approached him, he realised they were both vaguely familiar, as if he'd seen them somewhere but they'd never actually met.

St Etienne led them forward.

'Jordan, this is Guido.' She nodded to the clean-cut tallish blond in jeans, vest and a black suede waistcoat. 'And this is Bobbie . . .'

Bobbie was shorter and darker, and so dissimilar it was almost breathtaking. A slender slip of a girl, she was dressed

175

in the fashionable neo-Japanese yuppie-punk style: baggy cotton jacket, similar trousers, and a tab-collared shirt, all in a muted off-black grey. Her face was pale as milk, her lips and eyes painted scarlet and black respectively, and her hair a bushy back-combed soot-black mass.

Jordan, to his surprise, found them both strangely unthreatening. He made to rise, but St Etienne stopped him with a strong downward pressure on his shoulder; and when Jordan tried to resist this, he felt his own body fail him. Inexplicably, he was as weak as a kitten.

'Bobbie, Guido, this is our new treasure. This is Jordi.' The restraining hand slid from Jordan's shoulder to his face, and in a lightning, perfumed moment, his lips were engulfed in a wet, demanding kiss. And as St Etienne's mouth subjugated him completely, his head was forced back, his bare throat arched, and he felt the hand of possession cup his excited genitals.

She's showing them what I am, thought Jordan, dissolving, mortified, his hips bumping wildly against her grip. I'm just a helpless slave, a sex toy, an available fuck. The idea made his prick shudder and his arse go loose and open.

Then, as suddenly as it'd all begun, her mouth was gone.

But the cradling hand remained, and as Jordan fell back, gasping, he felt more exposed than if he'd been nude and spread-eagled, his whole body available to all. Unable to stop himself, he met the eyes of his two observers in turn, and saw excitement blazing in both their faces.

'Isn't he beautiful?' St Etienne said smugly, taking her hand away as if to show her friends what she'd done to this, their new toy. Jordan was acutely and humiliatingly aware of the many, many tell tales: his tousled, unbound hair, his flushed face, the rumpled state of his shirt, his pungent sweat . . . and his grotesquely bulging groin.

'Lovely,' murmured Bobbie, dropping to her knees, her blacklined eyes riveted to the straining zip of Jordan's jeans. Pale, perfectly manicured fingers reached toward the prize, yet tantalisingly, didn't touch it. 'Lovely,' she repeated.

Guido wasn't so reticent. He gave Jordan's erection a rough but friendly squeeze, then kissed him long, deep and hard, his tongue probing and diving as if searching for the lingering taste of St Etienne . . .

Jordan felt faint. Not only had he just been brought to orgasm at the hand of a true-blue leather-clad dominatrix, he was now actually enjoying being kissed by a man.

'Hey, break it up, you two.'

St Etienne's voice was firm but amused as she hauled her friend bodily off Jordan. Even in his dazed state, Jordan was struck by the strength that particular feat would require. Guido was tall, well-muscled and no mean burden . . . and St Etienne was, when all was said and done, a slender and rather fine-boned woman, despite her hard-edged fetishistic splendour . . .

And splendid she was. Unequivocally. Beside her Jordan felt like a sleazy, shagged-out male slut . . . The hot clinch appeared to have had no effect on St Etienne whatsoever, and as she rose smoothly to her feet, she made something go flip in the pit of Jordan's belly. No crease or wrinkle marred the perfection of her black leather garments; her strange red-blonde-brown hair was still secure in its sleekly gelled ponytail, and her razor-straight fringe still kissed the line of her finely-plucked brows. She looked unruffled and unruffleable, and Jordan felt a discreet thrill of challenge. Could he be the one to blow that total and unassailable cool?

'Let's take this into the playroom, shall we?' St Etienne said archly, already pulling Jordan to his feet.

'The playroom?'

Bobbie and Guido were grinning at Jordan's befuddlement.

'A special place where we can all get loose,' St Etienne went on, 'through there.' She nodded in the direction of a closed and unmarked door. All the other rooms in this apartment were open-doored and clearly accessible; this door screamed of mystery.

'Guido. The drinks, my dear. You know best,' St Etienne murmured, nodding in the direction of the well-stocked cabinet; and as the blond moved to comply, Jordan realised why he seemed familiar. Guido was a barman somewhere

– somewhere Jordan frequented and yet irritatingly couldn't remember the name of. Perhaps he'd met Bobbie in the very same bar? The question faded as he felt his hand enclosed in St Etienne's.

'Come into my parlour,' she said, smiling flirtatiously as she led Jordan towards the playroom.

It was a big area – a room that probably ran the whole length of the flat – and yet strangely cozy. Subdued, flame-effect lighting flickered from wall fittings; the carpet was thick and soft and the only furniture seemed to be two or three low tables and a scattered selection of vari-sized couches, each upholstered in a different shade of red velvet. At the focus of the room – the exact centre – stood one of boiling, blood-orange scarlet.

It was to this couch that St Etienne led Jordan, although she didn't encourage him, as yet, to sit.

Jordan stared dazedly around him, his whole body throbbing with awareness even while his mind was floating. Had he been drugged, fed some mind-bending aphrodisiac? He felt like throwing off his clothes, doing a wild dance, posing himself on the blood-red couch and adopting the lewdest, most obscene positions he could think of to excite and titillate this woman and her sexually sophisticated friends. He had an intense urge to masturbate furiously in front of them . . . To hold open his own buttocks and beg one of them, any of them, all of them, to probe him. He moaned, trying to rub his crotch against St Etienne's slender, black-covered thigh . . .

'Patience, baby,' she soothed, stroking the tangled hair back from Jordan's brow. 'I know you want it . . . and we do too! But there's no need to rush. Playhour lasts all night.'

Slim fingers moved over Jordan's face, exploring and caressing, then hovered at his mouth before entering and encouraging him to suck. Jordan did just that, but with little idea why. He suckled madly on St Etienne's first and middle finger for about thirty seconds, wetting the leather that covered them to the knuckle, and gradually realising he wanted them to be more intimate flesh. Knowing this he slurped harder than ever, bumping his crotch in time to his sucks, smearing himself against St Etienne, searching for the soft answer to his own hardness.

'Oh God, Jordi, you're amazing,' she gasped, no longer sounding quite so self-possessed. 'So responsive. You're pure sex. A perfect whore. I think I'm in love!' For a moment she seemed to melt into Jordan's own heat, then abruptly she pulled away, shaking her head as if to clear it. 'Hey, you little sexpot, go steady. It's time we had you nude . . . What do you think, my dears?' she enquired of Guido and Bobbie, both of whom, Jordan realised, were watching the exchange with close attention.

And now they both nodded, their eyes bright with anticipation. Jordan's fingers went shakily to his shirt buttons.

'No, no, no!' cried St Etienne, taking both Jordan's hands in hers. 'We'll strip you. We like to unwrap our treats ourselves.' She released her grip, yet Jordan still felt imprisoned, held by her darkly glittering eyes.

'Guido, will you do the honours with the drinks? You know what we all like. Jordi will have whisky, with a little dash of ginger ale and some ice. Bobbie, come here and help me undress Jordi.'

Jordan half expected her to snap her fingers. Click click click. St Etienne's orchestration of this drama was total, and her two friends slid so easily into their roles that it was obvious this'd all happened so many times before. Breathing slowly, trying to calm himself, Jordan knew instinctively that he was only the latest of many they'd initiated into their alternative world. He felt irrationally jealous.

But not for long.

In the blink of an eye St Etienne was kissing him again, holding his face between her two hands as she raped his mouth. The kiss was bruising, ache-making, all-encompassing; yet even as he almost choked on St Etienne's stabbing tongue, Jordan was aware of other hands working on his body.

His feet first. Totally passive, he stood on first one foot then the other as Bobbie took off his shoes and socks. Jordan moaned under his breath as St Etienne released his face, then slid one hand behind his head to keep up the crushing pressure on his mouth, and used the other to strip off his shirt with ruthless efficiency. Bobbie, meanwhile, was working on his lower half.

Jordan was fighting for breath, his jaw on fire, as his jeans slid down and he felt gentle urgings to step out of them. Then, suddenly, as if the knowledge that her prey was now dressed only in a pair of thin underpants was some kind of signal, St Etienne broke the punishing kiss and looked first at Jordan's throbbing mouth and then downwards.

Following the gaze, Jordan blushed throughout the whole of his body; there was a rampant bulge pushing out the fine blue cotton and an obscene spreading dampness from his recent ejaculation. Bobbie and St Etienne exchanged conspiratorial grins, and the latter nodded very slightly.

Obviously this was a pre-arranged part of their ritual. Obedient Bobbie fell to her knees and, to Jordan's delicious horror, pressed an open mouth to the wet patch on his underpants. He whimpered as her serpent-like tongue flicked his thinly covered tool. And he cried out again, long and pitifully, while she licked at the stain as if savouring the recently shed semen lodged in the cloth.

Jordan's hips had just begun their shameful involuntary pumping when St Etienne cuffed her young friend lightly on the head and pushed her away from her feast.

'Get off, you greedy little tyke. Didn't your mummy ever tell you? You take the paper *off* before you eat the lollipop.'

Bobbie smirked up at them both, pure devilment shining from beneath her heavily mascara-ed lashes.

'Now let's get a move on, shall we? Please proceed with your task, Bobbie dear. Jordi will feel much more comfortable without these nasty spunky panties.'

As St Etienne continued her lecture Jordan realised that despite his own feelings of humiliation and weakness, he wasn't actually the only submissive present . . . Bobbie was patently in seventh heaven when St Etienne ordered her about; the slight, black-clad girl was almost shaking with ecstasy as she shuffled forward on her knees to obey.

Simultaneously, St Etienne made a tiny gesture and Guido held out a tinkling icy drink in a heavy cut-glass tumbler. As he watched it being passed from hand to hand, Jordan felt Bobbie's cool fingers sliding away his briefs.

He kept his eyes steadfastly on the glass, fighting for some small scrap of poise; any second now he would be naked, his erection exposed like meat on a slab, while his three companions were still fully clothed.

'Quickly now, Bobbie,' St Etienne rapped out, and in one swift, graceless jerk the briefs were around Jordan's ankles. Like a pre-programmed puppet, he stepped neatly out of them, his cock bouncing as he moved.

He ought to have felt more comfortable now, out of his clothes, his swollen organ freed from its constriction. But he didn't. His lower belly cramped furiously and his cock felt like a great rod of lust, dragging heavily on his groin and balls. He looked down, then instantly away, appalled by his own slick-tipped hugeness . . .

'Oh my!' Bobbie whispered, and Jordan moaned at the impact of the young woman's breath on his red-hot shaft.

'Holy shit!' Guido gasped huskily.

St Etienne, for once, seemed robbed of speech; her large eyes sparkled moistly and her painted mouth noiselessly formed one word.

Beautiful . . .

The silence lasted for what seemed like eternity, and Jordan closed his eyes, accepting his erotic martyrdom. He sensed St Etienne moving, then felt her bare arm snake around him from behind, and a hand splay on his naked belly to draw their bodies close together.

I'm going to die, thought Jordan wildly, his cock screaming for the soft-skinned fingers and leather-clad palm that lay lightly across his abdomen.

'Please . . . my prick,' he pleaded, gyrating his hips, then realising with a sweet thrill that his behind was massaging the slight, tender bulge of St Etienne's sexual mound. He heard her faint sigh, then sighed in echo, moulding himself closer and fondling his captor's crotch with the cheeks of his own bottom.

181

'You angel,' gasped St Etienne, pushing herself against the offered crack, her thin leather trousers barely a barrier between them. Jordan's heart leapt, and in the midst of his powerlessness, he felt strong. Moving rhythmically, loving the swing of his own cock now, he thrust backwards in time to St Etienne's forward lunges, exulting in her low grunts of excitement, revelling in the hard press of her nipples against his back, the soft yielding texture of the flesh they crowned. Her breasts, lush and unbrassièred beneath her leather vest, were caressing him through the thin creamy hide. He made a noise of hunger and appreciation, and shimmied determinedly against her, rubbing his bare back against those two deliciously stiffened points.

'Oh no you don't, you little devil,' exclaimed St Etienne after a moment, swinging Jordan around and on to her hip, out of harm's way. 'I don't plan on coming just yet.' She paused a moment. 'Here you are, Jordi, sip this like a good little boy.'

Jordan felt the frosty glass against his lips, and, realising he was parched, he began to drink. The whisky and ginger mix was perfect; and having it fed to him like this was both gorgeous and demeaning. Happy tears squeezed between his closed eyelids, and he was sipping slowly and obediently, lost in his own submission, when another sensation impinged suddenly and shockingly on his consciousness.

His cock, surrounded by warmth and wetness, taunted by a voluptuous suction . . .

The glass was taken from his lips so he could look down. So he could watch . . . The tears blurred his vision, but nothing could blunt the pleasure in his aching loins. His prick was deep in Bobbie's rapturously gobbling mouth . . . he was being sucked off, his erection reduced to an amusing piece of stiffness for the entertainment of his companions.

'Drink again, baby,' whispered St Etienne in his ear as Bobbie's tongue seemed to be everywhere at once.

'I can't! I can't! It's . . . I –'

'Yes, you can . . . Now sip slowly . . .' The glass was at his lips again, and unbelievably, he was swallowing whisky, his throat moving in time with Bobbie's as the girl seemed intent on swallowing *him* whole!

And now, somehow, the drink was gone and St Etienne was murmuring babytalk endearments as she nipped and nibbled at Jordan's ears and neck. Delirious, yet feeling everything with pin-sharp clarity, Jordan shouted hoarsely as Bobbie's tongue dug at the tender spot just under his glans. His hips bounced crazily and he seemed to float, suspended between St Etienne's embracing arms and Bobbie's feverish grip on his thighs. The dark girl was like a terrier; no amount of kicking and writhing could break her suckling hold on his prick. In fact the more Jordan struggled, the deeper Bobbie seemed to engulf him, massaging the whole surface of her victim's tool with the moist interior of her mouth and throat.

'Oh God! Omigodomigodomigod!' screamed Jordan as another sensation joined the torment. Someone was delicately stroking his arsehole with a single moistened finger. Opening his eyes, he realised Guido was kneeling beside Bobbie, reaching underneath . . .

'I can't! I can't! Please! Oh God! Yes!' The finger ceased its cautious tickling, and began to push determinedly into his body. Jordan whined in bliss and horror as the digit slid through the stretchy membrane and into the rectum itself. He felt it waggle impishly inside him, just as Bobbie drew back to enclose just the tip of his cock and flick rhythmically at the hypersensitive groove beneath the head . . .

'Unngh! Unngh! Unngh!' The sounds were crude and ugly, and spittle rattled uncouthly in Jordan's throat as white-hot ecstasy rode the entire length of his engorged shaft. Fire seemed to backwash his whole belly and groin, and he wept and drooled as his semen pumped convulsively into Bobbie's waiting mouth.

And all the time, St Etienne was whispering brokenly into his ear. 'My angel . . . my little angel . . . sweet, sweet little angel . . .'

As the storm in his body ebbed, Jordan felt both mouth and finger withdraw, and at least two pairs of arms lift him on to the velvet couch. Only half conscious, he enjoyed feeling his skin being wiped with a damp, fragrant cloth, and someone very tenderly smoothing back his sweaty hair, then kissing him gently on his closed eyelids . . .

What the hell have I let happen to me? he mused, not unhappily, as his mind slowly regained its function. I'm just a toy . . . A body for them to play with. All of them, he thought, shuddering and reliving the feel of Guido's intrusive finger. Behind his still-closed eyes, he created a picture; himself, half-fainting in St Etienne's arms – with Bobbie's mouth glued to his crotch and Guido's finger up his bottom . . .

'Lovely,' he said, as laughter bubbled inside him. Almost purring with contentment, he wriggled luxuriously on the couch, loving its smooth, plushy texture against his back and arse.

'Do you feel good, sweetheart?' murmured a familiar voice as a familiar hand stroked his face.

Jordan opened his eyes, and it seemed the most natural thing in the world to take that hand and kiss it passionately. 'I feel marvellous,' he replied, pressing his open mouth to St Etienne's palm, licking her soft skin slowly and sensuously. 'I've never felt better in my life. Thank you. All of you,' he finished, looking at the three who'd just made love to him.

'Thank you,' answered St Etienne, ever the spokeswoman, as she ran a hand down Jordan's naked flank.

'But I didn't do anything,' Jordan said puzzledly, shaken more than anything by the renewed twitching in his prick – his response to St Etienne's fleeting touch. I've had two orgasms in the space of thirty minutes, he told himself. How can I be getting hard again so soon?'

'You three,' he went on shakily, 'you three made me come . . . but I haven't . . . haven't done anything for you.'

'Not yet,' said St Etienne, pausing to let Jordan absorb both the implications and the fact that she and her two friends were far less dressed now.

Jordan's prick leapt again at the sight of St Etienne half

naked. She'd stripped off her skimpy vest and beneath it were a pair of proud, delicately rounded breasts that looked both natural and yet strange when set above the gleaming silk-soft hide of her leather trousers. The whole effect was far more titillating, somehow, than total nudity, and Jordan's fingers itched to fondle her as she sat down on the couch beside him.

Guido was completely naked. He was sitting a few feet away: back resting against one of the other couches, legs splayed, eyes closed, happily and unself-consciously masturbating. There was a dreamy smile on his face as his cock thrust chunkily between his fingers. Bobbie, bare from the waist down – her loins a contrast of white belly and black snatch – was watching her friend intently. As Jordan watched, she popped out her red, pointed tongue and ran it round her mouth as if relishing another feast.

'Bobbie would live on spunk if she could,' observed St Etienne matter-of-factly, 'and it might actually be feasible, come to think of it. She gives the finest head in the whole City, to either sex.'

'She's wonderful,' said Jordan without thinking.

'That's right,' replied St Etienne, 'but what about you, Jordi? Wouldn't you like to show me how wonderful you are?'

Jordan looked into eyes that glittered with challenge. 'How do you mean?' he asked.

'Eat me out, Jordi. Give me some head . . . What's the matter, don't you think you can thrill me?'

'Yes! I mean . . . No! I – ' Confused, he couldn't formulate a proper answer. He loved the taste of cunt, and his mouth watered profusely at the thought of the woman at his side, but if she'd been muffed by the matchless Bobbie, what impact could *he* hope to make on her?

Suddenly a harsh groan speared both their attentions. Jordan sat up like a flash and he and St Etienne stared rapt at the spectacle of Guido's climax. The blond had climbed backwards somehow, and with his body arched out crablike from the couch, his pelvis seemed to hang in mid-air suspended from Bobbie's gulping mouth.

Jordan swallowed too, in pure amazement. Guido's pubic hair was jammed against Bobbie's lips and there was no doubt he was ejaculating deep in the girl's slim throat. Impossibly deep. Bobbie's eyes were bulging, her jaw painfully stretched and the muscles of her neck were rippling . . . but even so, while supporting her slight weight on one hand, she was managing to frig herself furiously with the other one. And just as Guido seemed about to flood her gullet with come, Bobbie herself started to climax; her slender hips bucking in time to the savage action of her fingers.

Stunned, Jordan turned away; but not before he'd seen Bobbie's throat undulating like a snake as it released the head of Guido's prick. 'I . . . I couldn't do that,' he stammered, his own mouth and neck aching sympathetically, as if he'd endured the act too.

'Nobody's asking you to,' said St Etienne gently, placing a forefinger under Jordan's chin and making him look up. 'Deep-throating takes years of practice to perfect. And young Bobbie's been doing it far longer than she ought. But –' she hesitated, and her eyes seemed filled with fire, 'what I want isn't so tricky, Jordi. A simple licking out will suffice . . . although I expect you to work hard, sweetheart. You understand that, don't you?'

It was an order, and for a moment Jordan couldn't speak. St Etienne kissed him gently on the corner of the mouth, 'Come on, Jordi, don't let me down now,' she whispered. 'I'm hot and juicy . . . And the others will do something nice to you at the same time . . .'

She hasn't come yet, has she? thought Jordan, feeling guilty. I've come. Guido's come. Bobbie's come. But not her.

'Please, oh God, yes. I want to suck you. I'll do anything you say,' he said, excited even as he said it. He tried to imagine what she might taste like. He wanted her to know – now! – he was hungrier for St Etienne than he'd ever been for a woman in his life.

'Oh God, you're a jewel!' she gasped, then kissed him deep and hard, 'Oh God, Jordi, do it! I want it now . . .'

Urgently, and with less than her usual grace, she scooted along the couch a little and spread her long, lithe thighs, 'Kneel between my legs, darling,' she ordered, and as Jordan complied, a great shudder ran through St Etienne's sylphine body, 'I can't wait to feel your mouth on me . . . Unzip me! Now! Do it, baby, do it!'

Kneeling, Jordan stared numbly at the apex of St Etienne's thighs, and the soft vee defined there. There was a succulent delta beneath that fine leather – a place to feed and suck. A place to pleasure and be pleasured at . . .

'Jordi, baby . . . Please!'

The novelty of it – St Etienne actually pleading – galvanised Jordan to action. Fixing his eyes on her face rather than her groin, he slowly and carefully undid first her heavy metal-trimmed belt and then the sleek-running zip of her trousers. White silk was visible in the created gap – delicate, womanly clothing beneath the brutal leather.

'That's it, Jordi. Now undress me,' St Etienne whispered. Taking her weight on her arms, she tilted up her pelvis, and Jordan was able to pull both her trousers and her silky undergarment – a minute lace g-string – down over her long sleek thighs, past her knees and bunch the whole lot inelegantly around her ankles. She panted and flung her belt out of the way, then pressed her booted feet together and edged her bottom towards the edge of the couch. Leaning back, she seemed to offer her cunt as a luscious, naked, anointed morsel for Jordan's delectation . . .

'Dear heaven,' whispered Jordan, overcome by the beauty of the sight before him: the glossy, tightly trimmed fuzz of pubic curls, the fat blood-filled outer lips, the soft rose-dark contours within . . .

She was the boss lady here, the tough power queen in her rough-house leather . . . but in the moist, fundamental place between her thighs, St Etienne was all soft, yielding woman. And to Jordan, this glistening patch of rumpled female flesh was a pure reassuring familiarity in a world that was so radically strange . . .

Suck me! Lick me! Devour me! it said, the palpitating

187

folds and rich musk-hot aroma reaching out like grace to ensnare him. Jordan bowed blissfully to obey its command, but within tongue-touching distance of St Etienne's swollen clitoris, he paused . . .

She was special and remarkable. Sensual and magnificent. Caught in the web of his own lust, Jordan wanted to give this goddess something worthy of her greatness.

Beautiful sex. Endless orgasm. Stunning cunnilingus that would rock even the mighty St Etienne in her tracks.

And yet how could he achieve his goal? She'd been ser- viced here by the very best . . . the most accomplished cunt-lickers in the City, including, almost certainly, the fey dark young woman who was even now resting from her labours over Guido.

Wetting his lips, Jordan reviewed Bobbie's comprehen- sive skills, then studied the delicate inflowing topography before him, the deep wine-red flower with its sweet crinkled petals that huddled beneath the tight hard bud of woman's utmost pleasure.

But even as he hesitated, the cunt before his eyes came flaunting towards him in a wanton thrust.

'Suck me!' she commanded, sliding long fingers into the creases of her groin to lift and separate the plump outer labia. 'Get your mouth on me now, you fuck, or I'll die.'

Jordan obeyed, half dying himself as he stabbed his tongue directly on to her clit. And as the lady lay back, released her own flesh and grabbed his head roughly in both hands, then proceeded unashamedly to hump his face, Jordan realised that gentleness and virtuoso subtlety were not her current requirements.

'Eat me,' she shouted as he threw his mouth into the musky oceanic maw of her slit and licked and sucked and slurped as if his life depended on it.

No cunt had ever tasted or smelt so delectable . . . Never had juices flowed so freely over his laving tongue . . . Never before had the flesh beneath his lips so quickly begun to flutter and pump in orgasm.

She howled in ecstasy, smashing herself against him. 'Chew me! Suck me! Drink me!'

Jordan complied, swallowing hard on the great tumble of slippery nectar that oozed and bubbled from her spasming hole. Liquid trickled over his chin and jaw as he mouthed and pulled on the hard, exposed bead of her clitoris. He was vaguely aware that she was smacking him deliriously about the shoulders and head, but he felt no pain as he supped at her lusting fountain of life . . .

Subdued by her own pleasure, St Etienne seemed to settle suddenly into a gentler more accepting response. 'Oooh baby . . . baby, you angel,' she cooed, as her hips wafted gently beneath Jordan's slobbering mouth. 'Oh, Jordi, my Jordi . . . You're beautiful . . . You're killing me, baby, you're killing me . . .'

Jordan was lost now to everything but St Etienne: her cunt, her flavour, her spongy yielding heat. The veins that throbbed beneath the silky fruitlike cleftskin, the pulsing tip of her clitoris, the juices that seeped so freely . . .

Intent on giving, the whole of Jordan's consciousness was centred in his mouth and his hands as they clasped her thighs . . . Only gradually did he realise that Guido and Bobbie were both now very, very close . . .

The others will do something nice.

He heard the promise over again now inside his mind and, feeling the warmth of two more bodies right next to him, he was more than ready when a pair of hands began to caress his buttocks. Which of them was doing it, he couldn't tell. All he knew was the touch was gentle yet firm, and that the cheeks of his bottom were being moved and moulded in time to the beat of his own hungry sucking.

The action was wickedly reciprocal, and the unknown fondler followed every tiny nuance of Jordan's mouth and tongue . . . Every push, every twist, every determined and delicate twirl. Each was echoed in the manipulations of his tingling rear, making the excitement he received feed the excitement he gave . . . Three fingers rode his anal crack, taunting and rubbing, doubling his delight in St Etienne's slit. His tongue danced over the silken flesh, revelling in its texture and liquidity and the rising tremble of yet another orgasm.

189

Triumph howled its siren song in Jordan's brain, and somewhere in the loop between mind, mouth and arsehole, he realised his cock had stiffened like iron. I'm hard again, he marvelled as he felt St Etienne pulsing against his mouth and hard fingers sawing ruthlessly at his anus. I've come and come and now I'm ready all over again. He bounced his bottom at the probing fingers, using the hole itself to beg for more, because his drooling mouth was full of St Etienne's puffy labia.

'You want something in you, don't you, baby?' she gasped, her voice distorted by pleasure. 'You want something in your arse, don't you, darling?'

Jordan grunted around the hot flesh in his mouth, waggled his bum furiously. Yes! Yes! Yes!

'Grease him, Guido,' ordered St Etienne hoarsely, pulling herself away from Jordan's mouth, then lifting him up so she could kiss where her cunt had been. 'I'm going to take you, Jordi my love,' she murmured, licking at Jordan's lips as if savouring her own taste there. 'I'm going to make love to you, sweetheart. I can do it . . . I'm going to open your lovely bottom, and thrust and thrust until we both come . . . I'm going to fill your arse, Jordi. Rape you. Take you. That's what you want, isn't it?' She drew back, stopped kissing with her mouth, and kissed Jordan's eyes with her burning gaze . . .

They held the shared look for what seemed like a lifetime and then St Etienne turned to Bobbie and ordered imperiously: 'Get it, Bobbie! You know what I need . . .'

Jordan could only wait. To speak his submission aloud would be too much. If he said the word 'yes' now, he'd come all over the couch and carpet. And he hardly dare think of what 'it' might be . . . although his boggled brain was already showing him a graphic picture.

With no will of his own, he let St Etienne drape him forward over the red velvet, then lift his hips slightly for Guido's ministrations. He felt something cool and slippery applied to the boiling groove of his bottom, then bit his lip, fighting orgasm, as more and more of it was worked deep into his trembling hole. A hand took his and held it supportively, and he turned and looked into Bobbie's painted face. Her eyes were gentle, her expression both understanding and encouraging.

'You'll be all right, Jordi,' she whispered, 'you'll be fine . . . You look beautiful.'

'Thank you,' Jordan mouthed, still unable to speak aloud. He felt indescribably rude like this: his arse offered up, the lovehole exposed and the passage open, gluey and slimed in readiness. He tried to relax even more . . . Any second now . . . Any second now . . .

Expecting to be taken from behind, he grunted with surprise when Guido half lifted, half pushed him over on to his back, laying him on the red couch with his bottom hanging over the edge, anus hovering in mid-air, prick waving, rigid and helpless . . . Totally vulnerable, he watched in wonder at the most extraordinary spectacle of his sexually active life.

St Etienne had finally stripped to the buff, and with one long dancer's leg canted elegantly up, the foot resting on a low couch, she was inserting one end of an artfully formed double-ended rubber phallus into her copiously moistened vagina. He saw her gasp as the giant *faux* penis slid in, watched her eyes close ecstatically as her half of it sank to its hilt.

And then, even though the dildo was lodged between her thighs and sticking out proudly like an ersatz erection, Jordan marvelled at the pure feminine beauty of her body. Nude, St Etienne was supremely female, her breasts high, her hips out-curved, her waist almost breathtakingly slim. She looked flowerlike, halfway to fragile . . . and yet the rubber penis was hugely gross and intimidating. Looking at it, Jordan shuddered, wondering how much pain there'd be. It seemed so long since that single, brief penetration in his teens, and even then the man hadn't been as big as this monstrous replica.

'Don't be frightened, Jordi,' St Etienne said quietly, moving over him, obviously aware of his fears. 'You can take it. I'll be as gentle as I can, Jordi, but God knows, it'll be a struggle with a body as tempting as yours . . .'

191

Graceful, yet urgent, she dipped, took Jordan's ankles in a firm grasp and placed them on her own shoulders – one on either side of her neck. Then, no longer seeming in any way frail at all, St Etienne slowly rose up again and Jordan felt his arse canting up off the couch, his hole offered and in perfect position to be fucked. His own living prick quivered as the dildo touched him and rested motionless at his entrance. The whole of his life and sanity seemed to teeter on a precipice . . .

'Oh God, please,' he heard himself say.

'Yes, my beauty,' murmured St Etienne, and Jordan felt pressure building on the membrane and his entire body being folded under the woman's almost supernatural strength. 'Give in to me, Jordi. Relax. Open up. I only want to love you!'

To love you . . .

That did it. Jordan moaned in wonder as his anus opened like a sea-anemone and St Etienne slid into him with perfect, pre-ordained ease. There was a moment of re-arrangement – their limbs remeshing – then St Etienne was climbing up and over him, forcing the clublike rubber cock even deeper into Jordan's bowels.

'Oh no! Ooooh! Oh! Please, no!' Whimpering in girlish distress, Jordan felt his guts churn rebelliously.

'Take it easy, darling,' St Etienne crooned in his ear. Did she know the feeling herself? Jordan wondered, trying to imagine St Etienne being fucked in her tight womanly arse.

'Relax, Jordi. It won't happen,' St Etienne went on softly, pushing even deeper, 'and even if it does, it doesn't matter. It won't be the first time.' She chuckled throatily, and Jordan gasped, feeling the mirth transmitted right through his possessed backside. The urge to defecate flared wildly, peaked in unthinkable delight, then subsided just as suddenly.

St Etienne, acutely aware, whispered. 'There . . . that's better, isn't it?'

'Oh yes . . . Oh yes,' sobbed Jordan, feeling only beauty now: a voluptuous heat and fullness that brought tears of joy to his eyes, and made him kiss and caress every part of St Etienne he could reach. There was a great sensation of distension, an unrelenting swollen-ness . . . Was it his own body or the pressure of the bung inside him? There seemed to be no boundary between them. They were two sets of loins entangled and touching at every point, possible and impossible. He pushed back boldly and knew, joyfully, that in a bizarre turned-about way he was thrusting into St Etienne's hot cave of a cunt. Aware of her pleasure, Jordan felt its echo in his prick – an organ that was warm and safe, twitching blissfully and sandwiched between his belly and St Etienne's . . .

'You're beautiful, Jordi,' she moaned, starting to move now, her strokes strong and sure as the fuck began in earnest. 'God, that feels fabulous. It's right in me . . . I'm fucking you and it's fucking me. Oh God, Jordi, I'm in heaven!'

So am I! screamed Jordan inside as St Etienne crushed his mouth in a kiss. Pierced by both tongue and dildo, he slid his hand into the sweaty cache between their two bodies and curled his fingers around his own throbbing tool. St Etienne swirled her hips, as if in approval, and Jordan began to wank himself in time to his partner's relentless thrusts. He wanted to shout and wail. The pleasure was like nothing he'd ever known; molten bliss flowed through his arse and prick in an endless cycle until he was one great ball of ecstasy from the waist down. Sobbing like a child, he surrendered to a huge spasm and felt his tortured cock leap, then disgorge semen all over his fingers, and his own and St Etienne's belly.

'Oh, my lovely Jordi,' St Etienne cried, pressing closer to the pulsing organ as if trying to caress it with her abdomen. 'It's so beautiful! So beautiful! Oh God, it feels so good.' Jordan didn't really know what she was praising – his arse, his prick, the spunk or the dildo – but he was beyond caring. He was as much a woman as she was now; he was a hole, a languid swimming rectum whose only purpose was to submit to his lover. Already adrift in his own afterglow, Jordan let his body react instinctively. His hands roved freely across St Etienne's sweat-sheened skin, pausing and retracing his path each time he heard a gasp of pleasure.

By letting himself go utterly loose and pliant, Jordan soon found he could reach into the tangle of their bodies to caress St Etienne's cunt and the crucial nub of flesh within it. He swirled a fingertip right on its throbbing peak . . . and was almost deafened by St Etienne's long howl of response.

Simultaneously, he was rocked and pounded by a series of percussive lunges that threatened to crush his pelvis and almost tear him in two. St Etienne wailed on and on like a banshee, and Jordan felt a great heat welling deep inside him, and more liquid spurting from his prick as the rubber phallus battered rhythmically on his sensitive prostate.

St Etienne's climax seemed to last several millennia, even though Jordan's half-blown mind said it was just mere moments, and her spastic jerks transmitted themselves remorselessly to his innards. But eventually she fell into stillness. Squashed and folded beneath her slumped body, Jordan found the discomfort strangely pleasing and lay perfectly still, unwilling to disturb St Etienne's blissed-out exhaustion.

'You little fool,' St Etienne mumbled at last, starting to lift herself off Jordan's awkwardly bent form. 'I'm smothering you, baby. Why didn't you say something?'

'I'm –' Jordan began, then groaned hoarsely as her movements jostled his bruised rectum. 'I'm fine,' he said through gritted teeth as he felt the dildo pop out of his abused anus.

'You're not,' she said softly, standing up, then leaning over Jordan and edging him tenderly into a more comfortable position on the couch. 'It's hurt you, hasn't it?'

Jordan nodded, trying not to move too much. His arse was really very sore indeed, and the rest of him seemed to have been in a wind tunnel for a fortnight. Suddenly very exhausted, he sighed sleepily, then smiled to himself as he heard the small plopping sound of rubber leaving cunt and the thud of a substantial object hitting the carpet. Seconds

later St Etienne slid on to the couch behind him and cuddled him close.

The sensation of being cherished was quite wonderful,
and seemed even more so when a voice whispered in his
ear . . .

'You were beautiful, Jordi . . . The best. I think I love
you . . .'

Jordan said nothing. He couldn't. Snuggling back against
the soft, sleek body of a most incredible woman, he shivered
under her stroking hands, breathed deeply of the scents of
sweat, cologne, cunt and semen, and savoured the feel of
a damply sticky pubis pressing into the back of his thigh.

Sheer heaven. In spite of his aches and pains, Jordan
began to drowse, only to be awakened after a couple of
minutes by the sounds of frantic movement and grunts and
moans of uninhibited pleasure.

'Just look at them!' murmured St Etienne in his ear, and
obediently Jordan opened his eyes.

A couple of yards away, Bobbie and Guido were fucking
like minks.

Jordan watched the scene blearily, too exhausted now to
get turned on, despite the raw eroticism before him. Guido
had mounted the gentle submissive Bobbie from behind and
was ramming into her small delicate cunt without mercy or,
it seemed, any degree of finesse.

But Bobbie didn't seem too bothered by the lack of
gentleness. As she flailed and bucked against the onslaught,
she was chanting Guido's name repeatedly and almost
gnawing the carpet in ecstasy.

'Would you like to do that next time?' St Etienne asked
quietly, stroking the side of Jordan's face.

'Do what?' he asked, feeling intensely sleepy in spite of
the inflaming sight in front of him.

'I don't mean fuck Bobbie, Jordi . . . I want to know if
you want to fuck me?'

'But she said . . .'

Who'd said what?

Jordan suddenly felt utterly tired and utterly confused.

Memories hazed. Someone had laughed when he'd said . . .
Said what?

'Jordi? Answer me, sweetheart. Would you like to fuck me?' St Etienne's voice was starting to sound strange too. Still soft and husky . . . but different somehow and more familiar than it ought to have been.

'Answer me . . . Come on, Josh, speak to me!'

Josh?

Who . . . It was all very weird now, but one thing at least was sparklingly clear.

'Oh yes,' he whispered. 'Oh yes, darling, I'd love to fuck you. I'd love to. Love to fuck you . . . fuck you . . . fuck you . . .'

10 *A Little Something on Account?*

. . . fuck you . . . fuck you . . . fuck you . . .'

'Very nice, Josh, I'll take it as a compliment. But will you please try and wake up now?'

What? What did she mean? Josh felt as if he were in limbo, floating in greyness, waiting for sounds and colours to start meaning something. They were all there – his senses seemed to be working – but he couldn't put anything together. Nothing added up. Or if it did, the sums were coming out wrong.

'Come on, Josh, open your eyes,' encouraged the voice that wasn't quite what it should have been.

Delicious lethargy still held him in thrall, scrambling all signals; even the pleasurable ones. He was adrift in a warm bath of sex, his prick exquisitely tingly and his arse loose and hot and stretched.

His arse? Oh God! Ohgodogodogod!

In a split second, Josh came awake, the bath turned icy and he *was* Josh again. The Josh who'd always believed *he* did the fucking . . .

Believed! What a joke. His subconscious . . . his 'Jordan' had just proved otherwise . . . and the visceral revulsion, the yearnings he'd always fought like hell, rose up to taunt him. His arse, his tight man's arse, had been opened and taken. He'd been fucked. He'd been well and truly shafted.

'Josh! Are you all right? Open your eyes!'

Couldn't she leave him alone? Still half on auto, he tried to strike out and found he couldn't. Struggling wildly, he opened his eyes. Saw the treatment room, the couch, the restraints . . . Saw Isis – the scarred flipside of the woman who'd just fucked his arse – and hated her.

'You bitch! Let me loose,' he screamed, wrenching at his bonds and murdering the white-coated woman with his eyes. 'What have you done to me?'

Suddenly, oh horror, oh fabulous horror, he felt a slow sliding sensation in his bowel . . . The thing that stretched his bum and felt so good was sliding out, its exit as gorgeous as its ingress.

'St Etienne . . .' he hissed, longing . . . Then caught a flash of white out of the corner of his half closed eyes.

Isis. She'd done this! She'd tricked him! She'd promised there'd be nothing gay, then given him something that was virtually the same . . . and in front of an audience.

'I'll kill you!' He jerked rabidly at the velvet-lined bonds and tried to throw himself up off the couch. But there was no point. Isis was already at his side. Poised . . . He felt a sharp pricking pain in his upper arm.

'I'll kill you,' he murmured, then felt a soft dark weight pressing down on his mind. 'I'll . . .'

Then the pain, the room, the raging fear – and Isis – were all lost in blackness . . .

Josh woke up.

Again.

And felt much better. He was still naked, but when he flexed his legs and arms, he realised he was free.

'Here, drink this,' said a familiar voice. Someone who was exactly who she should be this time, someone he really didn't hate at all.

Josh opened his eyes and sat up, then took a long thirsty pull at the glass of water Isis held to his lips.

'How do you feel now?' she asked quietly, putting the glass aside. Josh shuddered, looking into her hideous yet beautiful face and remembering two different yet equally disturbing dreams. One bizarre and delectable; one that terrified him.

'Better,' he answered sheepishly, 'and I'm sorry for what I said before. I don't know what got into –' He stopped abruptly and grinned. 'Let me rephrase that. I felt weird. I was scared and angry. I'm sorry I yelled at you. I don't know why I said those things . . .'

'I do.'

As Josh swung his legs so he could sit with them dangling over the side of the couch, Isis came and sat beside him. He was acutely aware of her heat, and the fact that her lovely body was just inches away from him. Astoundingly, his cock flicked slightly in response; and though a wave of joy accompanied the phenomenon, he concentrated on the nervous twisting of her pink-lined fingers to take his mind off it. He wanted answers now, not another erection.

'What do you mean?' he enquired, sliding his hands discreetly down his thighs to block her view of his crotch.

'It's my fault you went wild when you first came round.' Isis paused as if trying to decide what came next . . . and whether she dare speak of it.

What the hell's she done? thought Josh. The white smock rustled evocatively as Isis' uneasiness manifested itself in fidgeting and shuffling her trim backside on the couch. Josh eyed the extra inches of creamy thigh this revealed, then crossed his wrists over his own thighs to try to hide the inevitable.

Luckily Isis was unable to look him in the face. Or the crotch. 'Well,' she began again, 'you're probably the best and most reactive client I've ever had, Josh. I promise you I've never actually "gone under" with you, but I can tell by what you say, and by the readouts, that when you're experiencing a re-creation, it's all absolutely real for you.'

She glanced at him then, and Josh nodded. It *was* real.

'Anyway . . . seeing as how you responded so well, I thought I'd see if I could improve on that. So I did a bit of retuning to see if I could upgrade the "reality" even further for you.' She smoothed her palms down her skirt as if she were sweating. 'But it looks as if I might've gone too far. You had about a dozen orgasms this time . . .'

'Good God.'

His groin was starting to hurt again now, the stiffening triggered both by her female proximity and her extraordinary revelation. Surely, though, he hadn't come that many times in St Etienne's playroom?

'It sounds as if my body was having an even better time than my mind,' he observed, grinning broadly to reassure the worried-looking Isis.

'Oh yeah,' she said, lacing her fingers, still nervous, 'the response was excellent. But I took you so deep that it knackered up the return to "real" reality. The transition was too abrupt and it threw you into shock. I'm sorry, Josh, I'll have to retune for next time. Try to find a happy medium . . .'

'Don't worry. I'm okay now, aren't I?'

Isis nodded, clearly not all that convinced.

Josh decided to convince her. 'At first I was shit-scared. Being buggered . . . it felt so fabulous, more than the dead straight "het" in me said it ought to. That's what made me go nuts.'

'But why shouldn't it feel good? It's a very sensual experience, whatever your sex or persuasion. And if you're worried about being gay, Josh, I really don't know why. Most people are bisexual anyway, when it really comes down to it.'

'You're probably right there, Isis,' he said, unfolding his forearms out of his lap. 'Because I sure as hell still fancy women.' With a resigned laugh, he looked down at the fleshy crimson tower rising out of his groin. He was fully erect again, seeping pre-come as if this was the night's first hard-on, not at least the dozenth. And this time, he knew exactly why his tool was waving . . .

He wanted this strange, clever woman at his side. He wanted Isis more than he'd ever wanted anybody, male, female or even someone with aspects of both, like St Etienne. 'I'm sorry. I can't help it,' he said, flashing her a grin.

'You randy bugger.' She was laughing now, but obviously reassured. 'You never give up, do you?'

'This never does,' he replied, tapping his swaying erection. 'But I'm going to have to, aren't I?' he went on quietly, 'unless you've changed your mind, which I seriously doubt. I want you, Isis, but I'm obviously not going to get you. And anyway, I'm superstitious!'

'What on earth are you yattering on about?' enquired Josh's old imperious Isis, hopping off the couch and making him ache even more as a long expanse of shapely thigh was revealed in the process.

'Didn't you say I'd had twelve climaxes tonight?' He followed her off the couch, prick bouncing obscenely as he landed. 'If I come again, it'll be unlucky.'

'Go and get dressed, you idiot,' Isis chuckled and turned towards her computer console. 'I'll meet you back in the bar and we'll have a drink and decide where you go from here.'

Easier said than done, decided Josh later, back at his flat. He and Isis had had their drink and their chat, but it'd been strangely unilluminating. Isis had been charming, yet her real thoughts had been as veiled as her face often was. Josh had suspected she was still concerned about his post-adventure outburst, and behind her peculiar bi-coloured eyes, the scientist had already been at work on a solution . . .

'And she probably still is,' Josh muttered to himself as he got into bed and pulled the sheet across his naked body. Although she'd never fully explained how the sensory re-creator worked, Josh had formed the impression that a good deal of complex programming was involved; and while he was here, relaxed and comfortable between the crisp cotton sheets of his double bed, she was back in the treatment room, hunched over her computer console, squinting at a screen full of arcane figures . . .

The trouble, Josh realised, turning over restlessly, was that his own mind was now just as puzzling to him as Isis's screen would've been. Only wanting *her* remained constant; otherwise his hormones were in utter turmoil.

He'd been heartily glad earlier on that St Etienne and Bobbie hadn't returned to the bar. It had been difficult enough to look Guido in the eye. There was no way the blond barman could've known the contents of the latest 'adventure', but Josh had the weirdest feeling Guido was somehow aware of what had 'taken place'. He was a man who worked among a lot of sexy people, after all, and no doubt he was well versed in the art of observation. He was probably picking up vibes Josh was hardly aware of exuding . . .

I hope to God he doesn't fancy me, thought Josh, turning over yet again, then thinking of how attractive Guido's muscular, long-limbed body was, and how incredible he'd looked in Bobbie's mouth.

'Stop it,' he shouted out loud to himself, sitting up and switching on the light. 'For Christ's sake think about women!'

Which brought him back to Isis.

Who on earth did she fuck? She had to get satisfied somehow or where; she was mature, sexy and vital. She had all her juices flowing, and inevitably she'd need some action.

And he couldn't imagine her being short of suitors, in spite of her bitter comments about guys with *Phantom of the Opera* fetishes and suchlike. He pictured her humping some anonymous but lucky young stud, and his groin pulsed insistently.

Face it, Mortimer, you're hooked, he told himself resignedly. Easing down more cosily into the bed, he retuned his mental picture and replaced the faceless youngster between Isis's thighs with an image of himself.

The clarity of it all was frightening, pin-sharp and almost as real as an 'adventure'. Delicious frissions played up and down his tool; he could taste Isis's mouth as he kissed her, smell her perfume, feel the feminine solidity of her body as he rocked his pelvis and plunged into her moist, engulfing heat. Closing his eyes and sighing, in the real world, his hand drifted to his crotch . . .

It was almost noon when Josh reluctantly woke up, and he lay still for a few minutes, trying to decide whether he felt properly rested or still a bit out of sorts. His body felt sticky and distinctly grungy, and his penis faintly sore. A long hot shower followed by a herbal body rub sounded enticing. Better not be too vigorous around some parts of his anatomy, though. Not after last night . . .

It'd been nice though.

Refreshed, soothed and revived by shower, body rub, and a mug of strong coffee, in that order, Josh strolled at last into his small but elegant lounge, only to have his hard-won sense of wellbeing shattered by the red 'priority one' code flashing on his answermachine.

'Damn,' he growled, cinching his robe around him and taking a seat before the computer monitor. Personal callers couldn't engage this particular code, so it couldn't be any of his usual friends trying to reach him.

What about Isis? His spirits and his cock leapt when he realised that with her computer knowhow she could probably callifudge just about anything out of any system.

But both prick and hopes deflated when he punched in de-scroll and a familiar logo unfurled on the screen.

SOLARCORP MINING EXECUTIVE.
  PRIORITY TO J J MORTIMER — SENIOR ENGINEER
PHOBOS FACILITY . . .

The gist of it was, Josh thought glumly as he sipped his cold coffee some time later, that at midnight tonight he'd be at City Field hopping a shuttle to take him back to Phobos. There'd been a massive explosion at the mine and his expertise was required to set things right. Mercifully, there'd been no serious injuries, but the blast had damaged structures on which the whole camp depended; so, until repairs were effected, miners' lives were in jeopardy.

Josh sighed. He'd have answered this call even if he hadn't been obliged to, but having already signed up for his next tour because of the outrageous financial demands of Pleasurezone, an early recall was standard operational procedure.

He couldn't lay the blame at Pleasurezone's door. Not really. Yet as he weighed the Libidox capsule in his palm, his mind screamed 'no!' and his groin cramped in protest.

He checked the chrono. Yes, there was time. Pleasure-zone owed him. Isis owed him. The whole wild thing had cost so much he owed it to himself.

A little something on account, that's what he'd have. A last pleasure-splurge before Phobos. One last chance to get his rocks off before the placidity of temporary chemical gelding. Whistling a tune to himself, he started punching in the code . . .

At seven o'clock, almost wishing he had taken the Libidox, Josh finally got fed up of 'There is no one here to speak to you, please leave a message . . .' In between making his departure arrangements, packing his bags, and making other calls, he knew for a fact he'd tried to call Isis on seventeen different occasions. The computer had logged his attempts: seventeen connections, then seventeen tedious repetitions of that frustrating message.

'What the hell is she doing?' Josh switched off the screen in disgust, grabbed his leather jacket and was out on a travelway almost before he realised what *he* was doing. 'Mountain to Mahomet and all that stuff,' he muttered to himself, drawing a curious stare from a fellow traveller. Five hours left to take-off. He'd get that 'something on account' from Isis, even if it killed him.

And yet, as he patted his hair and checked his 'look' in La Selene's mirrored foyer, a still, small voice at the back of his mind subversively informed him it might be enough just to see her . . .

But she's not forced to be here, he told himself, pushing open the door to the main bar; and his heart sank as he scanned the sparsely filled room. Sevenish was early for a place that really lit up only around midnight . . . and he was only playing a hunch. Glancing towards the back of the room and the red baize door, he knew there was no way to pass through it without the correct entrance code.

Then, directing his attention back to the bar, the heart that'd sunk bounced up again.

Right in the corner, hard by the wall and half in shadow, there she was!

Perched on a stool and deep in thought, Isis was studying a thick sheaf of papers that spilled across the counter before her. As he watched, she took a sip of coffee from a cup at her elbow, then re-adjusted the granny glasses perched on the end of her nose, frowned, and made a swift annotation on the top sheet of her stack. The lady doctor was clearly hard at work, and judging by the fact she appeared to be mouthing curses, having her fair share of problems.

'Hi!' said Josh brightly as he slid onto an adjacent stool.

'What are you doing here? You're booked for Thursday, not tonight.'

'Charming. And it's nice to see you too, Isis,' replied Josh crisply, squashing his disappointment. Her lack of welcome hurt him, but, strangely, made him want her even more. She was imposingly sexy when she was fierce, and a scowl did incredible things to her scar. Frowning her displeasure, she was a pagan devil-goddess, a totem who could consume him alive as easily as look at him.

'What do you want, Josh?' she went on, ignoring his facetious greeting. Pulling off her glasses, she smoothed an errant lock of hair out of her eyes. The movement was slight and unstudied but it tautened her thin white shirt across her breasts, and made Josh's groin twitch like an obscenely displaced heartbeat. She was casually dressed tonight: plain shirt, jeans – and when Josh looked down – scuffed trainers on her slim, elegant feet. These were probably the reason she'd tucked herself away like this. La Selene had no dress code as such, but its clientele were usually clad in the height of current fashion.

'I . . . I just wondered whether you could fit me in tonight instead,' he began, and then, in the face of her continuing silence, he outlined the details of his recall.

Isis's disapproving expression softened as the account progressed, and as it did so, her whole demeanour became more sympathetic, and more sensual. Aching with need, Josh watched the subtle shift of her thighs as she relaxed on her stool. Oh God, how he longed to nestle there! The snug jeans clung to her fine curvy hips and slim waist; Josh followed the direction of that overstitched centre seam he loved so much . . . His mouth went dry, his penis wept.

'So you see,' he concluded, 'this is my last chance to party before Libidox makes me a temporary eunuch. I wanted to go out with . . . well . . . something other than being fucked in the arse as my last sexual memory.'

'Yes, I see your point,' said Isis slowly, picking up her pen as she did so and chewing its end contemplatively. Josh nearly groaned aloud, hardly able to believe what that absentminded gesture did to him. He saw – and felt! – her small red mouth enclose his aching prick . . .

'And under any other circumstances, Josh, I'd have been happy to oblige.' She abandoned the unappealing pen and nibbled her full bottom lip instead. 'But I've spent most of today overhauling the system, reconfiguring just about everything so you wouldn't get the screaming abdabs next time you wake up. It's all in bits, Josh. I only slipped out for a coffee break. I've got to go back in there now and put the entire shebang back together again . . .'

She cares! thought Josh exultantly. She really cares! The joy of it almost drowned his frustration.

Almost but not quite.

'Isn't there anything you can do?' He hated the whining tone in his voice almost as much as the patent fact of being a slave to his own screaming cock. God, he'd have to have something soon, even if it was only a trip to the lavatory to wank! 'What about that "something special" you had as a back-up? You know, last night.'

'It won't work, Josh. I'm recalibrating the whole system.'

You could let me fuck you instead, thought Josh savagely. Empty my balls into you . . . it'd do just as well.

But what he said instead was, 'You owe me something, Isis. It's Pleasurezone's fault I'm obliged to go. At least you could give me something on account.' He turned away, more angry with himself than her, and signalled to Guido for a drink.

When the drink arrived, he sank half of it, and stared moodily at the remainder as he listened to the scratch of Isis's swiftly moving pen.

He was just about to drink off, make his goodbye and leave, when he felt a soft and uniquely feminine touch on his arm. The writing had stopped, he realised, and when he looked down, Isis's long, delicately scarred fingers were pale against the dark leather of his jacket.

'There might be a way,' she said in a low voice, her odd, glowing eyes offering hope but only tentatively. 'It might be a bit rough around the edges, not quite as "real" as usual, but I might be able to wangle something. It'll mean some jury-rigging, Josh, but I'd like to try.'

'So would I,' he replied, halfway to heaven just from the pressure of her fingers.

'Let's go then. You haven't got much time.'

And it was the swiftest transition from bar to treatment room he'd ever made. No dawdling over erotica, no mental foreplay with books, tapes or artwork . . . A few essential minutes in the bathroom, a quick half-strip, and he was climbing on to the white leather couch, his cock swinging eagerly.

Isis didn't waste time either; she went straight to her computer in jeans and workshirt. As Josh settled himself into the now familiar mouldings, her fingers fairly flew over the keys, pulling up whole wodges of data, cancelling and rekeying, and blaspheming frequently and colourfully as she did so. Josh knew he should be scared, but his cock was an iron-hard column of need and he'd never been randier in his life.

She was still preoccupied when she moved swiftly around him, fastening the various straps. Josh could almost see the calculations taking place behind her eyes. She's so brilliant, he thought in awe, then laughed out loud, realising that the very idea of her dazzling intelligence had made him stiffer than ever. If only he could be the man to blow that incredible mind. He laughed again, remembering that he'd longed for something quite similar with the 'adventurous' version of St Etienne!

'What's so funny?' she enquired, turning to press a key.

'Nothing,' replied Josh shakily as the cleverly placed leather covered ridges began to open his arse in readiness.

Swiftly and impersonally she lubricated him, then, with another keystroke, sent the probe sliding into his rectum.

'Ooh yes,' he hissed, bearing down hard.

Penetration . . . he loved it. There was no hiding the fact. The phallus felt cool, and, though quite inert, reminded him vividly of St Etienne and her amazing artificial penis.

Relaxing into the delicious sensation, Josh tried to ignore the sounds of agitation coming from the direction of the console.

Isis knew what she was doing, didn't she? Josh told himself not to worry and had no problem obeying. Revelling in a well-stuffed arse and a rigid and gloriously tingling tool, he closed his eyes and let all questions float from his mind. Passive, yet trembling slightly, he felt Isis return and give him his shot, then place the softly lined eyemask carefully in place. Next it'd be the cuff on the tip of his penis . . .

Josh felt himself drifting away, cocooned in warmth, exquisite stimulation and total darkness . . . He smiled behind his mask, completely unconcerned. She'd said it would be different this time, but she *had* promised him pleasure and he trusted her completely.

Tap tap tap . . . Her genius fingers still flowed busily across the keys.

'You stupid fucker!' An angry voice. Another wild fusillade of keystrokes . . .

'Isis?' he queried blindly, not worried for himself but saddened to hear *her* self-recrimination.

'Don't worry, Josh, you'll get your adventure.' Sounding very odd now, a combination of defeat, resignation, and spinemelting erotic mischief, she continued, 'In fact, it's about to start any minute!'

This was a very peculiar state; half in, half out of the Pleasurezone. He still couldn't see, but he knew something special was happening . . . *The* 'something special'? Visuals would cut in soon, and his electronically deluded mind would take him flying free of the bonds that held him . . .

Or would they?

Hovering in the warm, dark peacefulness, Josh sensed a presence beside him, heard soft rustlings and breathing . . . The dream lover was close now, very close, caressing his face, his belly, and – ooh! – his cock . . . It was the weirdest adventure yet, he observed in a fragment of lucidity, but there was nothing to complain about. A pair of bare thighs were suddenly and delightfully astride his own. He couldn't see a single thing, but his cock said a hot sex was suspended above him like a sizzling vapour.

There was a long sigh, sweet and breathy in the empty air, and simultaneously he was engulfed! His tool was sunk upon by warmth and wetness, enclosed in a grippy sleeve that hugged every trembling millimetre of his flesh and rippled around him like a heavenly syncopated wave.

The ultimate cunt.

'Oh God!' he crooned, untroubled by either darkness or his bonds. The unseen caressor had him in paradise, wherever or whatever that might be. Simmering on the edge of an orgasm, Josh neither knew nor cared.

'Not quite,' said a familiar but flustered sounding voice, and Josh laughed out loud again.

In triumph . . .

The woman above ground her body on to him in ever-decreasing circles . . . a tricky-bitch attempt to distract him from what he now already knew. Then with his arse speared and cock about to explode, he felt her lean forward and unfasten his hands . . .

'Go on,' she murmured huskily, 'you might as well take the mask off . . . Although you'd be doing yourself a favour if you didn't!'

'No way,' said Josh, groaning in a fight for self-control. Some diabolical inner muscle was massaging the head of his cock, and the strong thighs that flanked his hips were rocking him gently on the probe. His cock jumped wildly in its sheath, but he bit his lip bloody, pushing back the inevitable for just a little longer. He'd see a face when he came! And he'd see her seeing it.

Limbs twitching, his body at war with a violent urge to come, Josh reached up and slowly tugged off the mask.

Eyes still closed, he flung it away. The moment of revelation was nigh, yet he savoured the torture of anticipation.

When his eyes flicked open, the first thing he saw was the juncture of their loins: hair tangled together, a mesh of his jet black and her red-gold-blonde. She was more auburn below, he noted wonderingly, fiery like the liquid flame that licked his smothered cock.

Teasing himself, he panned up over an ever-so-slightly rounded ever-so-very kissable belly, the tender erotic dink of a navel . . . then sighed at the sight of her ripe, lace-covered breasts. Mentally stripping off the sheer fabric, he cruised on and up the slim column of the loveliest throat he'd ever seen till he reached a beautiful, wryly smiling face – a face with an orchid-cunt scar and glittering, unnervingly disparate eyes.

'Sorry. It's kinda beauty and the beast time,' whispered Isis, leaning over to stroke Josh's cheek before touching her own. She still had on her thin white shirt, and its open panels brushed his chest as she moved.

'I see no beast.' He ran his fingers across the cups of her flimsy bra, lingering over the hard tips beneath, and smiling as she gasped. 'Be naked for me, Isis. Please?'

Her face clouded a little, then she shrugged and shucked off her shirt. Josh reached up and unhooked the bra's tiny front clasp, and she slid the garment away with a grace that left him speechless. A few hair-fine pink scarlines criss-crossed her arms and trunk – obviously the cause of her frown – but her breasts were perfect, with high, delicate globes, creamily opulent and crowned with puckered, berry-brown nipples. Josh's tongue ached to caress them . . . his lips to suck . . . his teeth to nip gently . . . He put up both his long hands and rubbed her, then fought for breath as she wriggled in response, swivelling herself mercilessly on their double impalement.

'You witch,' he hissed, loving the voluptuous agony of it. 'Trust *you* to find a way to fuck *me* too.'

'Neat trick, eh?' She shimmied again, and Josh moaned, his fingers closing roughly on her breasts. He'd wanted to be so gentle if this'd ever happened, but she was driving him crazy. Squeezing his cock with her incredible innards and at the same time raping his arse with all the power her cousin had . . . in dreamtime.

Isis grunted, covering his hands with hers as she tilted her body slightly and mashed her clitoris against him.

'I wanted this all along, you know,' she said, breathing unevenly now. 'I wanted it the first moment you came into La Selene. I was watching you from the shadows. I told myself I was nuts! I couldn't get over the idea of climbing on top of you . . . Just like this . . .'

'Then why didn't you do it before?' he demanded, tears springing to his eyes at the incredible sensations.

'You know why,' gasped Isis, fucking herself silly on his rod, pushing her breasts at him for further mauling. 'Oh God, I love that,' she keened as he pinched her. 'Shall . . . shall I unfasten your feet?'

'No! Leave 'em! I like it . . .' His fettered ankles gave him purchase as he arched his pelvis up off the probe, and, grabbing Isis summarily by the hips, slammed her cunt down hard on his cock. It was like being in her up to her throat, and with a great shout, Josh felt his cock convulse and spew out its tribute deep in her body . . .

'Isis! Oh God! Oh God!' he bellowed, yowling at the top of his lungs as she matched his action and jammed him back down onto the phallus.

White lights burst softly behind his eyes, and his loins entered another universe . . . Never . . . never before like this . . . His semen poured like a molten river inside her, bubbling between his flesh and the shimmering walls of her climaxing cunt, oozing between their bodies, soaking the mingled hair . . .

From a great distance he heard, 'Josh Josh Josh' like an incantation and felt her nails score cruelly into his arms. 'Ooh Josh! Ooh God, I'm coming,' she wailed, her distorted words making far less sense than her boiling, thrashing body.

Then nothing seemed to make sense anymore. Overloaded nerve-ends tumbled Josh into a dark soothing void.

211

He slept . . . but in the soft black nothingness he knew there was still an Isis . . .

'Was that a mercy fuck?' he enquired drowsily sometime later.

They were in a bed together at last, tucked away in Isis's pocketsized living quarters which opened off the Pleasurezone suite. Josh had never even known of the place's existence, but now he acknowledged it as a miniature paradise. And he smiled, thinking of how they'd stumbled, dazed, naked and sticky, from the fateful white couch and its banks of electronic wizardry to the plain uncluttered simplicity of this tiny room.

'I might ask the same of you,' replied Isis, sitting up and giving him the straightest look she was capable of. Josh saw small bruises marring her peerless breasts, and, feeling faintly guilty, raised himself up to kiss them.

'I don't suppose there's anything I can say to make you believe you're beautiful, is there?'

She shook her head but smiled.

'Well, you are to me, and I don't want to argue about it,' he said decisively, 'and if I didn't have to go and mend a mine in about – ' he glanced at the small bedside chrono, 'two hours, I'd spend the next week right here in this bed *showing* you how beautiful you are.' His mouth settled on a breast again, and Isis whimpered softly as he slid his hand between her legs. Working steadily and rhythmically, pacing lips on nipple to finger on clitoris, he brought her quickly to another powerful climax, enjoying the abandoned honesty of her groans as much as the beauty of her magnificent body.

'But what am I going to do with you when you get back?' Isis asked when she'd caught her breath.

'Fuck me senseless, I hope,' he retorted, hugging her close and pressing his thigh into the sopping place between her legs.

'No . . . Yes . . . Oh bugger! I will, but what are we going to do about Pleasurezone? I owe you four adventures . . .'

'I'll take it in straight sex. I'm not fussy,' Josh smiled ruefully. Adventures in the Pleasurezone were amazing. Incredible. But after what'd just happened he'd swap everything he'd spent so far – ten times over! – for the time to have a long, slow and very, very conventional screw with this remarkable woman beside him.

'Don't be silly. I owe you thousands!'

'I'm serious. You're worth thousands.' Reckoning swiftly, he decided that the next fifteen minutes, spent in the missionary position, could well settle his account with Pleasurezone for good.

He checked the chrono again. One and a half hours left.

'Isis . . .' Gently but insistently he urged her back against the pillows. 'What about another little something on account?'

'The bank's open, Mr Mortimer,' she answered with a low throaty chuckle. 'Welcome to the Pleasurezone.'

Manoeuvring quickly, he replaced his thigh with his erection and pushed. Then pushed some more . . . then plunged . . . then drove deeply home.

'Yes!' he murmured, as Isis' hands slid around and gripped his arse. He felt her nails cut his skin, and her juicy cunt caress his cock.

Loving the little pain as much as the big pleasure, Josh smiled into the scented softness of her neck and began to thrust . . .

Oh God, it was adventuretime again!